WHEN WE WERE ANIMALS

ALSO BY JOSHUA GAYLORD

Hummingbirds

AS ALDEN BELL

Exit Kingdom
The Reapers Are the Angels

WHEN WE WERE ANIMALS

Joshua Gaylord

DEL REY

1 3 5 7 9 10 8 6 4 2

Del Rey, an imprint of Ebury Publishing
20 Vauxhall Bridge Road,
London SW1V 2SA

Del Rey is part of the Penguin Random House group of companies
whose addresses can be found at global.penguinrandomhouse.com

First published in the US in 2015 by Mulholland Books, an imprint of
Little, Brown and Company, a division of Hachette Book Group, Inc.
First published in the UK in 2015 by Del Rey

www.eburypublishing.co.uk

A CIP catalogue record for this book is available from the British Library

ISBN 9781785030949

Printed and bound by Clays Ltd, St Ives plc

Penguin Random House is committed to a sustainable future for our
business, our readers and our planet. This book is made from Forest
Stewardship Council® certified paper.

For my mother,
who, when as a child I woke from nightmares
and asked her how dark it was outside, replied, smiling,
"Pitch black."

There was a mean trick played on us somewhere. God put us in the bodies of animals and tried to make us act like people. That was the beginning of trouble....A man can't live, feeling himself from the inside and listening to what the preachers say. He can't do both, but he can do one or the other. He can live like we were made to live, and feel himself on the inside, or he can live like the preachers say, and be dead on the inside.

    —Erskine Caldwell, *God's Little Acre*

The youth gets together his materials to build a bridge to the moon, or, perchance, a palace or temple on the earth, and, at length, the middle-aged man concludes to build a woodshed with them.

    —Henry David Thoreau

All truth is crooked, time itself is a circle.

    —Friedrich Nietzsche

I

CHAPTER 1

For a long time, when I was a girl, I was a very good girl.

You should have known me then. You would have liked me. Shy, undergrown, good in school, eager to please. At the dinner table, especially when my father and I went visiting, I didn't eat before others, and I sometimes went without salt because I was too timid to ask anyone to pass it.

They said, "Lumen is quite a little lady."

They said, "She's so quiet! I wonder what's going on in that mind of hers."

I did all my homework. I ate celery sticks as a snack. I went to bed early and knew that the shrieking outside my window had nothing to do with me at all.

———

SOME PEOPLE SAID the moonlight shone stronger there. Other people said it was the groundwater, a corrupted spring beneath the houses, or pestilent vapors from the abandoned mine shaft in the woods. (It's impossible to know exactly what you breathe—I think about that sometimes.) Once upon a time, Hermit Weaper explained to me and some other girls who had wandered onto his property that there was a creature who lived in the lake, and that this creature crept slyly into town once a month and laid eggs in the open mouths of the youth, and that was why we behaved as we did. Lots of people speculated. I didn't. I don't. I don't for the same reason I don't try to guess why houseflies fly the way they do, capricious and bumbling. Some things just are, and there's nothing to be done but smile the world on its way. Some people—though not as many anymore, since faith has become quaint as magic—even thought that the town was evil and being punished by God, like Sodom and Gomorrah, or Nineveh, or Babylon—poor cities! The truth is, nobody knew why it happened this way, but in the town where I grew up, when the boys and girls reached a certain age, the parents locked themselves up in their houses, and the teenagers ran wild.

It's been a long time since I left that place, and now I lead a very different kind of life. My husband is a great admirer of my cooking—even though I never use recipes. There is a playground attendant at the park where I take my son to play. Playgrounds now have rubberized mats on the ground, and the attendant keeps a watchful eye for potential predators—my son is safe, he doesn't even know how safe. I have friendly neighbors who are concerned about the epidemic of dandelions on our lawns. The checkers at the grocery store greet me as they greet everyone else, smiling and guileless. I'm a different person, mostly.

And it makes me wonder if one day I might be able to rediscover fully the child version of myself, before things fouled themselves up, when I was a little girl with commendable manners, when my father and I were two against the world, when my striving for goodness was so natural it was like leaves falling from trees everywhere around me, when I believed sacredness was to be found in many small things like ladybugs and doll toes, when I didn't have a murderous thought in my head, not even one.

———

HERE'S SOMETHING I remember.

I am six years old. I awaken in my bed to the pitchy darkness of night. The familiar glow of my mermaid night-light is gone, and there are sounds coming from outside in the street— screeches like those of predator birds, but human. There are people out there. And also rain. Thunder.

I call for my father. He comes in, carrying a candle in a crystal candlestick. He sets the candle on the table next to me and sits on my bed. His weight dimples the bed, and my small body rolls against him.

"You're dreaming, little Lumen," he says.

"No, I'm not," I say.

"How can you tell?" He is testing me, but his eyes tell me he is sure I will pass.

"I never dream about the night," I tell him. "All my dreams are daytime dreams."

"Is that true?" He seems pleased.

"Yes."

"Well, that's the sign of a pure spirit."

A blinding flash startles the room, a moment of clear sight in the blindness—and a moment later a violent crack of thunder. The earth is tearing itself apart outside. I picture the ground rent with gaping fissures. And the voices, howling crazy at the sky, the thunder, the apocalyptic sundering of the world.

"What's happening?" I say.

"Just a storm," says my father. He is a geologist. He knows about the currents of the earth. "Must've taken down a power line somewhere. The electricity on the whole block is out. Nothing to worry about."

The rain goes clattery against my windowpane. Then the voices again from outside. Feral cries. They sound not afraid, as I am, but rather celebratory—wanton, a word I am aware of.

"Who's out there?" I say.

"Just teenagers," my father says.

"Why are they like that?"

"That's just the way they are."

"Will I be like that when I grow up?"

"You? Perish the thought." It is a pet expression of his. Perish is to outlaw, but parish is also a place for pastors. It is a magical word, and it might protect me. "You'll be different. You're my good girl, aren't you?"

"Yes," and I am his good girl.

"Will you always be my good girl?"

"Yes."

Always is so easy to promise.

"Then there we go," he says and brushes my hair away from my forehead with his fingertips.

The pandemonium continues outside my window, and I reach out to touch the fine, shimmering angles of the crystal candlestick. That, too, seems magic, like a wand or a gemstone that holds power in its mineral core.

"Where did it come from?" I ask.

"It's old," my father says. "I found it in the credenza. It was a wedding gift to your mother and me."

Outside there are many voices at once, caterwauling in the

rain. They must be running past, because I hear them grow gradually loud then quiet again. I look at the window, expecting maybe faces pressed against the glass, a smear of pale skin against the dark. Yet there is nothing to see but the hazy reflection of candle flame.

My father must see my apprehensive gaze.

He says, "Do you want me to tell you the story of our wedding?"

"Yes. Was my mother's name Felicia Ann Steptoe?"

"It was. Until she married me, and her name became—"

"Felicia Ann Fowler."

"That's right."

"And did she wear long orchid gloves on her wedding?"

"She did."

I have heard this story many times before. It is a catechism between him and me.

"Show me the pictures," I demand.

But he shakes his head. "It's too dark. Tomorrow, when the sun comes up."

"Okay," I say.

Then I hush so he can tell the rest of the story. And he tells it, every detail the same and perfect. And he looks up to the ceiling as he tells it, as though it were a story of shadows narrated by his easy, ocean-smoothed voice.

And as he tells it, my lips form my magic word against the night—perish, parish—repeated intermittently, like the thread that quilts together many pieces of fabric, while outside the animal cries of teenagers join with the thunder to rattle the windowpanes.

———

THAT'S ONE THING. Here's another, from even earlier.

We are playing hide-and-seek in our big house. It is a serious game, because not even the third floor is off-limits. I run from room to room, looking even in places where I know he cannot fit—under couches, behind bookcases.

I climb the steps to the third floor, out of breath but happy. I am closing in, I'm sure of it. He's not in the bathtub, behind the shower curtain. He's not in the guest room crouched behind the desk. But I am warm.

I open the door of another room, one we keep shut, one used mostly for storage. There is a sound coming from the closet, a low, whispery sound. I've found him.

I swing wide the closet door, and there he is—there he is—clutching at a dress that belonged to my mother, and choked with tears!

———

THIS IS WHERE I tell you that I grew up happy. Motherless, I was treated nicely in school. I was complimented on my hand-writing (which remains picture-perfect to this day—many people believe I use a ruler to cross my Ts), and my diction, which inspired my fourth-grade teacher, Mrs. Markson, to declare that she had never seen a child so full of grace and refinement in all her years of teaching. English was my favorite subject, because I was a good reader—my father having early on in my life en-couraged me in the ritual of reading together every weekend afternoon in the backyard, I in a hammock slung between two oak trees, he stretched on a deck chair beneath the shade of the slatted wooden pergola over the patio. He would, every now and then, call out, "How's the book?"—and then I would be expected to deliver some thoughtful appraisal of whatever I was reading at the time. Positive or negative—it didn't matter, as long as my critique was grounded in some personal, authoritative interpretation. "I'm not sure why they use farm animals as characters instead of people," I might say. "I don't see the advantage in it." And he would nod, satisfied that a position had been taken one way or the other.

But I was also good at math and science, which led me to believe that my left brain and my right brain were perfectly in balance with each other, that I had an ambidextrous intellect, and that someone with my gifts ought to think very hard about what she really wanted to *do* in life, because there would be so very many options open to her.

The only subject I didn't like much was history. I couldn't be bothered to care about the kings and queens and pilgrims and soldiers who lived so long ago and had nothing to do with my little town and its peculiar ways.

But I was a very dedicated student—even in history class—because my father took great pride in my academic successes, and I wanted to please him. It was difficult for him, having to raise a child on his own, and sometimes he seemed stricken, and I certainly didn't want to add to his already considerable grief. So I did the best I could, and my best turned out to be very good indeed.

And of course this: my mostly female teachers seemed to like my father quite a lot. I watched them moon over him, and he was a lesson to me about what women ought to admire. When they praised me in his presence, their words redirected the compliments toward him. "She is a marvelous reader. You can tell she's been raised to think critically." Or: "She's at the top of her class. It's obvious she has a wonderful support system at home."

You can't take these things personally. My father puffed out his chest with pride, and the look he gave me as he received these adulations was payment beyond measure for my hard work.

As a reward for a good report card and as long as it wasn't a full moon, he would take me to the drive-in movie theater. We got there early in order to find the ideal space in the center of the lot. Then, until the movie started, I was allowed to run back and forth over the rows of tarmac dunes constructed to raise the front ends of the cars to a proper viewing angle.

During the movie, we ate from a bag of popcorn on the console between us. Sometimes a young couple in the car next to us would steam up their windows, and I was embarrassed. But if my father noticed, he never let on.

So it was a simple matter to shut myself off from the mortification of witnessing the private acts that might be taking place everywhere around me.

———

THEN IT WAS the sixth grade and I was twelve and I had a best friend named Polly.

Once, we rode our bikes down to the lake. It was Worm Moon, so it must have been March, and we had gotten out of school early. The school always had late starts and early closings on the three days around a full moon. The purpose of the shortened hours was to give students plenty of time to travel to and from home without having to be caught outside while the sun was down—but Polly and I lived so close to the school that we could use those extra hours to adventure around town.

We pulled our bikes through a thicket of dense brush until we came to a little patch of beach that was unknown to anyone but us. In the summer we would have stripped off our clothes and dived into the murky water, but on this day there was a crispness to the air, and we pulled our jackets more tightly around us. We skimmed stones off the surface of the lake and spoke of many things, including Hondy Pilt, the slow boy in our class who only knew how to say a few words and spoke them in a loud, inarticulate voice, and Rosebush Lincoln, the girl who was rumored to have made him cry by cornering him in the boys' bathroom and making him pull down his pants so she could examine his boy parts. Rosebush Lincoln was in training to be a doctor.

Petey Meechum was also under discussion. Our school had square dancing once a week, and he was the boy who asked us each to be his partner (Polly seven times and me five) more often than he asked any other girl. All the girls wanted to be his square dancing partner, so Polly and I were pleased about our prospects for young womanhood. Petey Meechum's attentions told us we were on the right track, and they boded well for our futures.

"Do you think he writes about us in his diary?" asked Polly.

The "us" signified a political settlement. There had been some tension between Polly and me on this matter, and lately we had come to some vague truce by speaking about the boy's affections as if they were directed in equal measure toward both of us rather than simply toward one or the other.

"Boys don't keep diaries," I said. I wasn't sure if she had been joking. Polly was sometimes wry and sometimes frank.

"I know," she said. "How come you think that is?"

"I don't know," I said. "Maybe they don't care to dwell on things. Or maybe they don't need to write things down because they have naturally good memories."

"I bet Petey has an excellent memory. My mother says he's the marrying kind."

"The marrying kind? How come?"

"I don't know. She won't say. I think it's because he tucks his shirt in again every day after recess."

We sat on the sand, our legs pulled to our chests, and laughed into our knees. On my right, where Polly couldn't see, I traced my initials in the sand with my finger. Then I imposed PM over my initials and put two twigs in a cross over the top. When I stood up, I would have to remember to brush the whole thing out quickly with my sneaker before Polly saw, and if I did then the incantation would be complete.

I had brains, but I was plain-looking compared to Polly, who had powder-blue eyes and pretty blond hair she wore in a pony-tail. Me, I had mud-colored eyes and common brown hair, which was never the right length. Right then it was just below my jaw-line, and it flipped up on the ends—not in a cute symmetrical way but rather with both sides pointing to the right, so that I looked like a cartoon character in a soft wind. Plus I was puny for my age, the smallest girl in my grade, and freckled, and I wore glasses that were too big and round for my face. The only way I was going to win Petey Meechum from Polly was through magic.

But my magic had no time to work, because just then there was a voice behind us.

"You girls!"

We leaped to our feet and saw, emerging from the brush, the large shape of Hermit Weaper, whose cabin was on the other side of the lake past where the road lost its tarmac and became two rutted rows of bare earth in the weeds.

"You girls!" he said again and pointed his finger at us.

We ran for our bikes and began tugging them through the thick underbrush toward the road. He followed us, finger point-ing, his craggy face twisted into a furious jack-o'-lantern, spittle launching from between his dried lips, hanging in strings from his chin.

"You get on out of here!" he called after us as we struggled toward the road. We moved as fast as we could, but he followed us still, lurching his way below low-hanging branches. His left leg was crippled by some ancient injury, but to us that simply made his pursuit all the more monstrous—his lumbering sideways lope through the trees.

Then there was a crash behind us, and we looked back to see Hermit Weaper fallen against the base of a tree, pulling himself up to a sitting position. He had stopped pursuing, but we continued to break our way through the trees as though he were right behind us.

"Don't come back!" he cried, straining his voice to reach us as we got farther from him. "Worm Moon tonight. They'll get you sure! You don't stay inside, they'll hunt you down. They'll take your eyes, you hear me? An hour from now, this whole town goes warg. They'll eat your lungs right outta your chest! They'll pop your lungs like balloons and eat 'em right down! You hear me? Don't come back!"

When we reached the road, we got on our bikes and pedaled hard all the way back to my house. It wasn't until we were safely inside that we realized the sun had already set and the streets were quiet. We had lost track of time at the lakeside.

My father said it was too late for Polly to go home. He said she would stay the night, and he called her parents to tell them so.

That night Polly and I huddled under the covers of my bed and speculated about the world of those who were older than we.

We both knew that Hermit Weaper was just trying to scare us back home. But Polly couldn't let go of his words.

She said, "I don't want my lungs eaten." Then she added, "I don't want to eat them, either. I mean, when we're older."

"Don't worry," I said. I reveled in her nervousness, because it made me feel more keen than my friend. "I'm sure we'll acquire a taste for it."

"Ew," she said, and we giggled.

"Would you rather—" Polly started, then rephrased her theoretical question. "Let's say it's a dark alley. Would you rather meet up with Hermit Weaper or Rosebush Lincoln's brother on a full moon?"

Rosebush Lincoln's brother was sixteen.

"I don't know," I said. "I guess the Hermit."

"I'd rather Rosebush Lincoln's brother."

"Don't say that."

"It's true. They don't really hurt people, you know. It's not true what the Hermit said. They don't eat your—they don't hurt anybody. Except maybe themselves. And each other."

I liked it better when we talked of such things in the fairy-tale terms of lung-eating. It was easier to cope with. If you talked about hurt in the abstract, it was a deeper, more echoey well of a thing.

"They could hurt you," I insisted.

"Not on purpose. They're just teenagers. We'll be like that too one day."

I didn't tell Polly that I had already promised my father I wouldn't be like that. She would have taken it as disloyalty. Much later we tried to sleep, but there were the voices outside. I couldn't forget what Hermit Weaper had said. In my mind there was a picture of Rosebush Lincoln's brother, handsome Billy Lincoln, and there was a hollow cavity in my chest, and where my lungs should have been there was nothing at all, and one of my lungs was actually hanging between Billy Lincoln's teeth, half consumed, deflated and bloody, like a gigantic tongue—and I couldn't breathe, because all my breath was caught in Billy Lincoln's grinning mouth.

———

MY HUSBAND DRIVES us home from the Petersons' party. This is just last night.

It's 12:15, and we are late in relieving the sitter. Jack is itchy with liquor, and he says to me, "You were—you were the sexiest wife at that party."

"Jack."

"No, I'm serious. I'm not kidding around. No one can hold a candle to you."

"I thought the lamb was overcooked. Did you think so? Everyone complimented it, though. Janet prides herself on her lamb."

Then Jack pulls the car over to the side of the road and turns off the ignition.

"Do you want to fool around?" he asks.

"Jack, the babysitter."

"To hell with the babysitter." It's his grand, passionate gesture. He must have me, here in the car, and the rest of the world can burn. "I'll—I'll give her an extra twenty."

The silliness of family men. I chuckle.

He takes offense. "Forget it," he says and goes to start the car. I've hurt him by not being sufficiently quailed by the blustery storm of his sex. It's funny how many ways there are to hurt people. As many ways to hurt as there are species of flower. Whole bouquets of hurt. You do it without even realizing.

"Wait, Jack. I'm sorry."

"Why did you laugh?"

"I don't know. Maybe I was nervous. What if someone sees us?"

"Let them," he says.

So I reach up under my skirt, hook my underpants with my thumbs, and pull them down. He unzips his pants, and I straddle him. While he quakes and gurgles beneath me, I gaze out the windows of the car. The road where we've stopped is indistinguishable from any of the others in the area—a quiet residential neighborhood with sidewalks and shade trees. In truth there is no danger of being caught. The residents of this area are good and decent people. Their lives, after midnight, consist of sleep or the late, late show on television, played at a low volume so as not to wake the children. The streets are empty. The mild breeze dapples the sidewalk with the shadows of leaves in lamplight. But there is no one out there in the dark. No one.

Jack moves under me. I hold his face to my bosom, I kiss the top of his head. In a few moments, he is finished.

He wants to kiss me passionately to show that his love for me doesn't end when his sexual urgency does. He's a nice kisser after all these years.

He rolls down the windows for the rest of the drive home.

On the way, he points to the sky.

"Look," he says. "A full moon."

"I know," I say without raising my eyes. The car drives along in the quiet, fragile night.

"What do you call that one? Octopus Moon? Spanky Moon?"

"Blowfly Moon."

"Blowfly. That's my favorite one!"

I've told him very little about my childhood or the town where I grew up. What little I have told him—for example, that we had names for the different full moons—he finds quaint and charming. He pictures me as a prairie girl, maybe. Or a Mennonite.

His stuff is leaking out of me, a funny, unbothersome tickle between my legs.

In another part of the country, in the small town where I grew up, at this moment, there are packs of young people stalking the streets, naked, their pale flesh glowing, their breath coming fast and angry, their limbs filled with the quivering of strength and movement. Many, tomorrow, will wake torn and bruised.

When we get home, Jack apologizes to the babysitter and gives her extra money. Then he drives her home. While he is gone, I go upstairs, where my son is sleeping. He wakes when I come into the room, reaching toward me, wanting to be picked up.

I look down at him for a few moments, all that wee human greed and desire. I refuse to pick him up, but eventually I do kneel beside his bed and recite to him a rhyme I learned when I was a little girl.

Brittle Moon,
Beggar's Moon,
Worm Moon, more . . .

Pheasant Moon,
Cordial Moon,
Lacuna's bore . . .

Hod Moon,
Blowfly Moon,
Pulse Moon—roar!

Prayer Moon,
Hollow Moon,
Lake Moon's shore.

First you kiss your mommy,
Then you count your fours.
Till you're grown and briny,
Better stay indoors.

He waits eagerly for his favorite part—the part about roaring—and then he roars. He wants to do it again, but I tell him no. I turn on his night-light, which the babysitter has forgotten. Then I leave the room and shut the door behind me. In the upstairs hall, there is only the sound of the grandfather clock ticktocking away.

I have become a mother. I have become a wife.

Soon Jack returns home. We prepare for bed without much talk. I check the locks on the doors downstairs. It is a thing he always asks when I slide into bed next to him. "Did you remember to check the locks?" he asks. And I say, "Yes," and I can see by the expression on his face that he feels safe.

It starts to rain outside, the droplets of water sounding little tin bells in the gutters. Jack begins to snore next to me. The grandfather clock chimes one o'clock.

And what if I were to forget a lock one night? What if I were to leave a door wide open, casting angled shadows in the moonlight? Nothing would happen. In our neighborhood, there is no one out there in the rain, not a single person squalling under the stormy black.

All our skins are dry.

I WONDER ABOUT it sometimes—what kind of girl I might have been, what kind of woman I would be now, if I had grown up somewhere else. California, for instance, where teenagers have barbecues on the beach and bury bottles of beer halfway in the sand to keep them upright. Or New York, where they kiss in the backseats of taxicabs and lie on blankets in the middle of parks surrounded by buildings taller by far than the tallest tree.

Would I now be one of those women on television who are concerned about what the laundry detergent is doing to their children's Little League uniforms? Would I love my husband more or less? My son?

As a teenager, would I have been one of those girls who go to the mall and defend themselves, all giggling, against boys—huddled together like a wagon circle in the food court? Would my great concerns have been college and school dances and fashion?

In my town, expensive clothes were not held in high esteem. Girls bought cheap. Dresses, they tended to get torn apart.

It's impossible for me to make the connection between who I am now and who I was then—as if I died long ago in that town and resurrected somewhere else, with a brain full of another girl's memories.

Except that I miss my father.

They said I had his mind.

Polly admired him as well. She always told me it was okay that I didn't have a mother—that I didn't really need a mother because I had the best father in town. He made Polly and me grilled cheese sandwiches with ham and the tomatoes from the garden that he and I had cultivated with our own hands. Polly liked hers with cocktail toothpicks sticking out of each quarter. He called

19

her Sweet Polly and said that when the time came she would have so many boyfriends she would never be able to choose just one and would have to marry a whole passel of them.

He stood smiling, tall and skinny at the kitchen island. She glowed for him.

———

SUMMERTIMES, POLLY CAME to my house, and my father would greet her at the door.

"Sweet Polly!" he would say. "Lumen's upstairs."

The long, hot days of July, he would turn on the sprinkler in the backyard, and we would put on our swimsuits and play in the dancing water. The sprinkler was on the end of a hose, and it shot a Chinese fan of water in a slow back-and-forth arc that we liked to jump through. The only rule was that every fifteen minutes we had to move the sprinkler to a different part of the lawn to assure balanced coverage. Polly never remembered, but I always did.

We were the same age, but at thirteen it was clear that Polly was developing before I was. Her swimsuit swelled at the chest where mine was loose and puckered. She stood almost a full head taller than I did, and she did cartwheels through the shimmering water, her long limbs a dazzle of strength and nimbleness. When I tried to cartwheel, my body didn't move the way I wanted it to, and I came toppling down into an awkward crouch.

After a while we were tired and simply lay on our stomachs in the grass, liking the feel of the fan of water as it intermittently showered us with cool needles. We lay in single file, our faces just inches from each other, our chins supported on our fists.

"Shell didn't look so good when she came home this morning," Polly said.

Shell was Michelle, Polly's sister, who was fifteen and a half. She'd begun breaching just two months before. The previous night had been the last night of Hod Moon.

"My parents found her sleeping on the lawn this morning," Polly went on.

"With no clothes on?"

"Yeah."

This was something I still could not fathom—the exposure. For as long as I could remember, my father was very careful about knocking on my bedroom door before he entered so that I would not be walked in upon as I was dressing. How did one nude oneself before another person—before the world?

"And also," Polly said, crinkling up her face, "she was beat up pretty bad."

"Really?"

"Yeah. There were bruises and cuts all over her. Plus—"

Polly went silent for a moment. She pulled up some blades of grass and opened her fist to let them fall, but they were wet and stuck to her fingers.

"Plus," she went on, "she was bleeding. You know?"

I said nothing. I was paralyzed—as though I were standing on a precipice, stricken with vertigo, unable even to pull myself back from the edge. This was large, multitudinous. My mind was a color, and the color was red. The needling water on my back felt like it was falling on a version of me that was a long, long way away.

"They put her in the bathtub," Polly said. "I stayed with her when they went downstairs. The water, it turned pink. She says she doesn't remember anything, but I can tell she does. I think she remembers all of it."

For a time, we were both silent. She picked the wet blades of grass off her hand, and I watched her. It was time to move the sprinkler, but I had to know more, and I couldn't break the spell the conversation had put me under.

Finally I mustered the courage to ask a question:

"Did she get pregnant?"

"No," Polly said. "She told me they put her on the pill before she went breach. She said all the parents do it."

I thought about my father. It was difficult for me to imagine him giving me that kind of pill. How would he do it? He could make a joke out of it, bringing it to me on a burgundy pillow, as though I were a princess—and we could pretend it meant nothing. We could pretend my secret and shameful body had nothing to do with it. Or maybe it wouldn't be necessary. I was determined to skip breaching altogether.

"And she said something else," Polly went on.

"What else?"

"See, I was sitting on the toilet next to the tub, and she closed her eyes for a long time, and I thought she was asleep. I was just looking at the pink water and all the dirt that was in it. There were little leaves, and I picked them off the surface. She was so dirty. She came back so dirty."

"What else did she say?"

"So I thought she was asleep, and there was this little twig in her hair and I wanted to take it out for her. So I went to take it out, but when I tried she grabbed my wrist all of a sudden and gave me a look."

"What kind of look?"

"I don't know. I didn't like it."

"Was it angry?"

"No. Not exactly. More just...I don't know. Like a *jungle* look, you know? But it was only for a second, and then she let go of my wrist and smiled at me. That's when she said it. She said it's all right. She said it's nothing to be afraid of. She said it hurts, but it's the good kind of hurt."

"The good kind of hurt?"

"That's what she said."

I didn't want Polly to see that I was confounded by this notion, because she herself seemed to have accepted it as an obvious and universal truth, the potential goodness of hurt. It was important to Polly that she be in the know about all things adult, and she lived by the rule that performance eventually leads to authenticity. So it was difficult to tell what she actually understood and what she was only pretending to understand.

For my part, I squirmed uncomfortably in my ill-fitting swimsuit. These things seemed entirely detached from the books I read, from the math and science I was so adept in the mastery of. I sometimes wondered (as I sometimes still do) if I had gotten off track somehow, if maybe I wasn't as natural as those around me, if perhaps my life were unjoined from the common lives of others.

The way my teachers looked at me, I suspected they could tell I didn't belong. Especially Mr. Hunter, the drama teacher for the high school kids, whose curious and fearsome gaze I was sure followed me wherever I went.

The sprinkler splashed us with its rainy metronome, and there we lay in the growing shadow of my big house, the two of us, blasted through with the abject discomfiture of our tiny places in the world.

We were fourteen by the following summer, and Polly had developed even further, her hips having shaped themselves into curves—which I thought must have been in some way responsible for the new saunter in her walk. There was still no shape to me at all. I wore colorful dresses and put ribbons in my hair as evidence that I was, in fact, a girl. I stood naked before my bedroom mirror and, with the intention of luring out my stubborn and elusive womanhood, recited Edna St. Vincent Millay poetry I had learned by heart. I smeared honey on my chest, believing it might help me grow breasts. Honeybees are industrious—they can build anything. But the poetry seemed not to possess any magic, and my father found the sticky honey-bear bottle on my nightstand one morning and explained that it was bad for my teeth to snack on it in the middle of the night.

Over the previous year, Polly had begun spending more time with Rosebush Lincoln and the other girls from school. She never excluded me, and I made a concerted effort to join together with all the girls when they sunbathed by the lake or got a ride into the next town to go shopping at the thrift stores. But Rosebush always made it clear that I was only to be tolerated because I was allied with Polly, that my visa into the world of Rosebush Lincoln was temporary and most definitely revocable. I was put on notice.

When there's nothing else to do, you can always watch the birds. The finches, their twitchy and mechanical little bodies—they go where they want to go, driven by impulse and instinct. The finch does not dwell in consideration of its nature or the nature of the world. It is brazen and unapologetic. It hammers its little bird heart against the blustering wind, and its death is as beautiful as its life.

———

IT WAS THAT year, that summer, that I followed the other girls to the abandoned mine. What did they used to mine there? I want to say gypsum, because gypsum is a lovely word and a gyp-

sum mine is a pretty thought to have. It was on a different end of
the woods from the lake, and the entrance to it was at the base of
a small overgrown quarry. The parents of our town instructed us
to stay away from the quarry because of lurking dangers, but it
was always beautiful and peaceful to me. In certain seasons there
was rivulet of melted snow that came out of the mountains and
trickled irregularly down the stony sides of the quarry and ran
finally into the mouth of the mine. If you went there alone, you
could just listen to that plink-plonk of water and be tranquil. You
could lie in nests of leaves, all those dying oranges and reds, all
those deep browns that come from what green used to be, shaded
by the old-growth trees that leaned over the lip of the quarry, and
you could be nothing at all.

The mouth of the mine itself was weeded over with sumac
and creeper vine, and there were two sets of mine-cart rails
that emerged from the opening like tongues and ended abruptly
on the floor of the quarry. You could wonder for hours about
where those tracks went. Miles of underground passages beneath
the town, maybe a whole underground city, with tunnels that
opened in your basement! I explored our basement once, looking
for an opening into hidden Atlantis—but all I found were forgotten mousetraps with hunks of dried-up cheese.

It was almost exactly a year after my conversation with Polly
under the sprinklers, and her sister, Shell, was still breaching.

"I don't think she's ever going to stop," Polly said miserably.
"What if she doesn't stop before I start?"

"You? But we're only fourteen."

"It's not unheard of. My parents said it's not unheard of. It's
different for different people. Plus I'm developing early in other
ways."

"Well, I don't think it's going to happen yet."

"It better not. My parents are going to throw a big party for her when she's done. That's how relieved they'll be. They said I'm not going to be half as bad as her."

It seemed as though this were a source of disappointment for Polly.

So when she came to my house on a weekday morning in July, telling me that everyone was going to the quarry and that we should hurry to join them, I followed her. If I didn't follow her, I reasoned, I might be left behind forever—a child who simply misses the chance to grow up.

So we took our bikes, pedaling hard and purposefully. On other days we might have been leisurely about our pace, weaving in lazy arcs back and forth across the empty roads. But that day was different.

Arriving at the quarry, we saw four girls already there—Adelaide Warren, Sue Foxworth, and Idabel McCarron with her little sister, Florabel, in tow. We scrambled down into the quarry, bringing tiny avalanches of white silt pebbles after us.

"Where's Rosebush?" was the first thing Polly said as a greeting to the other girls.

"I don't know," said Adelaide. "Look what we found."

We all gathered in a circle around the thing on the ground. At first I couldn't figure out what it was—a wispy thing like smoke or frayed burlap, it moved with the breeze. Hair. It was a long skein of mousy brown girl hair.

"It was ripped out," Sue said.

"How can you tell?"

"Look."

She reached down, gathered its tips into a bunch, and picked it up. Dangling from the base of the lock was a scabby little flake that I quickly understood to be scalp skin.

Florabel shrieked and started running in circles.

"Shut it," her sister said.

"Whose is it?" Polly asked.

"I don't know," Sue said. "Better be a local girl."

A fierce territoriality is the by-product of uncommon local practices. Whatever happened in our town was manageable as long as it stayed in our town. We were not encouraged to socialize with people from elsewhere. We were taught to smile at them as they passed through. Every now and then some teenager from a neighboring town would get stuck here during a full moon—and the next day that outsider would usually go home goried up and trembling. That's when trouble came down on us—authorities from other places going from door to door, kneeling down in front of us kids trying to get us to reveal something. But for the most part, people left us alone. Ours was a cursed town to outsiders.

Just then there was a sound in the trees above, and we gazed up to find Rosebush Lincoln standing next to her bike on the lip of the quarry.

"I'm here, creeps," she said and let her bike fall to the ground. Strapped to her back was a pink teddy-bear backpack whose contents seemed heavy enough to make it an awkward process to climb down to the floor of the quarry. Once at the bottom, though, she sloughed off the pack and came over to where we stood.

"What's that?" she asked, pointing to the hair that Sue still held in her fingers.

"Hair."

"Uh-huh," Rosebush said. "I know where that came from. Mindy Kleinholt. My brother says she's been going around all week with a new hairstyle to cover the empty spot. Happens."

Rosebush shrugged with a casual world-weariness that made her seem thirty-three rather than fourteen.

Sometimes the thunderclouds gather overhead, and sometimes your haughty cat refuses its food, and sometimes you are
partially scalped in a moonlit quarry. Such things are a matter of
chance and hazard.

Rosebush, whose lack of interest in the hair made everyone
forget it at once, unzipped her teddy-bear backpack to reveal
what she had been struggling to carry: six tall silver cans of beer
connected at the tops with plastic rings. She set the cans on the
ground before us, stepped back, and presented them with an ex-
pansive gesture of her arms.

"Behold," she said. "My brother stole it from the grocery
store, and then I stole it from him."

"It's double stolen," said Adelaide, crouching down in front of
the beer and running her finger in a delicate circle along the top
edge of one of the cans. She was fairylike, always, in her movements. "It's still cold," she added.

"It's iced," explained Rosebush. "We have to drink it before it
gets skunked."

So she passed around the cans to the other girls. I took one
but found it difficult to open, so Polly opened it for me.

"Where's one for me?" Florabel said.

"You don't get one," said her older sister.

"Cheers, queers," Rosebush said, raising hers.

Everyone drank. I lifted mine in imitation of drinking, but I
didn't let much get into my mouth. Just enough to wet my lips
and tongue. The taste was awful, like moldy carbonated weed
milk. The other girls crinkled their noses as well.

Rosebush lectured us.

"You have to drink it fast," she said. "Hold your nose if you
need to."

"I'm going to enjoy mine throughout the afternoon," said Sue.

"Me too," said Adelaide.

"Suit yourselves," Rosebush said and shrugged.

We sat on the stones, holding our cool cans of beer. I stopped pretending to drink from the can, because nobody seemed to be paying attention to whether I was or not. Instead I put my fingers in the icy trickle of water running down out of the hills.

At one point the conversation turned to boys, and Rosebush brought up Petey Meechum.

"We nearly kissed the other day after school," she announced.

"What's nearly?" asked Sue.

"Nearly," Rosebush repeated in a tone that suggested any further calls for clarification were forbidden.

"He once told me I had pretty hands," said Adelaide, then she held them up for the benefit of any admirers.

"Anyway," Rosebush went on, irritated, "Petey Meechum is the kind of boy who puts girls into one of two categories. You're either a potential lover or you're a permanent friend."

At the words "permanent friend," her gaze landed on Polly and me. Polly looked down, submissive. I made my face blank, like cinder block.

"How can you tell the difference?" Adelaide asked.

Rosebush seemed about to attack, but then she shrugged it off, as would a predator that grows bored with easy prey.

"Believe me," she said, "when you're nearly kissed by him, you can tell."

Then she addressed me amicably.

"On a related topic, do you know who I heard was actually interested in you, Lumen?"

"Who?" I asked miserably.

"Roy Ruggle," said Rosebush.

"Blackhat Roy?"

29

"He's only got eight toes," Polly contributed. It was well known that Blackhat Roy had exploded two toes off his right foot when he was trying to modify a Roman candle with a pair of pliers two years before.

"But he's dark," said Rosebush, "like Lumen. And he's more her height. Also, he never goes to church, and neither does Lumen. You know, I sit right next to Petey in church. He tells me about his grandmother who died. Did he ever tell you about her, Lumen? You can tell by the way he talks about her he knows about pain. To endure suffering—it's the most romantic thing of all, don't you think?"

———

TO ENDURE SUFFERING. I wonder how much people really endure. They talk about heartbreak, and they turn their faces away. But heartbreak is really the least of it, a splinter in the skin. Hearts mend. Most tragedy is overcome with prideful righteousness. The tear on the cheek, like a pretty little insect, wending its way over your jaw, down your sensitive neck, under your collar.

I wonder how much suffering my husband has endured. Or Janet Peterson, with her dry, overcooked lamb. They are easily horrified, easily disgusted. They turn their heads away from the simplest and most mundane adversity.

On the other hand, to be bound by your own fate, to feel the eager lashes of a grinning world all up and down your nerve endings. To bleed—to make others bleed. To know there is no end of things. To become something that you can never unbecome. There are in the world sufferings that are not stage pieces but rather whole lives.

Rosebush Lincoln. I was shut to her that day.

Yet those words of hers, even now, recall to me the lovely, hungry smell of autumn leaves.

———

JUST AS ROSEBUSH Lincoln was extolling the virtues of endured suffering, there was a sound in the trees above the quarry, and we all gazed up to find a boy on the verge—as though we had conjured boyness with our witchy voices and manifested a puerile sprite from the morning dew itself.

"It's Hondy," said Rosebush. "He must've followed me all the way from town."

Hondy Pilt held the handles of his bicycle and stared down at us in his misty and bloated way. He said nothing. Hondy Pilt rarely spoke, and his eyes never looked at you exactly—instead they looked right over your shoulder, which made you feel that you were just some insufficient forgery of your real self and that your real self was invisible, somewhere behind you.

So Rosebush invited him to join us, and for the next hour she forced him to drink beer and she put wildflowers in his hair and she told him to sit a certain way so that she could use his bulky body to prop up her own and gaze at the clouds above.

I felt bad for Hondy Pilt, but he didn't seem to mind being used as Rosebush Lincoln's lounge chair, and I wondered if that was his particular magic—to be still content with the world in all its pretty little injustices.

It wasn't long before Rosebush got a new idea—which was to send Hondy Pilt adventuring into the abandoned mine. We all looked at the mouth of the mine, weeded and overgrown, a dark void chipped out of the earth, like the hollow well of a giant's missing tooth. We had heard stories of our older brothers and sisters spelunking the mine with flashlights, discovering networks of underground rooms, rusted mining equipment, bottomless shafts easily stumbled into. Our parents warned us against the mine, because a boy once lost his way in the maze of passages and never came back out—but every time they tried to board up the entrance, the breachers, who did not like to be disinvited from places, would tear it open during the next full moon.

"I don't know, Rosebush," said Idabel. "I don't think it's a good idea."

"Come on. Hondy wants to do it. Don't you, Hondy?"

She raised him to his feet and wound her arm in his so that they looked like a bride and groom, and the boy smiled at the sky.

"Ro'bush," he said in his indistinct way.

So she led him to the mouth of the mine, and we all gathered around, too—because nobody could stop Rosebush from sacrificing Hondy Pilt to the mine.

"Go on, Hondy," she said. "Go on now."

He looked into the darkness, then at his own feet, then in the direction of the girl at his side.

She encouraged him with sweeping hand gestures.

"Go on," she said. "Bring me a treasure. Find me a gold nugget."

And he went. While we all watched from the mouth of the mine, he moved forward step by step.

"Rosebush," Idabel admonished.

"Shush," said Rosebush, her eyes never leaving her knight errant. In fact, the farther he went into the dark, the more intent she became, her fists clenching themselves into tight balls, her breath coming faster, an expression on her face like some excruciating ecstasy. I could hear her breathing.

He stopped once, turned, and looked back at us, as if to be reassured.

"Warrior!" Rosebush called to him in a strange, whispery voice.

Then he moved forward again, slowly, until his form was lost completely to the dark.

We waited. A caught breeze blustered through the quarry, rustling the dried sumac, blowing strands of hair in a ticklish way across our lips. We used our fingers to tuck the hair behind our ears, and we waited.

Then, from the deep echoey dark of the mine, we heard a hiss, a monstrous, spitting hiss. Then Hondy Pilt's voice, a low, whining complaint, followed by quick movement—a crash, the sound of feet advancing fast in our direction, his voice again, miserable and high—and behind it all that feral hissing.

Then we saw him disclosed from the dark, his panicked bulk running toward us.

And then we believed in monsters, hissing creatures like aged demons unearthed from the dry crust of the world. We ran. The woods came alive with the sound of our shrieks. Birds fled and crickets hushed, and we turned and ran from the mouth of the mine, squealing, across the floor of the quarry and up the opposite slope, our fingers digging into the loose gravel for desperate purchase.

We were halfway up the side of the quarry when we heard a loud cry of pain below. Hondy Pilt had emerged from the mine at full speed and had tripped over Rosebush Lincoln's pink backpack. He now lay curled into a ball and howling on the floor of the quarry. It would get him. He was a goner now—food for the beasts of the earth—and we left him and hid behind the trunks of trees.

Except that then, beyond him, we saw emerge from the mine the monster that had chased him out of its den, hissing and spitting the whole way. It was a possum. Assured that its home was no longer in danger, the creature turned and scurried back into the dark depths of the mine.

Sometimes it happens this way. Your greatest fears in the dark turn out to be nothing more than angry rodents and zealous girls with pink backpacks. Or nothing less.

———

IT WAS ALL discovered. Hondy Pilt's forearm was fractured from his fall in the quarry. He would have to wear a cast for the next three weeks, and Rosebush Lincoln would be the first to sign her name on it in pink marker. We suffered little in comparison. Our palms were covered with tiny abrasions from our quick scramble up the side of the quarry. But it was nothing a coat of stinging Bactine couldn't fix.

Our parents discovered we had been drinking beer, and they intuited that we had been responsible somehow for Hondy Pilt's accident.

The orchestration of blame was intricate and devious—it was decided that I would take the blame for everything.

After we delivered Hondy Pilt back to the hospital in town, Rosebush Lincoln took me aside to have a talk.

"You have to say it was you," she said, her voice casual but uncompromising.

"It was me what?"

"The beer. And Hondy, telling him to go into the mine. It has to be you."

"Why?"

"They won't do anything to you. You're too good."

I didn't say anything.

"Look, Lumen. It was an accident. I like Hondy. I didn't want to hurt him. I'm already in trouble for a million things. My parents'll kill me. They're not nice. They're not like your dad. Please."

So I did it. While I held my hands palm upward over the sink and my father poured hydrogen peroxide on them, I told him it was all my fault.

"Is that right?" he said.

"Yes. I brought the beer. I told Hondy Pilt to go inside the mine."

"Really? Where did you get the beer?"

"I stole it."

"Stole it!" He smiled down at me. "So you're a thief now, are you?"

"Just that once."

I looked down at my palms, the hydrogen peroxide foaming in all the cuts.

"And you made Hondy Pilt go into the mine?" he asked.

"Yes."

"Why?"

It had never occurred to me that someone would ask why I had done the things I claimed to do—just as I had never thought to ask Rosebush why she was Rosebush. Why ask? People are like characters in books. They are defined by their actions—not the other way around.

"I don't know," I said pathetically.

The smile never left his face. He narrowed his eyes at me, trying to puzzle through my gambit.

"So . . . well, all these moral lapses—I guess you should be punished."

"I guess so."

"Let's see." He pursed his lips and tapped his chin with his fingertips. "What time is your curfew?"

What he meant was between full moons. Everyone had the same curfew when the moon was full: sundown.

"Ten o'clock."

"All right, then. Let's make it nine thirty for the rest of the week."

He went back to tending my palms, rinsing away the hydrogen peroxide and bandaging the cuts.

But something wasn't right. The reason he didn't know what time my curfew was because I was almost always home for the night by eight o'clock, hunched up on one corner of the couch, reading a book. His punishment was absurd—not a real punishment. And that's when it occurred to me: he didn't believe my confession. He was humoring me.

My suspicions were borne out the next day when Rosebush Lincoln confronted me on the street outside the drugstore where they sold colorful ices.

"You were supposed to take the blame," she said.

"I did," I assured her. "I did. I told my dad I did it."

"No, you didn't."

"I swear."

"Then how come I'm the one being punished for everything? How come Idabel's mom told my mom I was a bad influence?"

"I don't know."

"You're a liar." She pointed one long finger at my chest.

"I'm not. I told my dad it was me." I paused. "It's just—I don't think he believed me."

Rosebush Lincoln looked disgusted.

"Oh, that's just great. You can't even convince people you've done something wrong when you *try*. Just stay away from me from now on."

———

AT THAT AGE we didn't know what we did. Or, rather, we understood that it was impossible for things to go any differently. We were too young to change the course of bodies in motion.

My husband, Jack, he's a schoolteacher, but a new kind of schoolteacher, a kind we didn't have when I was a child. He works with kids who are At Risk—as though safety were such a common commodity that you could easily hang a tag from all those young people who didn't possess it. He has one girl—Natalie, who prefers to be called Nat—who sneers and curses and spits sunflower seeds at his shoes while he's trying to have regular, humane conversations with her. She has been sent to the principal's office many times for fighting with boys and other girls. She, too, knows about tearing out hair.

Trying to get her to rationalize her behavior, Jack asks her why she does the things she does.

"I don't know" is her reply. She says it as though the question is an absurd one and has no true answer.

I am curious how she would respond if I had my hands squeezed around her throat. (Would her muscles grow taut, wild?) But I also understand the authenticity of what she says. People like to talk to teenagers about consequences. They like to explain how certain actions may lead to reactions that are un-desired. But this is the wrong conversation to have. Teenagers understand inherently how one thing leads to another—but to them the point is moot, because the action that initiates its conse-quence is just as inscrutable as the consequence itself. The mouth that spits at my husband might as well not be her mouth at all. His shoes might as well be anyone's shoes, the room a room far away in some other nondescript American suburb.

That is the way of the young. They see something we don't: the great machines that turn us, indifferent to our will, this way and that.

So I wasn't angry at Rosebush Lincoln for asking me to lie to my father. And I wasn't angry at her when she shunned me for not having lied well enough. And I wasn't even angry about the things she did to Hondy Pilt. All she did was play her part in a tableau that, as far as I was concerned, couldn't have gone any other way.

Sometimes, when I was a girl, I climbed onto the roof through the gabled window of my second-story bedroom. From the chimney peak, I could see all the way up and down the street. It was as tall as my world got, and it was wonderful. Those summer evenings, I would lie on the sloping shake, securing myself with the soles of my sneakers, watching the stars come out. From my meager height, I beheld the whole entire world as I knew it. And what could be bad about all this?

CHAPTER 2

My name is Lumen. My father says my mother gave me the name because it means light. I am a light, and I light the way. That's what the North Star and guardian angels do. But my name also means this:

$$\Phi_v = I_v \cdot \Omega$$

Φ_v is me, Lumen. Lumen as a unit. I_v is how many candelas. Candela is another beautiful name. I wish I knew someone named Candela so we could be Lumen and Candela, and we would define each other in measurements of light. The mathematics of illumination. Ω is another unit, steradians, but that is an angular measurement—it defines the direction in which a light is shining. If the light is democratic, if it is loving and gentle and good, if it doesn't prefer one angle over another, then the equation becomes even more beautiful:

$$\Phi_v = 4\pi I_v$$

Because there are four pi steradians in a perfect, all-encompassing sphere.

Here I am, now matured to fifteen years of age, and my grades are excellent, the best in school, and I am also smaller than all the other girls in my class, delayed in my growth—stunted, even—and I stay in the library after the final bell rings to look up my name in the large, dusty encyclopedias.

Who could know me? Not my mother, who was dead before I remember. Not my friends, who seem to have found their way into an idea of adulthood. Maybe not even my father, who is generous to a fault and believes so heartily in the errorlessness of me that I wear myself out with being his good daughter. So maybe these books know for certain who I am. They seem so absolute about what they know. They etch my name in perfect symbols. They draw lines to define me, they show how Lumen equates to other delicious little glyphs. I want to be the precision of these equations. Then I could justify who I am.

So yes, there I am in the library, turning the pages of encyclopedias. My ankles itch under my socks. Many of the other boys and girls in my class, Polly included, have gone down to the lake to swim. The boys have tied a rope to a tree branch that overhangs the lake. They swing out over the water and drop in, like dumplings. Once in, they make a game of submarining their way to the girls and grabbing their legs to startle them. Some boys flip the girls head over tail. When this is done, the mandate of the flipped girls seems to be initial outrage followed by affable censure. I have gone to the lake, too, on occasion, but mostly I sit on the shore and watch. When I do go into the water, I wait patiently to be pinched or tumbled by the underwater boys—but perhaps I am prey too meager for their tastes. My hair stays dry.

I love the smell of the encyclopedia. When no one is looking, I bury my nose deep into the crease of the binding and
breathe in the book. No one else does this. I do not witness
any of the other students sniffing the pages of *Great Expectations*
when the paperbacks are handed out in our English class. Me,
rather than putting my nose to it, I casually fan the pages with
my thumb, which sends into the air the pleasant aroma of wood
pulp and ink.

In the library I sit at a carrel, the farthest one in the back corner, and I search through piles of books looking to understand
my name. The dictionary does me little good, but I have no hard
feelings toward it—I love the way the pages are thumb-notched
to make the finding of particular letters easier. If you look at
each page individually, it has a unique half-moon cutout at the
edge.

In another book I find this, which is the equation for lumi-
nance, which I take to mean the quality of luminousness, the
quality of me:

$$L_v = \frac{d^2 \Phi_v}{dA \, d\Omega \, cos\theta}$$

I recognize again my symbol, the superimposed I and O together. One and zero. Something and nothing. On and off at the
same time. I look up the Greek alphabet to discover what my
symbol is called. It is phi, and it can be pronounced either fee or
fye—which are the first two syllables of the giant's song as he
is threatening to eat Jack, who went up the bean stalk: Fe-fi-fo-
fum, I smell the blood of an Englishman.

Blood. It always comes back to blood. You start with light,

and you end with blood. But not mine. I am fifteen, I sit in the library with my itchy ankles, and I have not gotten my period yet. I am the last of anyone I know. I am afraid of blood, disgusted by it, and maybe my own fear has suppressed my bleeding.

I go back to the equations, which are black-and-white, pure and lovely.

I find another equation. The best one yet:

$$I_v = 683 \int_0^\infty \bar{y}(\lambda) \cdot \frac{dI_e(\lambda)}{d\lambda} d\lambda$$

It's the equation for luminous intensity. That's how much calculation is required to measure the intensity of me. You see how my symbol, the phi, is gone? The candela is still there, but the lumen is nowhere to be seen. Maybe that means you can't measure the intensity of a thing in relation to itself. You have to put it against others and measure the difference between the light given off by each one.

You have to put Lumen in the lake and see how still she stands, skimming the surface with her pale palms, embarrassed at the flatness of her own chest, noiseless and inert amid the raucous clamor of other boys and girls.

———

MANY OF THE people in my grade went breach that year. I stayed home and studied. Many of the girls acquired and lost a series of boyfriends. I listened to old records my father told me he listened to when he was my age. Many of the bodies around me in school seemed to be undergoing some torturous flux—people coming to school not just with red pimples on their faces but also with rips and tears in the overused skin of their arms and necks. They were savaged. My skin remained smooth and unscored.

Polly came to my house one day, the second day of Worm Moon, and showed me a large purplish bruise on her arm.

"How did you get that?" I asked.

"I don't know," she said.

"How could you not know? Does it hurt?"

"It happened, Lumen," she said. "Last night it happened. I went breach."

"You did?"

"Look."

She showed me again her bruise.

"What was it like?"

"I don't remember very much."

They said you remembered the breaches better after you had been through a few of them. Very few people could remember their first.

I looked at the bruise, and she displayed her arm proudly.

"It looks like a hand," I said.

She tried to twist her head around to see it better.

"See?" I said, pointing at the pattern. "One, two, three, four. Like fingers."

"Someone probably grabbed me?"

"Maybe."

"I'll ask around. Maybe somebody else remembers."

"Do you have anything else?"

She blushed. She knew what I was asking.

"I don't think so," she said. "I don't know."

Then I told her something that was a lie.

I said, "I wish I could have been there with you."

I had no desire to go breach. The thought of running wild,

that mortification, made me clammy and sick. But I was trying to be a good and decent friend.

She believed what I told her. Most people my age looked forward to the breach. It meant you had become something else. You were no longer a child. You were a true and natural person.

Clutching my shoulder with her hand, she reassured me.

"It'll happen for you soon," she said.

I looked down at my diminutive frame, my bony, nondeveloped chest.

"I don't think so," I said.

"Sure it will. Probably next month. Then we'll go out together."

I turned away, but in the mirror I caught her glancing apprehensively at my stubborn body.

"It's going to happen soon," she reiterated. "It happens to everyone."

Of course that was the common thinking. It happened to everyone in our little town. But I wasn't so sure it *had* to be that way. Though Polly couldn't see them, my teeth were clenched tight inside my mouth. She didn't know it, but I had made a determination many years ago that I still clung to as though it were a fierce religion. I wouldn't go breach. I wouldn't do it.

My mother hadn't, and neither would I.

I wouldn't.

———

IT WASN'T SOMETHING I could look up in books, so in order to learn more about the process I had to undertake a course of research that involved keeping secret notes on the things I heard from others. Of Polly I could ask questions directly—and she, before her own breach, provided much information from her experiences with her sister and her sister's friends. I could query my father on a few details, but it made me uncomfortable to speak with him about such things. Some of the teachers talked about it in school, but their approach to the topic was more abstract than I would have preferred. Ms. Stanchek, who taught us sex ed, referred to it obliquely and in cultural terms, citing breaching as one of the "many local customs that play a large role in determining how young people are introduced to adulthood." She went on to say, "Some cultures are very protective of their young people and try to keep them shielded from life as long as possible. Other cultures"—and here she winked at us—"drop you right into the cauldron to see if you can float." I wrote down her words verbatim, because her analogy was baffling to me. If you found yourself in a cauldron, whether you floated was not the issue.

Mr. Hunter, who taught English during the day and drama after school, referred to breaching in his discussion of *Lord of the Flies.* "If you want to understand these characters," he said, "think about how you feel when the moon is full. We might be mysteries even to ourselves. Do you know what you're capable of? Do you really know?"

His eyes fell on me, and my stomach went sideways. I looked down, focusing on my pencil tip pressing hard on the white paper. He was an outsider, having moved into our town only around five years ago. He couldn't truly understand our ways, but he liked to speak of them in provocative terms. I liked him and didn't like him at the same time. There was something in him that I needed magic to ward off.

When my notebook on the subject of breaching was filled, about halfway through my sophomore year in high school, I felt that I had a fair understanding of the process—even a larger and more nuanced understanding than many of my peers, who were going through it firsthand. I had filled in the details little by little over the years, assembling the mystery of it as I would a jigsaw puzzle—certain aspects of the picture becoming clear before others.

Here's the way it worked.

As a general rule, when people in my town reached a certain age—anywhere between thirteen and sixteen—they ran wild. When exactly this would happen was a mystery. For some boys it coincided with their voices getting deeper; for some girls it came with the arrival of their first period—but these were rare harmonies. Our bodies are unfathomable. They resonate with so many things—it's impossible to know what natures they sing to.

When people breached, they cycled with the moon. When the moon was full (usually three nights each month), those who were breaching went feral. The adults stayed indoors with the younger children on those nights, because in the streets ran packs of teenagers—most of them naked, as though clothes were something they had grown beyond—whooping and hollering, crying out violent and lascivious words to each other, to the night, to those holed up in houses. They fought with each other, brutally. They went into the woods to engage in acts of sex.

My father referred to the full-moon nights as bacchanals, but a bacchanal, I learned from the encyclopedia, had to do with Dionysus, the wine god, and it refers specifically to drunken revelries. The breachers were almost never drunk—unless they had gotten drunk before the sun went down. Their indulgences came from a place deeper than wine or virtue or vice.

The mornings after the full-moon nights, the breachers found their ways home and were tended to by their parents, who understood that this was the way of the town and there was nothing to be done about it. Sometimes people got hurt, sometimes seriously—and it was accepted that the damage was simply a physical corollary of the deleterious effects of getting older and being alive in the world. My town had a certain secret pride in that it refused to cosmeticize the realities of adulthood.

And of course the breach was temporary—it was just a stage. It occurred only three nights a month, and for each individual it lasted only for around a year. After that time you were a true adult, and the next time the full moon rose you stayed inside with the others and listened to the howls in the distance and were only just reminded of your time in the wild.

Some people called it coming of age—as though you were ageless prior to that time, as though aging were something you enter by going through a doorway. Did that mean that coming of age was the beginning of dying? I looked it up in the encyclopedia—all the cultural and religious rituals associated with coming of age. In Christianity there were confirmations, in Judaism bar mitzvahs. The Apache had a process called na'ii'ees—which was a beautiful word to look at—but that was just for girls, and I never found what the boys' equivalent was. The Amish had their Rumspringa—and this was as close to our breaching as I was able to find. The sober toleration of wildness. The trial by fire. The wide-eyed gaze upon the violent and colorful sins of the world. Some of the articles I read directed me to something that seemed at first to have nothing to do with coming-of-age rites: mass hysteria. Some people believed that such rituals were related to the kind of localized group thought that led to the Salem witch trials. For my part, I never knew how you could tell an illegitimate witch from a real

Jesus or vice versa, so I was always careful to give concession to any magic that might be at hand.

I asked my father why it was called a breaching, and he did not know. It had just always been called that, he said.

I found nothing about it in the encyclopedia, of course, but right where the article on breaching should have been there was instead an article on breeching—which was a rite of passage for boys who grew up in the sixteenth and seventeenth centuries. It was called breeching because it was the first time in their lives that the boys wore breeches, or pants. Up until that point they wore little dressing gowns. I was tickled by the idea of all those mighty men in history, like Louis XIV, growing up in dresses—I had not known such a thing occurred. Breeching happened earlier, though, between the ages of two and five. Still, it was considered a significant moment in the boys' development into men.

So I liked thinking our breaching was related somehow to that antique practice.

Of course the difference in spelling must have been significant. I looked up breach in the dictionary. "A legal infraction." Definitely. "A break or a rupture." Plenty was broken, plenty ruptured. "A fissure made in a fortification." That one stumped me for a while until it occurred to me that the civilized world, the daytime world, is a kind of fortification against nature and night and brutishness—then it made sense.

But it was the fifth definition of the word that intrigued me most. Apparently breach is also the word for what a whale does when it breaks the surface of the water and leaps into the air.

I wrote that in a box in my research notes, and I drew a picture of a whale bursting from the surface of the ocean. It seemed at odds with the other definitions, and yet at the same time not.

When I slept I dreamed of whales, huge seabound creatures, mustering their power, changing their course, diving deep and then swimming up in a straight vertical, from the dark depths of the ocean floor through the murk to where the light penetrates, up farther and farther, their bodies all muscle in the act of violating the logic of their natural home, thrusting themselves upward, crashing through the surface, feeling the unwet open air on their barnacled skin, taking flight for one tiny moment—taking flight.

———

THEN IT CHANCED to happen that my life became joined with the lives of others.

That's how it occurs, just like that, like the passage of midnight, the hand of the clock creeping past the midpoint of twelve. The minute before midnight and the one after are practically the same, except that they are a full calendar day apart. That's what happened to me. One day things were different.

It was in the tenth grade, and it happened, really, because of Blackhat Roy Ruggle. It was during lunch in the cafeteria, and I was sitting at the table next to Rosebush Lincoln's when he approached her. Rosebush was in tears because earlier in the week her father had initiated divorce proceedings against her mother and had gone to live in a house the next town over, and earlier that day she had also received a C on an English paper.

"What is she crying for?" said Blackhat Roy to anyone who would listen. He was gypsy dark, with black hair that was always a little greasy. He was short, but there was an inherent ferociousness in him that you wouldn't want to see any taller. There might have been something handsome about him if it weren't for the nastiness.

Rosebush tried to ignore him.

"No, seriously," Roy went on, declaiming in a loud voice that hushed those within its range. "I want to know. What is she crying for? Is she worried she won't get into Notre Dame? And then what? What's a Rosebush who doesn't go to Notre Dame?"

"Stop it," said Rosebush, hiding her face in the crook of her arm and allowing herself to be comforted by Jenny Stiles, who had the shortest hair of all the girls in school.

"Oh, wait—I get it," said Roy. "See, the last time I got a C, the principal gave me a fucking trophy—so I guess it's all relative. And what she's worried about, see—what she's worried about is that if she gets a C, then that's her first step to becoming like me."

"Cut it out, Roy," somebody else said.

"Stop it," said Rosebush.

But he leaned in close to her.

"Take a look, Rosebush. It's your future talking. After you fail out of school, we'll get married and have a barrelful of kids. We'll feed them cat food and squirrels and pray every night before we go to bed that little Festus won't burn down the neighbor's house. My father's hit the road, so you won't have to deal with him getting drunk and groping you at the wedding. Hey, wait a minute—do you think that's why your dad left? Shame? Do you think he'll give a toast at our wedding?"

"Stop it, stop it, stop it!" cried Rosebush. She stood suddenly, escaped the grasp of Jenny Stiles, and began beating her little fists against Blackhat Roy, who backed away slowly, hands in the air to show he was not fighting back—a cruel, bemused expression on his face.

Then, as I watched, others intervened. Petey Meechum was there first, pushing himself between Rosebush and Roy.

"Stop!" he said to Roy. "Leave her alone, asshole."

There was a sudden stillness as everyone waited for Roy to explain himself. He looked around, and a sourness crept into his face. What he said was this:

"Cunt."

That was another magic word, I realized that day, because of the power it had over people. They cringed as if struck, as if that single syllable were a weapon more powerful than teeth or fists. It was a dangerous word.

Blackhat Roy walked away then, but I heard something else that maybe no one else heard. It was something he said to himself, under his breath, while everyone else was rushing to Rosebush to comfort her.

"She doesn't get to cry," he said.

I didn't understand what he meant, but then again I did. Still, I felt sorry for Rosebush and her gone father and her C.

It was the very next period when I did something I never would have done if I had had the time to really think it through. The class was history, and we were taking a test. Rosebush sniffled miserably over hers. Me, I answered the questions without much difficulty. It was all material that I had put on flash cards for myself earlier in the week, while, I imagined, Rosebush's father had been moving from room to room in his house identifying what was his and what was his wife's.

Blackhat Roy was also in that class, and when he asked to use the bathroom I had an idea. I waited two minutes, then asked if I could use the bathroom as well.

Outside the room, I turned left down the empty hallway toward the boys' room rather than right toward the girls'. I could smell the smoke coming from the restroom, so I knew he was in there. There was a fire alarm on the wall to the left of the door, and then I watched my hand rise up and pull the red lever down.

I ran the other way down the hall so that I could be seen emerging from the girls' room while everyone poured into the hallways amid the screeching bells.

Funny. Sometimes the whole world moves just for you.

But why did I do it?

For one thing, it saved Rosebush. The history test, having been compromised, would need to be rescheduled. But that wasn't really why I did it. Not really.

What happened was this. The principal called Blackhat Roy into his office and accused him of pulling the fire alarm. No one thought to accuse me of anything, even though I was also out of the classroom at the time the alarm went off. I was Lumen Fowler. I was a good student. I was childlike of stature, and I was unimpeachable.

They couldn't prove Roy had done anything, but they didn't need to. In the process of being accused, he grabbed a glass paperweight from the principal's desk and threw it through the window of the office onto the lawn outside, where it almost struck a fourth grader passing by. That was enough to get him suspended for two weeks.

Rather than simply being subject to them, I had wanted to know what it felt like to *be* one of the forces in this world.

———

BUT PETEY MEECHUM saw. The next day he found me tucked into the back carrel of the library, where I liked to be with my books.

"You did it," he said. "I saw you."

I panicked. I gathered my books, stuffed them quickly into my knapsack.

"Why did you?" he said. "I just want to know. Did you know he'd get in trouble?"

"I don't know," I said, trying to get around him. I didn't like being cornered.

"Wait a minute," he said as I pushed my way past him. "I won't tell anyone," he called after me. "I just—I didn't know who you were."

Of course we had known each other for many years, but he meant something bigger. See how easy it is to become someone else? It happens all of a sudden—just like that. A ticktock of motion.

So who am I now?

———

THE YEAR THAT Polly went breach, I had not yet figured out that life sometimes requires contingency plans for the loss of those close to you—that the more people you have buffering you against solitude, the less catastrophic it is when one of them disappears. Among people my age, I only really had Polly—and when she went breach, I no longer had her. She didn't turn on me. It's not that. She had simply been initiated into a corps I wasn't part of. More frequently than not, our casual conversations in the school hallways (usually on the topic of test scores and the relative fairness of teachers) were interrupted by other students who shared giddy stories with Polly about what outrageous things had occurred during the most recent full moon. These others acknowledged me always with a curious, questioning look in their eyes, as if they were too embarrassed to admit they didn't know my name.

As it turned out, though, Petey Meechum, who had also not

yet gone breach, had taken a strange interest in me after the day I had run away from him in the library. Except he liked to be known as Peter now, in the same way that Rosebush, perhaps as a result of her parents' divorce, was demanding that she be called Rose. Apparently we were outgrowing the names of our childhoods. I was always Lumen. There was no evolution in my name. Well, there wasn't until later, after I had left the town behind—and then I started calling myself Ann. Ann Fowler. I'm sure there are hundreds of Ann Fowlers in this world. You would have no reason to single me out. My husband, he believes Ann is my only name and that I have no middle name. He knows no Lumen. It is a secret I keep from him, because when he comes home he tells me about the troubles of his day at work—and Ann Fowler is a remarkably good wife.

So it was Peter Meechum who frequently came to my house to study in the afternoons. Unlikely as it was, popular Peter Meechum came to me for help with geometry. Golden-haired Peter. Peter, whom all the girls ached for in school, and somehow he had delivered himself to me. Peter Meechum in my very own home, where I would make us a snack of carrot and celery sticks and French onion dip. I would pour him a glass of orange juice, and he would drink it all in one long gulp—and then I would pour him another, and he would make that one last awhile.

I wondered how long it would be before he discovered any number of other taller, prettier girls to help him with math. But somehow one of my childhood incantations had borne him to me, and I relished it with the desperate appetite of someone fated to die the very next day.

"It's an offense to my masculinity is what it is," he would say dramatically. "My having to be taught math by a wee girl."

He said it in a way that made me not mind being called a wee girl.

"We'll have to compensate," he went on. "After you explain tangents, you have to promise to let me beat you at arm wrestling."

"Tangents are easy," I would say. "It's just relationships. Angles and lengths. If you have one, you also have the other. I'll show you."

In my room, sprawled out on the carpeted floor, I drew diagrams for him on blue-lined notebook pages.

"How do you draw such straight lines without a ruler?" he asked. "Your triangles are amazing."

He ran his fingertips lightly over my triangles, as though geometry were a tactile thing.

"They're perfect," he said.

"They're not perfect."

He eyed me.

"Maybe you don't know what perfect is," he said. "Those right there—that's what perfect looks like."

That was something about Peter. His language made things happen. Things became funny when Peter laughed, and they became ridiculous when he labeled them so. He seemed, somehow, to belong prematurely to that category of *adults*—people who drove the world ahead of them, like charioteers, rather than being dragged along behind.

The truth is, I was in love with him—Petey Meechum, who was now Peter, who held a carrot stick in the corner of his mouth like a cigar while he was lying on his stomach on the floor of my room complimenting my triangles.

He sighed heavily and rolled over onto his back. He raised his arms toward the ceiling and used his splayed hands to make a triangle through which he peered, squinting, at the overhead light.

"After I graduate high school, I'm leaving," he said.

"Where are you going?"

"New York."

I didn't ask why New York. He would tell me without my prompting him.

"It's like a city on fire," he went on. "The streets are always smoking from underground furnaces."

"Steam," I said. I couldn't help myself.

"What?"

"It's not smoke. It's steam."

"How do you know?"

"I looked it up once. I saw it on TV and wondered what it was. There's a steam-heat system under Manhattan. Sometimes it leaks."

His hands fell to his chest, and he was quiet. I felt bad for knowing more about his dream city than he did.

"What will you do in New York?" I asked, trying to resuscitate his vision.

"Lumen, don't you ever feel like you want to leave?"

"What do you mean?"

"I mean this place. This weird little town with its weird little traditions. Other places aren't like this, you know."

"Every place has its own ways," I declared reasonably.

He rolled over again, back onto his stomach, and there was something beseeching in his tone when he spoke again.

"But don't you ever just want to get out? To go somewhere else? To be somebody else—even just for a little while?"

I looked down at the triangles in my notebook. The secret to drawing straight lines is that you use your whole arm, not just your hand and wrist. My father taught me that.

"I like it here," I said.

"What do you like about it?"

I wasn't prepared for follow-up questions. Part of me always resented having to justify my likes and dislikes. Other people didn't have to. No one ever asked Blackhat Roy what it was he liked about hunting knives. Everyone just knew he kept a collection of them, all oiled and polished, in his bedroom.

"Come on," I said to Peter. "You have to understand tangents. They're going to be on the test tomorrow."

———

"I NEVER SEE you in church," he said on another afternoon.

My father and I were not churchgoers—but we had frequently driven by when services were being let out, and I wished sometimes to be among those enlightened folk who had occasion to dress in finery in the middle of a plain Sunday morning.

Peter had taken to removing his sneakers when we were studying together. He tucked the laces neatly inside and set them side by side by the door. I liked seeing them there—that one touch of alien boyness that transformed my bedroom into something less than familiar.

"My father never took me," I said.

"Do you believe in God?"

"Kind of."

"You kind of believe in God, or you believe in a kind of God?"

I didn't know what to say. How do you tell a boy who takes off his shoes in your bedroom that God is a thing of the mind—but a very, very lovely thing of the mind? I stuttered along for a few moments before he let me off the hook.

"You know, I didn't used to believe in God."

Joshua Gaylord

"You didn't?"

"Huh-uh. For a long time I didn't. And then one day I did. Just like that. Does that ever happen to you? You're going along, minding your own business, seeing things the way you've always seen them—and then all of a sudden those things look different to you?"

The way he was looking at me made me wonder if he was talking about something other than God. Or if maybe God and the way he looked at me with those voracious boy-eyes were related. I wanted more of it. His boy-eyes—his godliness, which I felt deep down, like a surge.

Then he leaned back, as though something had clicked shut all at once.

"Never mind," he said. "I'm just feeling philosophical today. If you can help me pass this geometry test, I'll give you a present."

"What present?" I pretended to shuffle through the pages of my textbook, because I didn't want to show him that I was out of breath.

"I don't know—I'll build you a house on the lake."

"On the east shore, so I can watch the sunsets?"

"Sure. And another on the west shore so you can watch the sunrises. And a canoe to go back and forth between them."

"Just a canoe?"

"Come on, I already built you two houses."

"Fair enough."

———

IN SCHOOL, ROSE Lincoln leaned over to my desk during history.

"I heard you're tutoring Peter," she said.

I said nothing.

"Well, is it true?"

I shrugged. "We just study——" I had meant to say, "We just study together," but the *together* suddenly sounded, in one way or another, too complicit and damning.

"It's okay," she said with a laugh. "You don't have to be embarrassed. It's not like he's interested in you or anything. You know Peter——he's a flirt. The other day he told me I looked nice in yellow. He let Angela Weston give him a back rub in the cafeteria. Carrie Bryce said he brushed her butt when she walked by him in the hall. And you know it doesn't mean anything. I mean, I look so like hell in yellow. It's just the way he is. The reason he likes me is that we understand each other."

I wrote Rose Lincoln's name in my notebook and spent the rest of the period crosshatching over it until it was an ugly blotch of shiny ink that bled through to the other side of the paper——and I thought that would do for a curse.

———

BUT I FEARED that what Rose Lincoln said about Peter and me was true——that I was just a functionary to him.

It was a few weeks later. We were in my bedroom, and he was looking at a framed picture on the wall. The picture was of my mother and father when they were very young and just married. Peter had been spending the afternoons with me in my bedroom, and we had played many games of Parcheesi between studying sessions——but he had made no move to kiss me.

"What's it like not to have a mother?" he asked.

I had learned that afternoons make boys profound——the long, slow crawl of light between the shutters, the lazy dust motes in the doldrums of the air. Boys are affected, unconsciously, by such things. You can see it in their eyes. In the sepia light of dusk, they are traveling.

"It's okay," I said. "She died when I was too young to remember her, so I never really felt the loss of anything."

It was my stock answer when people lamented, unnecessarily, my motherlessness.

"Does your dad talk about her much?"

"I don't know," I said, not knowing what constituted "much." It was true that he used to speak to her frequently at night, after he closed his bedroom door, as though it were his personal version of prayer. If I put my ear up to the door, I would hear him relating the events of the day, the progress of my evolution through girlhood. But he hadn't spoken to her like that in a long time. Once, when I was little, I listened so long at his door that I fell asleep. After having your ear pressed against doors and walls for a while, you don't know exactly what you're listening to—maybe just that low, oceany hum of your own blood. It lulls you. He found me there in the morning, called me his beautiful stray, lifted me in his arms. I clung to him.

"Do you want to see pictures?" I asked.

"Sure."

The old albums were in the attic, and I thought that such a dark, cramped place might inspire kissing. I felt bad about using the memory of my mother in that way, but I reasoned that she also would have wanted me to be kissed.

Peter was quite a bit taller than me, so I had him unfold the attic ladder from the ceiling in the hallway, and up we went. I knew right where the boxes with the albums were, because I had helped my father organize the attic just the previous summer. It had been my job to create all the labels. It was warmer up there in the attic, and Peter and I sat side by side, with our backs propped up against old suitcases, an album resting open half on his lap and half on mine. Our shoulders touched.

"This is my favorite picture," I said.

"That's baby you?"

"That's baby me."

Most family pictures show the mother holding the baby while the father sits proudly by—but this one was the opposite. In it, my father, looking lean and dapper, had me bundled up in his arms. He was sitting in the easy chair we still had downstairs in the living room, and next to him was my mother, perched upon the arm of the chair, looking radiant and aloof, the skirt of her dress draped perfectly over her knees. Her smile was something I couldn't describe, except to say that it seemed to be queenly in the way that queens remind you of situations grander than your own puny life could conceive.

"She looks like you," Peter said.

"Does she?" I was pleased. "I think we have a lot in common. Maybe that's why she died."

"Huh?"

"I mean, I know it's morbid, but I think that sometimes. Maybe she had to die because we were so alike that the world couldn't tolerate both of us in it."

"That's . . ." he said, looking uncomfortable. "That's a really weird thing to say, Lumen."

But it didn't seem weird to me at all, and I was hurt by his response.

"Anyway," I said.

We were quiet for a moment. Then he said:

"So what do you have in common? I mean, other than your looks."

61

"Well, she didn't go breach—and I'm not going to, either."

He looked at me sideways with suspicious eyes.

"It happens," I went on. "Not very often, but it does happen. My father says she was all lit up—he says she carried the daylight with her. The moon, it couldn't have any effect."

"I never heard of that."

"Well, it's true—whether you've heard of it or not. Some people just aren't the same as other people."

"Hm." I could tell he still didn't believe me. "And how come you think you won't go breach, either?"

"We have the same blood. It stands to reason. Plus I can just tell."

"But your father, he went breach."

"Yes."

"So you could be like him."

"I don't know," I said, shrugging. "I can just tell."

It is always a young girl's dream to have a boy believe in her most colorful fantasies. You paint landscapes with your humble heart, then you seek to populate them with boys who will understand.

But then he underwent a quick change—as though he were brushing off the topic altogether. He clambered around so that he was on his hands and knees in front of me. I sat with my own knees pulled up protectively to my chest.

"Let me see," he said.

"See what?"

But he didn't answer. He was looking at my eyes, examining them. He moved his head from side to side, as though to get multiple angles on the subject of my eyes.

"What are you doing?" I asked.

"Shh."

He kept looking, then he seemed to spot something—as

though he had discovered a minuscule village somewhere in the core of my retina.

"Huh," he said.

"What?"

"You're right. Daylight."

That's when he kissed me. At first I held my breath, unsure about what I should do. Then when I finally breathed, I wondered if I should keep my eyes open or closed. His eyes were closed, so I closed mine. That's when my other senses took over. I could smell his skin and that boy shampoo that smells like mowed grass. He pushed himself against me, and I touched his arm with my hand—squeezed his arm as if it were mine, as if our bodies were forfeit to each other's—and then my hand was even on his neck, where there were little hairs, and I was allowed to touch them. I heard a tiny voice, like that of a squeak-mouse, and then I realized it was my own voice, and I thought how beautiful that sometimes your body knows what to do on its own.

At that time, I had a way of thinking of myself as a castle or a tower, something with many spiraling cobblestone steps that became secrets in themselves, winding around each other like visual illusions. The pleasure was in the climbing, the intricate architectures of thought and purpose. But it was on a rare occasion such as this when I could feel something else, something beneath the foundation of the tower, a rumbling in the earth itself that shook to delightful danger all those lattices of cold, cerebral mortar.

———

I HAD LOST track of time in the attic, and when we climbed down the ladder I was surprised to see that a pale, dry dusk had infiltrated the house while we weren't looking.

"Uh-oh," I said.

"What?"

"Prayer Moon. It's the first night."

Peter went to the window and gazed up at the sky.

"It's still early enough," he said. "I don't live that far away. I can make it."

"No, you can't. The moon's up."

"But look—it's quiet. I can make it. They wouldn't bother with me much anyway."

But my father, arriving home, wouldn't hear of it. He called Peter's mother and told her he would stay in our house for the night. There was plenty of room—such a big house for just my father and me. The couch in the upstairs den folded out into a bed, and I got sheets from the linen closet and made it up.

It was the first time there had been a boy sleeping in the house, and I wanted to assure my father that nothing untoward would happen. I found him in the kitchen while Peter was watching TV in the den.

"I told Peter he shouldn't come out of the den after ten o'clock," I said. "You can check on us if you want. Any time you feel like it."

My father grinned in confusion and shook his head.

"I'm sure everything will be fine," he said. "I trust you, little Lumen."

That was nice to hear, but at the same time I had recently grown irritated by the idea that I was so invariably trustworthy. Hadn't I just spent the afternoon in the attic kissing, of all people, Peter Meechum? Hadn't I kissed right through sunset?

"How come you trust me so much? None of the other parents trust their kids so much."

He smiled again, gently. And again there was something in it I didn't care for. Was it condescension?

"Well," he said, "you've never disappointed me yet. Never once. Such a perfect record earns you plenty of trust. Besides, you're fifteen."

I wasn't entirely sure what the fact of my age had to do with anything, but I had an impression—and he turned to the sink immediately after he'd said it, as though embarrassed.

He made spaghetti and meatballs for dinner, and Peter and I were responsible for the garlic toast. Peter made a big production of spreading the garlic butter on the bread, and I topped it with the ocher-colored seasoned salt.

We listened to music during dinner—as we often did during the moons. That night it was the opera *Turandot*.

"The opera's about a princess," I explained, because I had read the libretto the previous year. "She refuses to marry any man unless he answers three riddles first. If he answers any of them incorrectly, he's put to death."

"I guess she has her reasons," Peter said, and I couldn't tell if he was joking.

"She's a princess of death," I said with great seriousness. "It's her nature."

After dinner Peter and I watched TV in the den upstairs, sitting side by side on the couch that had been made up as his bed. We turned the TV loud so we wouldn't hear anything from outside. After a while we fell to kissing again.

It surprised me how quickly the whole thing became mechanical. I found myself too aware of the way our lips met, mapping out the movements of his tongue in my mouth. First he would kiss me square on the mouth, then take my lower lip between his two lips and leave a cold wet spot on my chin that I wanted to wipe off. Then he would turn his head sideways a little, as though passion were all about angles. (If we had been able to kiss with one of our faces turned completely upside down, I suppose that would have been truly making love.) Then he would leave a trail of ticklish kisses from the corner of my mouth up the side of my face to my ear, the lobe of which he took in his mouth. Then a bite or two on the neck, which I didn't know what to do with. Then the whole thing started over again.

The problem was that I was thinking about it as it was happening, picturing it in my mind as though I were a disembodied viewer standing off to the side—and from that perspective the whole thing looked ludicrous. I kept thinking about my father, who trusted me implicitly, and what he would have seen had he come into the room during that mess. Not disappointment, not exactly. But it would have given him reason to remind me again that I was fifteen years old—which was a repellent thought. Had he come in at that moment, he would have seen his daughter succumbing sloppily to teenagehood—whatever preposterous versions of love or curiosity or risk such a state implied.

Then Peter's right hand slid down from my neck to my chest and rested itself on the embarrassing nodule that was still in the process of becoming my left breast.

He froze suddenly. At first I thought it was because he was disappointed with what he'd found there. He lifted himself a few inches from me, his hand still on my chest, and gave me an intent, querulous look.

That's when I realized he was waiting for me to stop him.

I had been so studious and removed from the whole situation that I had forgotten the role I was supposed to be playing. I was the good girl. The girl being groped and salivated upon in the den of her own home was the good girl. You were safe with her, because she didn't allow anything to get out of control.

"I guess we should stop," I said.

"Okay," he said. "Sorry."

But he didn't seem sorry. He seemed relieved.

He levered himself off me, then we sat and watched TV for a while longer. It was half an hour before midnight when I told him I was going to bed. He said okay and leaned over to kiss me good night.

"I'm glad we went to the attic," he said.

It was a sweet thing to say, and the way he phrased it made me think funny thoughts — as though "going to the attic" were some kind of accepted rite of passage. Passage to the attic. I thought then that I knew something about rites, but I was wrong.

There are so many things about the world that might keep you laughing to yourself in the dark when you can't seem to fall asleep. Then again, alone in my bedroom with a hallway between us, the idea of Peter Meechum once again thrilled all my senses. I put my hand on my breast the way he had done it before, and it gave me little shivers all over.

I wondered why romance was a thing I felt in a truly visceral way only when I was alone. Maybe the cold, logical part of my mind closed doors to real people. Maybe I needed to be taught how to open those doors. And I thought that Peter Meechum very well could be the one to teach me.

We've all of us got an inward brain and an outward brain, don't we? When we are by ourselves in our rooms at night, unselfconscious and free, we are entirely different. That's when you might learn the most about instinct.

But the moon made its exceptions in our town. Here's another song from my childhood that I sing as a lullaby to my son.

Gather, young lovers,
In wind and in rain.
Cleave to the sky fires
That know not your name.
Unravel the day-screws
That tangle your brain.
Hold fast your white angel,
And cut it in twain.
   Hold fast your black devil,
   And cut it in twain.

And then, cut in two as we all are, can we ever take true account of ourselves? Or do we just lisp ourselves to sleep and dreams of freedom?

———

BUT THE NIGHT when Peter Meechum stayed over was also the night when a pack of breachers stood outside my window howling. It was well after midnight, and I had not been able to fall asleep. I heard them out on the street, mewling in the peculiar way they had, which made me think of lonely cats on backyard fences in the nighttime.

Mine was the only window that faced the front of the house. My father's bedroom and the den, where Peter slept, were both in the back—so they couldn't hear.

Then I heard my name, called snakelike and taunting from outside:

"Luuuuuuuuuumeeen!"

It was a girl's voice. It was Polly's voice.

Normally the breachers didn't bother with people who kept

indoors when the moon was out. They weren't malicious—they didn't stalk innocent prey. Normally they kept to themselves. They embattled each other if they battled at all. Some of them just liked to run through the streets—they kept on running until the sun came up. Others took to the woods and were lost in the morning when they woke. But by and large they didn't make assaults on those who stayed out of their way.

So this was something different—my name teased out in that manic hyena voice they all had.

"Luuuuumeen!"

I hadn't been sleeping anyway, so I went to the window and looked down.

There were six of them. They were naked, their skin pale and glowing under the light of the street lamps. They ran around in circles, testing the strength of their legs, the length of their arms. They hopped and ran and yipped and snarled. One of them grappled with another and was tossed into the shrubbery at the edge of our yard. When he got himself upright again, I saw there were perforations all over his skin from the brambles. He would hurt in the morning, but he seemed to feel nothing now.

In the middle of the pack, Polly stood very still, smiling up at my window. I didn't like her smile. I couldn't tell you exactly what it was. Her smile was the stillest on the street, but there was a breeze that blew strands of her hair across her face. She made no attempt to remove them.

When she saw me in the window, her smile widened—she even laughed, seeming to luxuriate in my witnessing her in such a state.

"Lumen," she said, seeming to breathe through her words, "come outside! Please, Lumen. Look at me. I want you to see me!"

The girl who stood in the street was not the girl I knew. Instead, she was some nightmarish inversion of the person who had played in the sprinklers with me years before. This girl was raw, viperous, glutted on nature and night. They all were. Like coyotes, they made mockery, with their bleating voices, of those who needed light in order to feel safe.

And yet they were all too human.

I had never seen Polly without her clothes on before. There was a sickly luminescence to her skin, as of a glowworm or one of those creatures that live so deep underground that they have no pigment at all. Her dropsy breasts—I could see that one was larger than the other, that the rusty nipples were more oval than circular, that they possessed the persistent misalignment of nature itself. There were red blotches on her stomach and legs, as though she were rash-broken, and I could see the freckles and moles that dotted her body—even a patchy birthmark that looked like someone had spilled coffee on her hip. The triangle of her pubic hair was discomfiting in the way it grew partly onto her thighs and up her stomach. While I watched, the breeze blew a chattering of tiny leaves down the street, and one of them got caught in her pubic hair—where it remained as long as she stood there.

Then she started to call my name in various ways, feeling it in her mouth, tasting the varietals with which she might be able to permute my personhood were I down there with her.

"Lumen," she called. "Lumenal . . . Laminal . . . Lamen . . . Lamian . . . Labian . . . Lavial . . ."

It seemed, at first, like a child's game—but the way she said the names made them sound obscene. They were versions of my name—if my name were some vulgar tropical fruit whose juice ran down your chin and whose pulp got stuck between your gnashing teeth.

As Polly continued her catechism, another of the breachers took notice and came to stand beside her. It was Rose. I didn't know if it was just because Rose had a different kind of body or because she cosmetically altered it, but her patch of pubic hair was smaller and shorter than Polly's—and as a result it masked less, and I could see the ugly fleshy nubbins of her vagina.

I wanted to look away. I really did. But there are some things in this life that demand your sight, your vision. This was a scene played out particularly for my delectation. There was no one in the world, at that moment, apart from them and me. We existed on opposite sides of a pane of glass. But it didn't matter—I was in their thrall. And they seemed to be in mine. As though I'd become a lonely Rapunzel at the top of a tower.

The others started to gather, too, standing very still in a group and gazing up at me. They smiled their grisly smiles and called to me in words or moans or hisses. Blackhat Roy was there with his two missing toes, but he stood apart, crouched at the line of trees that was the beginning of the woods on the opposite side of the street. A boy I recognized as Wilson Laramy stood at Polly's side. Without seeming to think, and while still gazing up at my window, he reached blindly to his right, found Polly's wrist, and guided her hand down to his crotch. Without shame, and still repeating the prayerful tautology of my name, her left hand closed around his penis. Casual—it was all so casual. You would think they had no idea what nakedness was.

Then they were all there together, as though by the instinct of pack animals, all casting their lewd voices up at me, their skin spectral and yet hideously biological, bleeding, lurching cadavers regurgitated by the earth and sent wandering down the abandoned thoroughfares of our little town—and here they were, uncharacteristically still, all their unclean gestures pointed in my direction—as though to tempt me, as though to mock me for not being tempted, as though the land itself hated me for existing so dry and tidy above its fecund soil.

And that's when Polly started to laugh, high and hysterical—a harsh, shrieking laugh that had no sense in it. And when she laughed, the others laughed, too, and they started to split off from the group—as though suddenly roused into action. First one ran off down the street, followed by two more. Then another—until the only one left was Polly herself, who, when her laughter died away, licked her lips slowly, her tongue moving between her teeth.

Then she, too, turned to run down the street in the direction the others had gone—and I was left to stare at the empty street, the ratchety shadows of tree branches against the lamplight, the only sounds the ticking of the grandfather clock down the hall, the insistent tapping of a twig against the glass of my window, and the stiff flood of my own pulse in my ears.

———

THE BALD WHITE maggotry of it! The spitting, drooling indecency of it! I couldn't sleep that night thinking about it. I can't sleep this night remembering it. We live in an eggshell. We swim in phlegmy albumen—the world outside tap-tap-taps against our chalky home. I stand beside my marriage bed, staring down at my husband, who snorts with rough sleep. I am forever gazing downward at people who live in dream worlds. The breachers, too. They run through the night, but they run in sleep, they run undercurrents deep in memory. In the morning there is no shame because they were not themselves—or their selves were buried so deep that their waking minds are blameless for their nighttime deeds.

I don't sleep the way others do. I fear sleep—and I fear not sleeping.

Once the pack below had gone, I sat in my room, clutching at myself in the pool of moonlight cast through my windowpanes. My head was crowded with so many things it ached with fullness—Peter's compulsory kisses, his hot boy-breath, the pressure of his hand over my lung, like a medical examination, the hiss of voices in the street, the exposed reechy bodies of those I see in school every day, Turandot, the princess of death, my father declaring me fifteen—*fifteen!*—his embarrassed eyes focused on the project of scrubbing a pot in the sink.

So much shame. I live in an eggshell.

There is so much shame.

———

THE NEXT DAY, I saw Polly in school. She sat next to me in our biology class. She said she was exhausted and rested her head on my shoulder.

She asked me what was the matter. She said I looked worse than she did.

I told her I hadn't slept well.

She called me poor Lumen, and there was no hissing in the way she said my name.

I didn't like how people could be one thing at night and another thing during the day.

I asked her if she didn't remember the night before—coming to my window, calling my name.

She said she didn't remember a thing.

But I could tell by the way she said it that she was lying, and I told her so.

She shook her head and said in a voice filled with sadness but not apology:

"Oh, Lumen, these things—it's like they happen to different people. Other lives."

So we went on, scribbling away about centrioles and lysosomes and Golgi bodies and other microscopic organelles that committed invisible acts of violence and love upon each other many times every second.

CHAPTER 3

That was the year in my life when everyone I knew went breach, one at a time, little oily kernels of corn popping against the pot lid, until I was the only one left, a hard, stubborn pip in the bottom of the pan, burned black.

Menarche was my magic word that year. Before I went to sleep each night, I whispered the word thirteen times—once for each regular moon and once for the Blue Moon, just in case—hoping that mine would come. My father, he never asked a thing about it. He gave me a fair allowance. It was understood that I would be self-sufficient enough to purchase my own products and take care of myself when the time came. So he remained unaware that I was not bleeding like the other girls were.

At my annual checkup, I lied to the doctor about it. I told him I had my first period six months before. He asked if it was happening regularly. I told him yes, regular. Regular as could be.

Polly seemed particularly taken with her breaching. She painted herself with the new habits of womanhood—the tip of her finger on her lower lip when she was lost in thought, a languorous lean against the school lockers when she spoke with boys, fingernails colored somber browns and oxblood reds.

Peter went breach a few months after we kissed in the attic. I had wondered if I would see a dramatic change in him, but he was the same. I asked him about his breach nights, but he didn't like to talk about them. He said, "You shouldn't be thinking about me when I'm like that." If anything, he became all the more proper and gentlemanly to compensate for whatever it was he did when the full moon rose. I admired his rectitude, but it made me feel lonely, too—as though he were visiting me in some foreign country where I lived all by myself, and we were both pretending that the rest of the world didn't exist.

This truth is, I liked my strange country. But I didn't want anyone feeling sorry for me, as though I were in quarantine. Couldn't they see my aloneness was a freedom rather than a prison?

Once, though, Peter brought me something back from his breach night. He said, "Look. I found it by the river."

He put it into the palm of my hand. It was a little metal heart with a loop at the top, a charm lost from a bracelet.

"It's old," I said.

"How can you tell?"

"It's tarnished."

"See?" he said. "It was waiting there for a long time. Waiting for me to find it and give it to you."

"Thank you."

He smiled.

"I think about you," he said, "at night, when I'm out there."

"What do you think?"

"I guess I think about being near you. I think about how it's like there's a bubble around you."

"A bubble?"

"A big bubble. A block wide. It goes where you go — you're the center of it. And every object gets a little bit better while it's in that bubble with you. It's always very bright where you are."

And I *was* bright just then. I was breathing very hard. The only thing I could do was get myself as near to him as I possibly could, so I leaned in and put my head against his chest and listened to his heart.

———

HONDY PILT WAS an interesting case. He had first gone breach when Peter had, during the same moon, and the next day in school the breachers seemed to have a newfound respect and even admiration for him.

I asked Polly about it.

"I don't know what it is about him," she said. "You just want to follow him. He ran through the woods — I've never seen anyone run like that. I mean, Lumen, he was beautiful."

"Really?"

"I know it sounds stupid, but it's no joke. We followed him, and he took us to this clearing on the side of the mountain. Nobody ever knew it was there. He stood on this rock jutting out over nothing. If he fell...but he didn't fall. He put his arms out. Like the sky was his or something. I don't know. I can't explain it."

It was true — there was something different about him, something even I could witness during the day. He had always seemed like someone struggling against invisible forces, but now there was a peacefulness about him — as though he had arrived at a place and recognized it as a true home, as though he had discovered a back door into heaven and waited patiently for the rest of us to find him there.

I tried to speak to him. In the cafeteria a couple days later, I brought him a banana as an offering. I had always been kind to him—more than most, I believe. I said hello. I asked him how his day was going. Usually he smiled back and uttered a few guttural words of greeting. That day, though, his eyes didn't even meet mine. He was gazing upward, as though he could see the sky through the ceiling. He reached out and put his big hand over my little one, and he just held it there for a long time. I didn't know what to do, so after a while I took my hand back and left him there smiling to himself.

I had wanted him to share his secrets with me, but instead what I got was consolation. The last thing I wanted was to be pitied by Hondy Pilt.

Amenorrhea. I looked it up. That's what it's called when you don't get your first period by age sixteen. At first I wondered what it had to do with the end of a prayer—where you say, Amen. But then I realized it was probably "men," as in "menstruation," and "a," as in "not"—so "not menstruating," amenorrhea. That's the word I tried to counteract with my magic word menarche.

Where did all that blood go if it wasn't evacuating my body? I worried. Did it collect somewhere? Did I have a sac in my thorax that was growing larger every day with unshed blood? That was crowding my other organs? If not blood, what was my body spending its time in the production of? All flowered fantasies and brain work?

Two months after Hondy Pilt and Peter Meechum went breach, the second, smaller Parker twin went breach. That meant I was the only one in my grade who hadn't. In fact many of the people in the grade below me had already started going. It was something you couldn't hide. Your absence on those nights was noticed.

Polly tried to console me. She said it was a sign of great maturity to breach late. Rose Lincoln was not so kind. She said it was because I was underdeveloped, obviously — that I was repressing my womanhood. "You have to have a grown woman *somewhere* in you scrambling to get out," she explained. "How come you don't want to let her out? You can't stay a girl forever, you know. After a while, girlhood's just a shell for something else."

To Rose Lincoln I was a shell. A dry husk. One of those disappointments like cracking open a peanut only to find there's no nut inside.

I knew I wasn't going to go breach at all. But I hadn't known what it would mean — watching everyone else as though we were on opposite sides of a wide river. I could hear them frolicking in the distance with their puffed-out bodies and their bleeding wombs. I felt that I was waving to them from my exile. Sometimes someone waved back.

So I said my magic word every night, and I looked at myself in the mirror every morning to see if any part of me had grown.

Peter Meechum petted me like a poodle and was in constant care not to corrupt me with his newfound adulthood. I wanted his hands on me, but he was reluctant.

And one day after the last night of the full moon, Polly came to my house and told me that Wendy Spencer had gotten an empty soda bottle stuck up in her the night before. She lurched all the way home with it inside her, and the paramedics had to break it this morning to get it out.

"Can you imagine!" Polly said. "It was *stuck*. How deep must it have gone to get *stuck?*"

"Suction," I said, picking at the cover of my history textbook.

"What?"

"It's not how deep. It's suction. They probably had to break the bottom to let the air in."

"Oh. How do you know that?"

I shrugged.

"I don't know. It just makes sense."

And so that was something else for me to think about when I couldn't sleep.

Something was coming, and it had broken glass for teeth. I was running from it, hiding. But in the middle of the night, when I lay awake in my bed listening to the howling outside, I didn't know which I really and truly wanted: this life or that one.

———

I PLEADED WITH Mr. Hunter not to read my essay in front of the whole class, but he said modesty would get me nowhere in life. I said it wasn't modesty, it was just that I didn't like people reading my writing.

He gave me one of his curious looks, one that I could feel in my belly.

"You've got a toughness in you, Lumen. More spine than all of them put together," he said in a low tone. "Why do you hide it?"

I didn't know what to say. Why was he talking about my spine?

"If you want me not to read it," he said, "tell me not to. Don't ask, *tell*."

But I could say nothing.

So he read it aloud and told everyone to pay attention to the diction and the transitions. He didn't say it was mine, but everyone knew anyway. I hunched in my seat.

"You're an excellent writer," said Rose Lincoln after class. "You're a master scribe."

Later, in math class, when we were all supposed to be working through a sheet of problems, she leaned over and whispered to me.

"How's your boyfriend?"

"What boyfriend?"

"You know, Peter Meechum."

I hadn't thought about him as my boyfriend.

"Things got pretty vicious last night, you know," Rose continued. "He got into a fight with Blackhat Roy."

I had seen the scrapes and bruises on Peter's face, but he was avoiding me in school that day so I hadn't had a chance to ask him about it.

"Why?" I asked Rose.

"Why what, sweetie?"

"Why were they fighting?"

"Come on, Lumen. I know you're a little behind us, but you must've heard *something* about what happens. There is no why. Instinct. Besides, you know how Roy is. He's got a meanness you can't do much about. So Peter did what he had to."

I didn't look at her. I tried to concentrate on the math problem in front of me. But the lines and numbers seemed to wobble and blur.

"Anyway, Peter showed himself a real leader," Rose went on. "Like a warrior-prince, you know? His skin was smeared all over with blood and sweat—you just wanted to lick him. And he deserved something—I mean, for taking care of that little creep Roy. So I let him have me. To the victor go the spoils, right? That's me—I'm the spoils."

I stood up from my desk so suddenly that I knocked my book

and worksheet and pencil to the floor. Mr. Goodwin looked at me curiously. I picked up my things and put them on the desk, then walked quickly out of the room, down the hall, and into the girls' bathroom. I looked at myself in the mirror, my diminutive, ugly little self, and it wasn't until I could see my eyes filling up with tears that I knew I was going to cry. So I shut myself in a stall and unrolled thick wads of toilet paper to cry into. I made no sound. I'm a silent crier when I wish to be.

When I was done, I splashed cold water on my face and waited for the redness to lessen. I was in the bathroom so long that the end-of-period bell rang before I got back to the classroom. When I went in to collect my things, Mr. Goodwin asked me if everything was all right.

I told him yes, everything was fine.

Then, on an impulse, I added:

"I was cutting class."

Mr. Goodwin gave me a confused smile, as though he didn't understand the joke. Then he just shrugged it off.

"Are you coming to math clinic today? A lot of kids could really use your help."

———

LATER, WHEN PETER came to my house to study, I remained conspicuously silent about his injuries. At first he tried to hide them or distract me with questions from the textbook. But the more time passed without my asking about it, the more indignant he became.

Finally he said, "Aren't you going to ask what happened to me?"

I shrugged.

"I figure it happened when you were breaching last night."

"But don't you want to ask how? Don't you want to know if I'm all right?"

"Did you have sex with Rose Lincoln?"

His face changed. Whatever ire he had been fostering toward me was suddenly gone—replaced by twitchy panic.

"What?" he said lamely.

"You had sex with her."

"Who said that?"

"She did."

"Rose lies. She's lying."

"I don't think she is."

He didn't say anything. His eyes searched the room. He was in a panic about being caught. I hated him for making me feel sorry for him. He reached out to me, and I pulled myself back so violently that I banged my shoulder against one of my shelves and a pile of books came tumbling down. I was embarrassed and angry.

"Why did you do it?" I said.

"I didn't—"

"You *did*. I know what breachers do. They run in the woods. They beat one another up. They have sex together. Isn't that what happens?"

"Lumen—"

"I thought you liked me."

"I do. So much you don't even know."

"That's not what liking looks like."

"You don't understand. When you're out there . . . you don't—"

"Yeah, I know. I got it. I'm a girl. I'm a nice girl. I'm the opposite of Rose Lincoln. She's the kind of girl you have sex with, and I'm the kind of girl you do math problems with."

"Stop it. It's not——"

"Yes, it *is*. I know it is. You're a sweetheart with me. So kind, so gentlemanly." I was crying by now. I knew because I could feel the tears on my cheeks. And I was embarrassed, which made the tears come even faster. "I'm like the thing you worship. The thing you put on a shelf and dust every week. Don't take Lumen down from her shelf——you're liable to get your fingerprints all over her. Let's keep her from anything ugly. The ugly's just for grown-ups. She can't handle the ugly——"

"Stop!"

He said it loud, loud enough to jar everything into sudden silence. My father was downstairs, and I was afraid he'd heard it. I didn't like the idea of dragging him into my pathetic little-girl world. I listened for a few moments to the ticking of the grandfather clock in the hallway. Then I looked to the window. It was the third and final night of Hollow Moon.

"You better go," I said, sniffling and wiping the tears from my face with my palms. "It'll be dark soon."

"I'm going," he said. "But you should know——you're better than me. You're better than all of us."

"Well, maybe I don't want to be better," I said. "Get out. Just get out. You don't want to be a danger to me."

———

THAT NIGHT I stuffed cotton balls in my ears and pulled the blankets over my head. I went to beautiful places in my head. I was part of everything I touched, and the world was glad to have me on its surface. I imagined myself on top of a mountain in Switzerland. I looked out over the wide valleys and saw no towns and no roads and no travelers. There was no one around to be surprised or disappointed about what I was or what I was not.

I was alone and unfearful.

———

IN THE MORNING, as my father and I sat at the kitchen table—he reading the paper and stirring his coffee, I ignoring my unappetizing bowl of whole-grain cereal—I asked him what it was like to go breach.

"It's not something for you to worry about," he said, not looking up from his newspaper.

"You mean because it won't happen to me?"

I forget where it started, this mutual belief that I was unbreachable. Was it something he told me as a child? Or was it something I suggested to him that he picked up on? We had lived so long, he and I, with the consensual reluctance to give up the fancies of childhood—and now I didn't know if this was one of them. Simply put, we did not talk about such things.

"I mean," he said, "because it's not something to worry about. Like the weather. It's going to be what it's going to be, whether you fret about it or not."

I knew this to be true, but I wanted more information.

"But you went through it. Do you remember it? What was it like?"

He sipped his coffee and lowered the cup slowly to the table. Then he folded his newspaper twice and leaned forward to look at his daughter straight-on. His eyes were very large, with pale crescents of fatigue beneath them.

"Do you remember," he said, "when you were maybe five years old, and you asked me about death? You wanted to know where your mother had gone. You asked if you would die and if I would die, and I told you it was an inevitability, and then we looked up the word inevitability in the dictionary?"

"No," I said.

"It was one of those conversations you dread having as a parent. For years before it happens, you lose sleep trying to plan for it. But there it was. You wanted to know what it was like where your mommy was."

He shifted in his seat and cleared his throat. I recognized the symptoms of trying not to tear up. I looked down at my cereal to save him embarrassment.

"Anyway," he went on, "I told you I didn't know what it was like. And do you want to know what you said?"

"What? What did I say?"

"You said—very matter-of-fact, as though you were quite positive about it—you said, 'Wherever it is, it probably has curtains.'"

He laughed. I laughed, too. Though it sounded vaguely familiar, and I wondered if he had told me that story before. And if he had, why hadn't I remembered it? Sometimes we are mysteries to ourselves.

"And," he went on, "that's when I thought, 'That's my girl. Whatever comes at her, she'll be able to handle it.' My little Lumen."

He put his open hand on the side of my face, and I leaned my head into it a little bit.

I went to school, and my head was filled with that story all day. It wasn't until many hours later that I realized something.

He hadn't actually answered my question.

AFTER SCHOOL THAT same day, as I was riding my bike home, Peter met me by the side of the road.

"Come on," he said. The way he said it was not nice at all.

"Where are we going?"

"Just follow me."

His parents had given him an old Volkswagen on his sixteenth birthday, and it was parked a little way down a side road. He got in, started the engine, and waited for me to join him.

Sometimes people wonder why they do the things they do. I don't wonder. He was Peter Meechum, whom all the girls love, and I was nobody, whom nobody loved. He had given me a command, and I was particularly good at obeying commands. And I had never been invited into his car before. So I went.

I hid my bike in the trees by the road and got into the car. The interior smelled of rust and oil.

He drove into the woods, then turned off the tarmac onto a dirt road. It was cloudy, and there were no shadows on the ground. Everything looked flat, too close. You could suffocate on the grayness of the world. The road was unmaintained. Weeds grew up between the tire tracks, and deep divots jostled my body about inside the vehicle. A weathered road sign lay in the tall sumac, half buried by hard dirt. It announced that the road was a dead end. But everybody knew it was a dead end. Even I knew where this road led.

I looked at Peter, but his gaze remained sternly forward.

Soon the trees opened up, and the dusty sun shone down on the wide expanse of the quarry. Peter brought the car to a stop and shut off the engine. I wondered if he would force me to walk into the mine just as Rose had forced Hondy Pilt to do the year before. But he said nothing. The only thing to be heard was the wind groaning in the trees.

He opened his door and got out, and I got out, too.

"This way," he said.

I followed him around the rim of the quarry to a small grove where the streamlet from the mountain above collected into three small pools before continuing down into the mine. There was a grassy clearing in the grove, and when you were in it you felt protected and safe. That day, though, it was cold. A sharp breeze made a whistling sound through the grove. I shrugged myself deeper into my coat and crossed my arms over my chest.

"Now what?" I said.

"Lay down."

"How come?"

"Because I'm going to have sex with you."

The expression on his face was determined and dire.

When I didn't move at all, he took me by the shoulders and led me to the place where he wanted me to lie. Then he exerted a slight pressure with his hands, almost nothing, really, and down my body went as if by mystical coercion. Maybe he had magic-spell words, too, that he used to cast conjurations. You cannot always understand boys, the things they do. They act, sometimes, as though in thrall to severe but natural forces. They can be waterfalls or wind gusts.

I sat down at first, then he gave me another little push, and I lay back. The dry autumn grass tickled my neck. I stared up into the gray sky, circumscribed by the tops of needled evergreens. It felt like the sky was particularly low that day—a ceiling you could almost reach up and brush your fingers across.

Then Peter stood over me, looking down at me as though he were a giant and I was a poor little farmer at the bottom of a bean stalk.

"I'm going to have sex with you," he said again.

"No," I said—because that seemed to be the thing I was supposed to say.

"You said I was ugly."

"No," I said again. I wanted to reach up and run my fingertips across the sky. I thought it must be silky and lush. Maybe my hand would sink into it. I was no longer cold.

He kneeled down and leaned over me.

"Take off your pants," he said.

"No," I said. I could hear my voice saying it. It was a charming voice—I was charmed by it. I could hear myself saying it in the space between the trees. My voice there between those leaves that fretted and shivered.

Then Peter was unzipping my pants and tugging them over my narrow hips. When he got them to my ankles, he realized he had to take my shoes off as well, so he wrenched them off without untying the laces. It was a very awkward process, and I felt sorry for him—and I kept laughing inwardly at the girl whose body was being turned this way and that.

He must have gotten my underpants off, too, because I could feel the reedy grass tickling my bare bottom.

So there it was. The whole thing. The low ceiling of the sky above, the ticklish sumac beneath, and me sandwiched between the two, my bare lower half looking like a ridiculously pale chicken leg, I suppose, one sock tugged partly off my foot like a floppy dog ear.

Peter unbuckled his own pants and took them off. His underpants were plaid. He stood over me.

"Are you going to do it?" I asked.

"Do you want me to?"

"No."

"It's happening anyway."

"Okay."

He moved my legs apart and kneeled down between them. At first he just examined me with his eyes. Then he fell on me and started moving against my body. His muscles were rigid, his weight on me like a load of lumber pressing me to the ground. They were lurching movements, spasms of anguished effort. He did not kiss me at all. Before there had been lots of kisses and not much else. This was the reverse of that. So maybe kisses were the opposite of sex. Maybe they were the birth of the death of sex.

I thought, *It is happening. This is happening,* thinking, *All our days add up to one day, and then they become something else. The point on the number line where negative becomes positive. The future the mirror image of your past—everything contingent on this moment here, the great, holy zero. My zero to his one. My nothing to his something.*

It was happening. I was waiting for it to happen. I could feel his movements, rough, even angry, against the skin of my thighs. There was a certain pleasure in not having to do anything—in having everything done for you while you just waited. He struggled away, and I waited and felt the warm, stinging chafe of his efforts.

I waited. I knew to expect the pressure of him between my legs, but there was no pressure. Then everything stopped.

For a moment there was an expression on his face of physical industry—vulgar, beautiful things flitting through a heated boy-mind. But then his eyes met mine, and that strange violent desire drained out of his gaze. Instead of falling on top of me, he stood back up.

"Never mind," he said.

I sat up, suddenly embarrassed by my nakedness.

"What happened?" I said. The sky now seemed very far away, measureless compared to how small I felt.

"Nothing happened," he said. "Never mind. You said no."

He was shifting nervously.

"You couldn't do it," I said. It wasn't an accusation. It was something I was realizing aloud.

"I could have," he said. "I didn't. You said no."

I reached for my pants, which were all balled up in the weeds. I put them on, and neither of us said anything.

We drove in silence back to where my bike was stashed. He stopped and waited for me to get out. But I didn't get out.

"You couldn't do it," I said. I didn't want to cry in front of him again, but I could hear the tremor in my voice. "You couldn't even if you tried. I'm a nun."

"You're not a nun."

"Yes, I am. I'm a nun, and nobody wants a nun. Nobody dreams about nuns."

"You're not," he said, but his voice was tired, unconvincing. He just wanted to be away from me.

It was too late. In the woods, for a moment, he had been an animal, he had functioned by beast logic. Now, again, he was just a boy. Was it just that he wasn't able to be the bad man, no matter how hard he tried? Or was I the one responsible for his transformation? Was I the antidote for breaching?

Did I ensnare what the breaching set free?

———

WHEN I TAKE my son to preschool, Miss Lily, his teacher, takes me aside and tells me that he has been having discipline issues and that the day before it was necessary to separate him from the other children for a while.

As she speaks, I watch my boy run forward to greet his

friends. He seems happy enough. Though I know that signifies nothing. I know how love and hate grow from the same seed.

"I mean," Miss Lily goes on, "I'm sure it's not something to worry about. Usually it's only a form of expression. We just need to work on redirecting it. But, again, I don't see it as a reason for real concern, Mrs. Borden."

She knows me as Ann Borden. I used to be Lumen Ann Fowler. Then I left the town where I grew up and I became Ann Fowler to signify that I was a different person. Then I married Jack Borden and became Ann Borden. A life of vestiges.

"Mrs. Borden?" she says again.

"Oh, yes, thank you."

When I leave, I drive across town to the high school where my husband works. I am a good driver. I obey all the traffic signs. I am always respectful to pedestrians, with their breakable bodies.

I do not use the school parking lot when I arrive. Instead I park around the corner and walk to the side of the main building, where Jack's office has a window that looks out on a large grassy expanse with trees and benches and fiberglass picnic tables. I sit at one of the benches, where I can see into his window. His back is facing me, and I can see that he is hunched over his desk, scribbling away industriously. The hair on the back of his neck is closely cropped. Sometimes he has me do touch-ups with a pair of clippers after he comes home from the barbershop. The skin of his neck is burned slightly from standing in the hot weekend sun, watering the front lawn.

I sit on the bench cross-legged. The advantage of my spot is that it is behind the large trunk of an oak tree, so if he should ever turn to look out the window, I can simply lean back and be completely hidden.

When people enter his office, Jack stands and greets them.

Then he waits for them to sit before he does. His adult colleagues smile a lot when they are in his office—he must be a charming man. When his At-Risk students come in, they sometimes fidget, and their heads swivel twitchily. Jack leans back in his chair in these situations.

I pick at the bark of the oak tree while I watch. Underneath is smooth, supple pulp.

When the students begin to talk, I notice that he nods a lot and listens with his head a little sideways—as though his brain were weighed down with the careful consideration of their words. The students seem to respond well to it.

I try it, there on my bench. I angle my head on the pivot of my neck as though carrying the weight of big thought.

A sparrow whistles overhead.

A little later the tough girl, Nat, comes into his office. She sits with her arms crossed and glares at him. Once I think she sees me watching, but she doesn't say anything about it. I know the look on her face. She wants to rip away at things. I know the tips of her fingers tremble like eager claws.

I pick at the bark of my tree.

At home that evening, I listen to Jack speak of his day. I nod and hold my head at an angle while I'm listening, but I must not be doing it right, because he says, "What are you doing?"

I tell him that I'm just listening.

"You feeling all right?" he asks. "You're acting funny again."

I tell him nothing is the least bit wrong. I ask him if he would like more potatoes.

After dinner I wash the dishes in water so hot it scalds the skin of my hands. I think about Peter Meechum and the quarry. I think about the body of that little girl who was me, lying there in the tall grass. Someone knotted up in confusion, always.

———

THE WEEK AFTER Peter Meechum took me to the quarry, the snow came, and I began to wonder if maybe I was a saint—one of those people whom badness slips right off of. People like to talk about ducks and water, about how the two repel each other. Really, it's that ducks have oily feathers. So maybe my pores leaked holy oil. My father also told me that some places have competitions in which young men try to capture greased pigs. That's me, a holy greased pig, slickering away out of the fumbling hands of evil.

Peter stopped coming to my house, and he didn't look at me in school. He was angry at me for being too good to rape. Saints are nobody's favorite people.

The first snow of the year came on a night when there was no moon at all. It was dark as anything, and so quiet all you could hear was the hum of your own thoughts. The snow came six minutes after two o'clock. It fell faintly in the cones of lamplight, descending like fleets of fairies through the cold sky. I was awake—the only one in town, I was sure—and I was sure that those miniature fallen sylphs were for me and my personal delectation. They came for me, because nature likes a saint. They settled on my windowsill, they collected on the dark grass of my lawn, they danced and whirled in the wind gusts before my eyes. I put my hand to the windowpane to greet it, that first snow. By the time I woke in the morning, I saw that after the snow had come to me, it had visited everyone.

That afternoon I stayed in the library after school reading about saints in order to know better what I was up against. A few saints got teamed up with the divines for some help—like Zita, who compelled the angels to bake bread for her. But as it turned out, the world was for the most part unkind to saints. Some of them were derided, including Saint Pyr, who, as far as I could tell, didn't do much to deserve sainthood. The only thing he ever really did was fall down a well.

Then there was Alice, who suffered a life of agony because of physical ailments. She had leprosy, and she also went blind. The only comfort she received was in the form of communion. But even in that respect she suffered. She could eat the bread, but she was banned from drinking from the Eucharistic cup because of her contagious maladies. But she had visions, and in one of her visions, Jesus came and told her everything was okay.

Lucy had her eyes gouged out, and she carried them around on a tray. But she was honored with a feast, which used to take place on the shortest day of the year, but then got moved to December thirteenth. Girls cooked buns with raisins in the middle to look like eyes and carried them on trays. I promised myself to remember Saint Lucy and her dug-out eyes on the thirteenth of December.

Another saint, named Drogo, was so hideously deformed that no one could stand to look at him. He imprisoned himself in a cell and ate only grain and water. But there was something called bilocation, which meant that he could be in two places at once. Some people said they could see him harvesting the fields even though he was locked away in his jail. I wondered if his spectral self, the one doing the harvesting, looked any better.

I discovered that there was a saint named Illuminata, like Lumen, but I couldn't find anything else about her other than that there was a church dedicated to her in Italy.

Apollonia was treated particularly brutally. The heathens bashed out all her teeth. They threatened to burn her alive, but she didn't give them the chance to do it—she escaped from them long enough to throw herself into the fire of her own accord. She was a saint, though, so she didn't burn. The flames had no effect on her. But the story doesn't end there. Heathens, shown evidence of their wrongdoing, don't fall to their knees to beg the Lord's forgiveness. They remained undeterred. They dragged Apollonia out of the fire and decapitated her.

Here's another interesting case—Saint Etheldreda. She was known, commonly, as Saint Audrey, which is where the word tawdry comes from. See, after she died, women took to selling lacy garments in her name. Tawdries were sanctified things, holy garments. Then the Puritans came along and started looking down on cheap indulgences such as lace, so the word changed its meaning. Which just goes to show how you can't do anything to protect your reputation when Puritans get involved—or heathens, either, for that matter.

My favorite saint, however, must have been Osgyth. She was married to a king, even though she didn't want to be. She bore him a son, as was her duty—but then when her husband was away hunting a white deer, she ran off to the convent to become a nun. The white deer. That was important. Whenever they specified the color of something, it was important. I wondered what the white deer symbolized. Something worthwhile, I hoped, because the king lost his wife in the pursuit of it.

Anyway, she was killed at the hands of Vikings, and at the place where she was killed a spring erupted from the earth and continues to give water to this day. The tears of a saint, flooding the land. You could drink them up.

Like Apollonia, Osgyth had her head cut off. But a moment after she died, her body sprang back up (like her tears from the earth itself!). She picked up her own head and carried it to the nearby convent, where she finally collapsed.

This was not, so it seems, an uncommon occurrence among martyrs. There's a whole category of saints who carried their own heads around after death. There's even a name for them. They're called cephalophoric martyrs.

Walking home through the drifts of new snow, I thought about that image. I thought about it over dinner, when my father asked me why I was being so tacit that evening. I couldn't stop thinking about it that day or the day after that or the next day—or ever.

My virginity, my saintliness, like the new snow you hate yourself for tromping on. What saints do, I realized, is make everyone else aware of their lowliness. You were simply about the regular business of your day until the saint walks by and makes you reckon with your true state as a bristly animal wallowing in its own filth. That's why everyone attacks the saints' bodies—to prove they have them and are anchored by them. But what the stories tell us is that they're not.

Peter Meechum had wanted to prove my frail, chafable, blisterable bodiedness. But there I lay under the afternoon sky—like a floating fairy or an ephemeral saint, smiling with her head removed and looking on from somewhere else entirely.

But what about the saint herself? Does she miss it—that puny tag of a body, with all its feeble, quaking pains and pleasures?

I still see it when I close my eyes—Osgyth, her neck a stump on her shoulders, feeling around blindly on the ground until she finds the toppled loaf of her own head, carrying it with effort across the fields to the convent.

What is a body without a mind? A slave to the feral instincts of ugly nature. An inelegant organ of gristle and stupid mechanics.

But also, what is a mind without a body?

It is a useless curd, lost in the mud. Or a pathetic piece of jet-sam, bobbing in the spring-lake of its own tears.

———

NOW IT'S TIME to talk about Blackhat Roy Ruggle, who was no good.

I remember how he was in grade school, runty and dark, the teachers leaning away from him with sour expressions on their faces. I remember him cursing them under his breath, seeming very mature in his primal anger. It never occurred to me as strange, back then, that I equated obscenity with adulthood—as though we all grow inevitably toward the twisted and grotesque. Later, in high school, the administration tolerated him with weary resignation, because it was well known that his father had left when he was only two years old, that his mother was a drunk who survived on state aid, that the two of them lived in a shack with a sagging roof on the edge of town, and that he worked in a scrap yard in order to make money to buy things like cigarettes and booze—things that stank of angry manhood.

He came to school dirty, his clothes torn, his shoes tattered and repaired with duct tape, his hair unwashed. There was no fight he backed away from, no conflict he did not lick his lips at. It made no difference how big or small his opponents were—he gnashed his teeth and spit out vulgarities and burned himself bright and hot into a cindered black punk. Teachers avoided him because they knew their authority wouldn't sway him. Younger kids avoided him because they knew their weakness wouldn't, either.

No one was surprised when he breached early. No one was surprised that his breach lasted longer by far than anyone else's.

He had always been part animal, and he needed no moon to tell him that.

Me, I avoided him—which was not difficult. Our worlds had nothing to do with each other.

Until the day they did.

After the day in the woods with Peter, I had spent the next couple weeks mostly alone. I wore white as much as I could—because it was the color of sainthood and it was the color of the deer that Osgyth's king hunted and it was the color of the snow descending everywhere around me.

In school I saw that Polly spent more time with the boys who had already gone breach. They would often have her pressed in a corner of the stairwell or against the lockers, their bodies flush with hers. Sometimes Polly seemed embarrassed to be squished between these boys and the lockers—but other times she gazed at the ceiling with half-lidded eyes, and I could see that she was lost to them.

"Do you have a boyfriend now?" I asked her in French class.

"Oui et non," she said. "C'est compliqué."

"Are you happy?"

"Personne n'est heureux."

"Some people are. Some people are happy."

My voice pleaded with her to be again the Polly I had known just a year or two before.

But that Polly seemed to be gone for good. This one, the one who got put into reveries by being pressed up against lockers, slammed her book closed and shrugged.

"Not everything is about white picket fences," she said. "Portes blanches."

"Clôtures."

Mrs. Farris, our French teacher, looked over at us. I looked down at the passage I was supposed to be translating. When it was safe again, I looked at Polly. I apologized with my eyes, but with her eyes she told me that I didn't understand, that it was not the business of saints to stand too close to the vulgarity of real life. She told me with her eyes to stay wrapped in my white shrouds.

It was on that same day that I saw Blackhat Roy backed up against a wall in the alcove under the stairs by Peter and some of his friends. Such conflicts were never my concern—I was mostly concerned about avoiding Peter, who was facing Roy and not me. Out of the corner of my eye, though, I saw that Roy had fixed me in his gaze, as though I were more interesting than the group of boys threatening to assault him.

"If you're going to do it," I overheard him saying, "just do it, and shut the fuck up about it."

Even as he said the words, he was watching me rather than them.

I rushed around the corner out of his sight. I didn't know what his gaze meant, but I wanted to get out from under it.

It was later that day that Blackhat Roy spoke to me for the first time in my life. It was at the bike cage, where he leaned against the chain-link enclosure—it bowed with his weight. I walked by, trying to be nothing to him, trying to reduce myself.

"Hey," he said. "Come here."

I went over to where he stood.

I flinched when he reached out to me, but he just tugged at the white ribbon in my hair.

"What are you trying to look like?" he said.

"Nothing." This was untrue. We are all, in one way or another, trying to look like something—but we don't like to be called on it.

"You look like a Creamsicle."

"Creamsicles are orange, not white," I said victoriously. Then I chanced to look down and see that I had worn my orange winter jacket over my white cotton dress and white stockings. "Oh."

He tilted his head to the side and seemed to examine me. Then he leaned forward toward my neck and inhaled deeply.

"You haven't gone warg yet. You're late."

I said nothing. I wanted to run.

"Can you feel it? I remember—I could feel it growing in me before it came. Like a tumor or something. A sick feeling in your stomach. Your guts all rolling around. Then it came, and I wasn't scared anymore. Are you looking forward to not being scared?"

He did not wait for a response from me. He seemed to have something in his teeth, and he rolled his tongue around in his mouth until he got it. He plucked it out with two fingers and held it up to look at. It was a piece of pink gristle from the school meat loaf at lunch. He flicked it away and returned his gaze to me.

"Me," he said, "I'm fourteen months already. Longer than anyone else. Maybe I'll never come out the other end. That happens sometimes, you know. Sometimes you stay breach your whole life."

"I never heard of that."

He shrugged.

"Sometimes," I said, "sometimes people don't breach at all. They just skip it."

"Now we've both never heard of something."

Behind me I was aware that two freshman girls were walking across the parking lot. Roy grew silent, and his hyena eyes watched them until they were out of sight.

He leaned back and wound his fingers around the chain link

over his shoulders. This is where I'll admit that I'd never really looked at Blackhat Roy before. He'd always been an abstraction to me, like big human notions such as horror and courage and mortification. But now he was forcing me to look at him, all of him. Some people, when they're breaching, don't quite get back to their regular selves when the full moon is gone. For some, like Roy, their breacher sensibility follows them into the daylight, throughout the month, the entire year. This was the worst kind of breacher when the full moon rose—and between moons, even during the daylight, you could still see the feral radiance behind the eyes.

He had grown bigger—I never really noticed it until now. He was no longer the runty creature I remembered from grade school. He had a thick mop of curly hair that fell down over his wide brow. He was dark, and it looked like he needed to shave. When he drew his hand across his jawline, you could hear a gristly static. His teeth were crooked, and the way his lips curled into a smile made you feel complicit in all sorts of crimes—things you didn't even have names for.

His hands, wrapped around the metal ligatures of the cage, were scarred and dirty and short-fingered. The nails were worn down to almost nothing and one of them was ripped off completely, as though he had paws made for digging, hands for labor or violence.

"How come you didn't save me today?" he said. "How come you didn't rescue me?"

"I don't know."

"How come you didn't keep your boyfriend from attacking?"

I said nothing.

"Is it because you figured I deserved it? Because you thought I must've done something wrong? Is that the reason?"

I shivered, and my throat tried to close up. I didn't know what would happen to me.

"Yes," I said quietly.

"Well, you're right. Did you know it's considered bad manners to take a piss in somebody's locker? I guess we learn through our mistakes."

"I didn't do anything," I said, my voice pleading.

"Didn't you?" His teeth gnashed, and for a second I thought he would use them to rip my throat out. I would have run, but I was pinned in a way that was a mystery to me. "Guess what. I may be rotten, but I ain't the only one. I know it was you."

"What?"

"You pulled the fire alarm that one time. You did it. And I know why. Did you think I forgot about that?"

I didn't know what to say to him, this furious and filthy golem of a boy. What could possibly be shared between us, apart from fear and calamity? I wanted to be away from him—I wanted him back in his cell in the abstract part of my brain, where I could trace him in the safe trigonometric functions of my daily life. But he wouldn't go. Maybe he would do what Peter couldn't. Maybe he would attack. Even here at school, because the boundaries of wilderness and civilization were nothing to Blackhat Roy. I closed my eyes and waited for whatever would come.

"Don't worry," he said after a while. "Probably I won't hurt you. I don't get much joy out of hunting down defenseless animals. Not much."

He unleaned himself from the fence, stretched himself to his full length, and rotated his head quickly in a way that produced an audible crack in his neck. He started away, and I thought everything was over between us—but then, before he had walked very far, he turned back.

"But when you go warg," he said, "then you better watch out. Because I think I'd like to chomp on you a little." He smiled when he said it, as though he wanted me not to fear his threats but to savor them.

I didn't move until he was completely out of sight, then I got my bike from the cage and rode home fast. The icy air blasted my face, but I was not cold. My lungs burned sulfur, and I wanted to cry, but the tears wouldn't come. When I got home, I showered—and in my stomach, I could feel the deep bowl of my guts. They sloshed around as though I had all the violent seas of the world inside me.

CHAPTER 4

Just as the streets of our little town were plowed, another snow came and buried us again. People speculated that we were in for a rough winter. The lake froze early, and it froze wide. That year ice skaters could go farther out than they ever had before. I went skating myself, but I went in the early morning, when nobody else was there. I did spins and twirls, and I thought I must be the most elegant sight, a lone skater in the sunrise. When others began to show up, I glided to the shore and sat on a stone to remove my skates. They would always be surprised to see me. Their thought was to have been the first — but they weren't. Sometimes things work that way.

Peter continued to avoid me. And Polly spoke to me as though I were a child — when she spoke to me at all. As soon as the final bell of the school day rang, I rushed home to avoid any further contact with Blackhat Roy, whose eyes seemed to track me in the halls from one room to the next. I had somehow wandered into his domain, and now I couldn't escape. Once I had lamented being invisible, but now there was nothing I desired more than to be out from under his gaze. He seemed to know when I came into a room, because his head would swivel on his neck and those dark eyes of his would nail me to a wall. Even in the cafeteria, swarming with hundreds of moving bodies, echoing with a constant din—even there, when I walked through the doors, I could see that dusky, scabrous face of his looking through the crowd at me, a still-pale petal in an algae-covered pond.

So instead of looking things up in the library after school, where I knew I'd be discovered, I took my books to the deserted school auditorium and studied there.

I was very much enamored with maps that year. Maybe it was because my father was a geologist and was always looking at elaborate technical diagrams that made earthly landscapes look like strange outlined amoebas on the page. I sometimes thumbed through his books, tracing the curved lines with my finger. But really my interest was in conventional maps. I looked them up in old atlases. I followed their legends, exploring—mistaking, perhaps, the paper on which the world was printed for the actual world itself. I read books that had maps printed on their endpapers. As the events of the book unfolded, I would turn back to the endpapers and locate them on the map. I liked how the linear progression of time over the course of a novel could be condensed into a single map image, as though it were all said and done before the book even started—as though all of any person's life could be reduced to just a legend explaining some fixed map we could not see.

I drew maps in my notebooks during class. Sometimes simple maps showing the spatial relationships of the students in a classroom, maybe with arrows illustrating their various kinds of connections. Or sometimes complex maps of the entire school building, featuring dotted lines that traced my regular routes from class to class.

My father liked my maps. He said they showed a unique mind, the kind of mind that existed above itself and was able to see itself in context. Context, he said, was a very important thing. So I said the word to myself thirteen times that night before I went to bed, and it became one more in my arsenal of magic words.

What I was working on that day, sprawled on the warm wooden floor of the empty stage, was going to be a Christmas present for my father. It was a very large and detailed map of the town and all the places in it that were significant to the two of us. Like the drive-in where we used to see movies but didn't, for some reason, anymore. Like the tree in the cemetery under which my mother lies buried. Or the exact place on the freeway where we almost got into an accident and he had to pull over on the shoulder and tell me how much he loved me, how much more than anything else in the world I meant to him. I know it was a strange one to include, but it made sense in my unique mind, and I believed he would understand.

I made our house the center of the map. I drew it in pencil first and then in fine black pen to get as much detail as possible. You could even see into the upstairs window of the house if you cared to look. And there, framed in the window, was the teensy-tiny figure of a girl standing before an easel, drawing a map.

It was nice there in the musty auditorium, the sound of my scratching pencil echoey in the large space, the heavy, muffling curtains hanging loose over the hard wood. The moving air from the vents ruffled them slightly, and they rippled like vertical oceans. I liked the rows of unpopulated seats staring at me, their lower halves all folded up except one on the aisle that was broken and remained always open, a poor busted tooth in that grinning mouth. There is nothing to fear in such cavernous and sepulchral spaces. You fill them with the riots of your imagination.

Absorbed as I was in my map, I hadn't heard Mr. Hunter enter from backstage and leaped up when he spoke to me.

"What's that you're doing?"

"Nothing," I said and quickly gathered my materials, clutching my map to my chest. "Working. There's no play practice tonight." I knew the schedule, you see. I liked to know in advance where people would be and where they wouldn't be.

He stood with his hands in his pockets, gazing at me with a foreign, unreadable expression. Under a tweed jacket, he wore a button-down shirt that had come a little untucked over the course of the day. He looked younger than my father, but I couldn't tell by how much. He had told us that he grew up in a small town outside Chicago, and I had always wondered why someone from Chicago would come to a town like ours. He had a ragged growth of stubble on his chin, and his eyes always looked like they knew more than he was telling.

"You know," he said, "I've been wanting to talk with you."

"What about?"

"What do you think about trying out for the play?"

"Me? I can't act."

"Everybody can act," he said, shrugging. "Everybody *does* act." I didn't know what to say.

"The best kinds of actors are the ones who perform so often—so religiously—that they don't even realize they're do-ing it."

"I guess," I said.

He would not take his eyes from mine for a long while, and I found I couldn't take mine off his, either—as though some un-breakable current connected our brains.

Finally he breathed in deeply, stretched, and looked up into the rafters.

"Anyway," he said, "think about it. All acting is just lying. You know how to lie, don't you?"

I said goodbye and rushed out as quickly as I dared. The sun had gone down, and the overhead lamps had buzzed on in the deserted parking lot.

Everybody else believed they could see my very soul. So why did I feel so blind?

———

IT'S TRUE THAT I am a Christmas baby—or at least close enough to count as one. I was born on December 23, Christmas Eve Eve, and so I am one of that breed for whom the celebration of existence gets irrevocably tangled up with garlands and lighted trees and window displays. No one likes a Christmas baby. The occasion requires that people purchase two different kinds of wrapping paper. It is too much celebration altogether, and it makes people queasy with indulgence.

Throughout my young life, my father did his best to make my birthday special—so we never put up a Christmas tree until Christmas Eve, the day after my birthday. There was no talk of the holiday at all until that day.

This year was special, because it was my sixteenth birthday, and sixteenth birthdays put you in a different category from the one you were in before. In the morning, my father told me we could do anything my little heart desired. But actually I was feeling a bit unwell, and all I really wanted to do was stay indoors and make pizza and watch movies on television and pretend that the world outside didn't exist.

"Done and done," he said and made me waffles.

Then he brought me a little wrapped box and dropped it on the table in front of me.

"I've been saving it for you for a long time," he said.

I undid the wrapping paper at the taped seams (I'm not one of those people who tear through wrapping paper willy-nilly, as though ferocity of consumption equaled appreciation of a gift) and set it aside. It was a jewelry box, and inside sat a little silver locket with floral engravings on the outside.

"It belonged to your mother," said my father. To look at it seemed to pain him. "I gave it to her when we were sixteen. Now I'm giving it to you."

Inside there were two pictures that kissed when the locket was closed. One was of my mother and the other was of my father—both when they were my age.

"Her name was Felicia Ann Steptoe," he said, reciting the bedtime catechism from my childhood, "and she wore long orchid gloves at our wedding."

It occurred to me on that day that my mother was actually closer to me than if I had been old enough to remember her when she died. She existed entirely in my own brain—she was that close. She was lovely inside there, always posing, always beautiful. She was happy as could be.

I thanked my father for the present, throwing my arms around him and hugging him so tightly he pretended to choke.

"Now you just relax while I do the breakfast dishes," he said.

"Wait," I said. "I need to know something."

"What's that?"

"What time was I born? I mean, exactly."

"It was in the morning some time. I don't remember."

"Is it on my birth certificate?"

"I'm sure it probably is."

"Can we check?"

"On this day, we seek to indulge," he said, wiping his hands on a kitchen towel.

He went to the closet in his office and thumbed through the file cabinets to find what he was looking for. I followed him and sat in his desk chair, watching.

Eventually he found the manila folder he was looking for.

"Ta-da," he said.

Then he took a pale green document out of the folder and scanned it quickly with his eyes.

"Let's see," he said. "Here it is. Eight thirty-two, ante meridian."

I looked at my watch. It was half past nine.

"Congratulations," he said. "You're officially sixteen years old."

So it was true. I was a year older but still periodless.

I was officially a lot of things. Sixteen was only one of them.

———

THE DAY AFTER my birthday was Christmas Eve, and it also happened to be the first night of Lake Moon. There would be no carolers this Christmas, no midnight masses at the church. This would be a Christmas to stay indoors.

My father and I had much to do, since our preparations for the holiday only began that morning. We got up early and picked out a tree from the Christmas tree farm by the freeway. It was my job to stand back and determine its straightness while he secured it in the metal stand in our living room. We decorated and drank eggnog. We sang along to "Good King Wenceslas," which was our favorite Christmas song—and, as far as I have been able to tell, nobody else's favorite Christmas song in the world.

> *Good King Wenceslas looked out*
> *On the feast of Stephen,*
> *When the snow lay round about*
> *Deep and crisp and even.*
> *Brightly shone the moon that night,*
> *Though the frost was cruel,*
> *When a poor man came in sight*
> *Gathering winter fuel.*

We sat together across our small dining room table, and we drank cinnamon-scented mulled wine that had been heated in a saucepan on the stove. My father put a stick of raw cinnamon in each one—and even though the wine did not taste good to me, I liked to be drinking it with him, watching the steam rise from the crystal goblets set on the red tablecloth I insisted on using for the occasion.

After dinner my father put on a Motown Christmas album, and we danced together to "I Saw Mommy Kissing Santa Claus," and then we lit a candle for Felicia Ann Steptoe and put it in the window, without somberness, to invite her ghost to visit.

There were very few presents under the tree, but they were all labeled carefully nonetheless. We made sure that some of them—both for him and for me—were labeled "From Santa," because Santa Claus was the invisible third guest at our miniature holiday. The truth is, we made our aloneness into a gift and gave that gift to each other, and it was our true and main present to unwrap.

I ate fewer frosted sleigh-shaped Christmas cookies than I normally did, because my stomach was still bothering me. So I went to bed early and turned on the radio to be lulled to sleep by "Have Yourself a Merry Little Christmas"—and also to drown out before I even heard them the sounds that might be coming from outside. This was a holy night, a peaceful night, and I would not indulge those wild creatures in the street—not even for a second.

———

IT WAS WELL after midnight when I woke up. At first I thought it was the cramping in my gut that had woken me—I thought for sure my period had finally come. But then, surfacing into consciousness, I realized that the voice I was hearing in my ears was actually coming from outside, that it was the voice of Polly. She called to me from the pitchy night.

"Lumen! Lumen, help me!"

I got out of bed, drew the curtains aside, and opened the window.

The first thing I noticed was the quality of the air that blew into the house. It was frigid in my lungs, but it made me feel much better than I had been feeling over the past couple days, and I made a resolution to get more fresh air than I had been getting.

Polly was there, standing just below my window in the front yard. Strange, I thought, that the last time Polly came and stood under my window Peter was sleeping in the den two doors down and knew nothing of it at all. Now he was somewhere out there among them.

Polly looked roughed up. There were bruises on her face, little abrasions all over the pale skin of her chest.

She was naked, her legs lost to midcalf in the snowbank. As part of my research, I had been made to understand that breachers did not feel the cold the way other people did. I was told that their blood ran hotter during those nights. A girl of science, a daughter of facts, I hadn't entirely believed it until now. Like a beech tree, Polly's frail white body was planted, unshivering, in the snow, her breath coming in visible puffs between her bleeding lips, her skin varicolored by the string of blinking Christmas lights hung on the eaves of the house. While she may have been hurting from her injuries, it seemed the cold was nothing to her.

"Lumen," she said from the pool of lamplight in the street, "please."

"What do you want?" I called down in a quiet voice. The night below was utterly silent.

"Lumen, I miss you," she said. "Remember how we used to be?"

"What are you doing here?"

"It's Christmas Eve, Lumen. I'm hungry. My mother used to make me pancakes in the shape of elephants on Christmas morning."

Her mind was gone wild, her panicked eyes darting from one thing to another.

"Are you all right?" I said.

She sat down in the snowbank and pulled her knees to her chest, rocking back and forth slightly. She mumbled something I couldn't hear.

"What? What did you say?"

"My turn," she said. "They said it was my turn. Sometimes you bleed others, and sometimes you get bled. That's the way. It hurts, Lumen. Apples and cheese—I used to eat them when they were cut up for me. I used to be pretty."

"Who did it? Who hurt you?"

She looked up at me, confused.

"They did," she said simply. "All of them."

It made me feel sick to see her that way, but also angry. I found myself hating her a little also, despising her for being so frail outside my window. She made life—our lives—seem meager.

I could feel the spite bubbling up in me. It felt strange but good.

And then it was gone as quickly as it came, because below me Polly seemed to hear something that startled her. She stood suddenly and looked around.

"What is it?" I called down to her.

But she was no longer listening to me. Tensed like a threatened cat, she ran a few steps one way, stopped, listened some more, then ran a few steps in another direction and stopped again.

"What's happening?" I said. "Polly."

Her breath was coming faster now, and she ran toward the sidewalk and the street beyond.

"Polly, wait!"

I hurried out of my room and down the stairs as quietly as I could, so as not to wake my father, down the hall.

I opened the front door, and it occurred to me again that the blast of bitter night air was a relief. I was overheated, my heart going like crazy, my pulse driving in my ears, and the air seemed blissful and calming. I wondered, in some still part of my frenzied brain, if this was the same beatified air Jesus was born into so many years ago in his little desert manger.

Polly was no longer in the front yard. Now she stood in the middle of the street, her legs bent in a half crouch, poised to run

for her life at any moment. But the street was empty. I leaned out
the door and looked, and I saw nothing. She was spooked.

I felt bad about the little flare of intolerance I'd had for her
just a few minutes before. She was damaged. She needed help.

"Polly," I called in a whisper, which was as loud as I dared.

She seemed to hear me, because she turned her gaze in my direction for one little moment—a crisis moment of longing and
sorrow, regret and fear—then she turned again and ran as fast
she could down the street.

"Polly," I called again, louder this time, but she didn't come
back.

I took a few steps outside, and then a few more. It's a funny
thing, sometimes, what we find ourselves doing. I observed myself as I walked, as though watching the actions of a character on
television. *Oh, isn't it interesting what she's doing. I wouldn't have expected that of her.* When I came again into my own mind, I realized
I was standing in the middle of the snowy street in my pajamas
and my bare feet.

I couldn't see Polly anywhere. It was just me under the hazy,
big Lake Moon. I turned this way and that, and the only sound I
heard was that of my bare feet shifting against the icy surface of
the road.

I wondered about that—my feet—and why they didn't seem
to sting from the frozen pavement. I looked back at my house,
and it seemed smaller from the outside than it was from the inside—like a puzzle that strained your mind to think about.

In the sudden quiet of the empty night, I thought what a curiously wide place the world was—that you could stand in your
nightclothes in the middle of a street and be quite, quite alone.

And then something else happened. It started to snow. They
were gentle, quiet little flakes, like the dust or pollen of another

season. I raised my arm and saw the snow collect on my skin, glistening along all the fine, light hairs.

You find glory in the strangest places.

I guess I wasn't entirely surprised by what happened next. I guess I wasn't. My body told me I had already known.

They came out from behind the trees in the woods across the street from my house. They had been watching me, you see. They had been there the whole time—that was what had Polly so spooked. They came out slowly, their pale bodies steaming in the cold, their skin taut and waxy against the wooded void.

I did not retreat to the house. I watched myself not retreating to the house. It was a wonder.

They came and stood in a circle around me. Rose Lincoln was there, and she approached and stood so close that I could feel her steaming breath on my cheeks.

"You're lost," she said.

The others smiled. They seemed to have difficulty standing still for long. It was all girls. It was the first time I realized they traveled like that sometimes, separated by sex. It was a coven, a brace, a klatch. Marina Donald stood right beyond Rose, and I could see her fists clenching and releasing, eager for something to throttle. Sue Foxworth was there, too, looking distracted. She scratched at herself and gazed off into the woods as though she were already running through them in her mind.

Rose Lincoln took one long, languorous look up and down my body.

"Is this what you wear to bed?" she asked. My pajamas had pink and purple hearts on them. They were cotton. The bottoms had an elastic waistband. The top had buttons down the front. She reached out with her painted nails and undid the top button, then she undid the next.

She seemed to lose interest before the third. She sighed heavily and looked at the sky, the snow falling lightly through the air.

"You keep yourself separate," she said. "Away from us. How come? Is it because you think you're better?"

I tried to respond. I licked the coldness from my lips.

"I don't . . ."

But what did I mean to say? That I didn't keep myself separate? That I didn't know why I kept myself separate? Her accusation felt strange to me, because I had never seen myself as having any agency in my exclusion from the crowd. I was the one excluded by them—I was the one kept at a distance by everybody else.

Wasn't I?

"That's right, you don't," she replied. "You don't. I know you don't. All you are is what you don't."

Suddenly she reached out with both hands and ripped my pajama top open. The remaining buttons popped and clattered to the icy pavement.

The others in the group closed in more tightly around me. Marina and Idabel McCarron were on either side of me. Their laughter was grotesque as they took off my pajama top and let it fall to the ground. Then I was bare-chested before them. Their nudity was nothing—they seemed not to feel it. How could they not feel it? My chest had never been exposed to anyone before. I was aware of it—my own brute nakedness—and my awareness was an excruciating ache that went all up and down my spine.

"She's so small," Sue Foxworth said. The fact that her voice was not accusatory did not comfort me.

Rose Lincoln got closer. She paid no mind to my bare chest. I tried to back away from her, but the girls behind me did not allow escape.

"It's Christmas," Rose said, her voice almost a whisper in my ear. "Don't you want to tear something down?"

I shook my head.

"No," I said. My voice was tiny and unconvincing. I tried it again, stronger. "No."

"No what?" Rose said. "What are you saying no to? Do you have any idea? Or is it just that saying no makes you feel safe?"

I wasn't hearing her. I shook my head and said it over and over: "No, no, no, no."

I came unfrozen and brought my arms up to cover my chest. Then I turned away from Rose and began to push my way through the bodies, feeling against my bare torso their bony protrusions, their ungainly knobs of skin and cartilage, their joints, their breath and fingers. But I made myself into a dart, and I kept pushing through.

They laughed. I could hear them laugh, but only from a great distance.

Behind me, Rose said, "What are you feeling right now, girl? What's your body telling you? Huh? What are you feeling in your guts? In your lungs? In your muscles? Inside those pink pajama pants?"

That's when I broke through. The bodies fell aside, and I stumbled with the sudden lack of restriction. I fell to the asphalt, coming down hard on my hands. Then I was up again, and I was running. But not toward the house. The house was behind me. I was putting everything behind me. I ran down the street in the opposite direction from the one Polly had run. I could hear their voices laughing as I ran. I wanted them behind me, too.

Except they were following. They ran, too, hooting and hollering as they went. They snarled and called out in obscene ways. I thought I could hear Idabel's high-pitched laugh, hysterical, like a mongrel in the gullies. Some of them barked like dogs and gnashed their teeth together as though they would eat me alive if they caught me.

The snow came harder, but I cared nothing about freezing. It felt good, those pinhead flakes against my bare skin. *It is snowing on my body,* I thought in some calm part of my brain. *Snowflakes are melting against my bare skin. Such a strange feeling—so unlikely!*

I ran. I ran past all the houses with their bright, cheerful Christmas decorations, their strings of lights, their plastic Santa Clauses on the front lawns. I ran past the crèche in the Sondersons' yard, the little baby Jesus nested in hay, overlooked by Mary and Joseph and the three wise men with their gifts from far away.

It made me think of the North Star. I would follow it. I would run to it—I would capture it in my hands. Where might it lead me? Were there new messiahs to be found? Or would it just lead me into the wide open—the deserts of wind and black? And I thought that would be all right, too. Running through space like that, feeling as though your legs would never stop working.

They were still behind me, though more distant now.

At the place where the road turned ahead, there was a trail I knew of. It went up over a hill and down into a little valley and then deeper into the woods. It would take me away. To where I didn't know. I didn't care. Away was the only place I wanted to be, and I didn't care what it looked like.

I launched my body up over the embankment and onto the trail, and I kept running. The snow felt like a static charge on my skin—the branches of the trees tore at me—the frozen pebbles of the trail dug into my bare feet. It was nothing. This was nothing. I could breathe right for the first time.

Lumen. There was Lumen, and there were the places people

did not go. And Lumen would go to those places. She would leap over fences and crawl through mud. She would climb up on rooftops and call crazy with every little branch of her lungs.

It was a holy night. I ran. My father slept soundly in his bed, somewhere far behind me, and I ran. Elsewhere in the world masses were being performed and stock was being taken of the glories and regrets of life—and it was nothing to me, because I ran.

My sore legs ached with the same splendid vigor. I relished the soreness, as I did my burning lungs.

I was naked in the woods. It was a beautiful outrage.

I had started running in order to escape Rose Lincoln and her pack. Then I was running to put things decidedly behind me, to seek lovely new emptinesses. Then I ran to outpace the nagging of my ticklish brain. Then I just ran.

II

CHAPTER 5

We live on a cul-de-sac. Our house is at the very end. During the days, when my husband is at work, the cul-de-sac becomes a playground. The mothers sit in front of their houses on lawn chairs and watch their children playing in the dead-end street.

Lola King lives next door. She is from New York and has very little patience for the provinciality of our burg. She has befriended me. She brings her lawn chair to my yard and sets it up next to mine. She also brings a pitcher of frozen daiquiris and two frosted glasses and even paper umbrellas to stick in the top. Her husband got into some sort of trouble back East.

"Cocktail time, darling," she says, a cigarette dangling between her lips.

The other neighbors don't approve. Particularly Marcie Klapper-Witt, who lives three doors down from me. She wears sunglasses so we cannot see that her judgmental gaze is always upon us. Lola raises her glass to toast her.

I smile and am delighted.

The children run in circles. They draw on the pavement with

oversize chalk. They shoot at one another with water guns that look like colorful missile launchers. My son is among them, and to watch him is to acknowledge how impossible it is to stay one thing for your entire life. Much of the time I stare at the clouds.

My son is four years old. He will not run wild and naked in the streets when he becomes a teenager. He will not hack away at the old, tired physical world just to watch it bleed. He will drink to excess with his friends. At most, he will urp up his dinner, drunkenly, on front lawns and then escape in shame. He will fumble awkwardly at the apparatus of girls' bodies. He will be stubborn and recalcitrant. He will slam doors. But he will not run savage through the night, coyote-like, enamored of his own power to sunder and tear. He will not drink hot blood. This town is a very safe town. We have a neighborhood watch, a community league, and I am on the PTA.

But he does bite, my son. He has a problem with biting. According to the other mothers, he is too old to be biting.

Marcie Klapper-Witt brings my son before me one day. She has his arm clasped in her fist, up by his shoulder. His elbow is bleeding, and he is crying.

"Mrs. Borden, your son bit my daughter," says Marcie Klapper-Witt.

"He did?"

"Yes, he did."

"But his elbow is bleeding."

"Fancy pushed him down after he bit her. To get him off her."

Fancy Klapper-Witt wears a tiara everywhere she goes. Her favorite thing is posing for pictures.

"Did he hurt her?" I ask.

"He *bit* her. He's really too old to be biting. You should look into that, Mrs. Borden. They won't let him into kindergarten."

"I'm very sorry, Marcie," I say. "It won't happen again."

Lola smiles up at the other woman.

"Cocktail, Marcie? It takes the edge off."

But Marcie Klapper-Witt marches off without saying another word.

I lean forward to talk to my son.

"Marcus, did you bite Fancy Klapper-Witt?" I ask.

He nods.

"Do you hate her?"

He shakes his head.

"Do you like her?"

He nods.

"Do you like her so much you want to eat her all up, like the wolf in Little Red Riding Hood?"

He nods.

"That's what I thought."

He sniffles. The tears have made streaks through the layer of dust and grime on his face. The blood from his elbow is smeared across his forearm.

"Does your elbow hurt?"

He nods.

"Here," I say. "Look."

I use my thumb to take some of the blood from his elbow and paint it in two horizontal bands across his cheeks.

"Now you're a warrior, Marcus," I say. "Do you want to see?"

He nods.

The tray Lola brought the daiquiris on has a mirrored bottom, so I hold it up for him to see.

He is pleased by this and goes off to play again.

Lola turns to me.

"No Neosporin?" she asks.

"What?"

"For his elbow. Aren't you worried about infection?"

I shrug.

"Bodies can withstand a lot of damage," I say. "If you lean on them, you're surprised how much they can take."

Lola laughs and clinks my glass with her own.

"Darling," she says, "you are a shooting star among drudges. You're just so *ethereal*."

I can feel my mouth grinning, though I am embarrassed.

"Well," she goes on, "that little Fancy bitch had it coming. I guarantee it won't be the last time in her life that some man tries to take a bite out of her."

I stare at the clouds and listen to the cicadas make their repetitious song, and when the sun starts to go down, all the mothers gather their children into their houses. Lights come on in windows all up and down the street.

Lola calls her own children to her.

"Come on, brats! Assemble!"

Then she, too, goes indoors.

I'm the only one left outside when my husband comes home. He parks in the driveway and climbs out of the car. Our son is asleep on the lawn, curled up on the grass like a house cat.

"What are you doing out here?" Jack says.

"Enjoying the evening," I say.

"Aren't you cold?"

"Not to speak of."

"Do you want to come in now?"

"I suppose so."

But the answer to his question is really much more complicated than that.

THEY WERE WRONG, all of them. You do remember some things—fragments that gnaw at you—the sense of becoming another animal altogether. That Christmas Eve, I remember myself in the woods—a delicious kind of lostness that was dizzying and joyful. I was alone, I believe, the entire night. I felt large, bigger than the trees that towered over me. Wider than the sky at its widest. I was the center of all I observed. There was nowhere to get back to because I carried all of myself with me. I was my own home.

But I did return to the house. Somehow I did. I woke in the backyard at dawn. I was naked, curled at the base of a rhododendron shrub, the powdery snow melted into a fragile, concave nest around my body.

I was cold. I was starting to feel the cold again.

I crouched there, trying to assess the situation. My mind was still muddled, and part of me still felt bold and unapologetic. But that part was quickly diminishing.

It was still very early. No one was out. I sprinted across the lawn, around the side of the house, and in through the front door, which was still unlocked. Inside I stopped and pressed myself against the wall, breathing hard. I listened, but the house was still quiet. The heat ticked on, and the wall vents rattled faintly. My father had not woken up. I crept up the stairs to my room, where I got a robe out of my closet and wrapped it around my body.

Lying on the bed, I tried to sleep, but my muscles ached and my head was spinning—and I didn't want to sleep, because I felt the opposite of tired.

So I took a bath in the bathroom down the hall. I made the water as hot as I could bear it, thinking to sweat out whatever was still in me from the night before. I was meticulous. I pried out all the dirt that had collected under the nails of my toes and fingers, I scrubbed the soles of my feet raw trying to get rid of all the yellowed mud caked in the creases. I picked pine needles from my hair, and they floated like miniature felled trees on the meniscus of the tub water. Sap knotted my hair in places, and I had to wash it three times in scalding water before I could dig out the coagulants with a plastic comb.

There was a knock on the door.

"Merry Christmas, little Lumen!"

"Merry Christmas," I called back.

"You're up bright and early. Ready for presents?"

"I'll be down in a minute."

I stood, dripping dry on the bathmat. Wiping the mirror clear of condensation, I looked at the girl I saw there. Judging by her looks, her scrubbed pinkness, you would never know where she'd been.

Back in my bedroom, I dressed in red and green, as was the tradition with my father and me. I avoided looking at the windows, because I did not want to think about the snow and the trees and the clear sky of morning. I wanted to be inside and think inside thoughts. I wanted to feel the comfort of walls around me—and to speak the delicate languages of family and society and tradition.

Downstairs, my father and I took turns opening presents. He was eager to see me excited, and so I was excited for him.

He took many pictures of me, but I vowed never to look at them.

It hurt too much to think how completely the girl in those pictures was not me.

———

THE LAST GIFT I gave him was the map I had drawn for him.

Until this very moment, I have never told anyone about it—not even my husband. Sometimes you hide away a memory because it is so precious that you don't want to dilute it with the attempt to recount it. Sometimes you hide a memory because the disclosure of it would reveal you to be a different person from the one others believe you to be. And sometimes you may hide a memory because it inhabits you in some physical way, because its meaning is inexpressible and dangerous. That is this memory—evidence, baleful proof—just the recollection of him opening my gift.

He unrolls it on the ground, kneeling before it like a supplicant, head bowed, prayerful and quiet.

What he says is, "You did this," and his voice is full of wonder and admiration. He does not bother to thank me. It is a gift beyond thank yous.

Using his fingertip, he travels from one place to another on the map, and at each location he pauses to examine the detail. It is as though he lives, for the moment, in that map, as though he and I are travelers on a different plane.

That plane is a place where you can redraw yourself from scratch.

The pen lines are so perfect, so straight and lovely—who would ever want to cross them?

———

I HAD TWO visitors later that day. The first was Polly. We stood, shivering, on the sidewalk, because I did not want her in my house. The space inside those walls was suddenly precious to me.

"Are you having a good Christmas?" she asked.

"I guess." I shrugged.

"Did you get good presents?"

Her face was still splotchy with bruises.

"Are you okay?" I said.

"Oh, this'll go away. It happens."

"Come on," I said. "Let's walk."

"Where?"

"I don't know. It's Christmas."

"It's cold."

"It's not so cold."

In truth it was very cold indeed, but I liked the punishing feeling of the icy wind. So we walked slowly down the middle of the street. There were very few cars out, but when one came we stepped aside and let it pass.

We said nothing for a few minutes. She seemed to be waiting for me to confess something, but I didn't feel like confessing.

Eventually, she said, "So?"

"So what?"

"So last night."

"Yeah."

"It finally happened."

"Uh-huh."

"Everyone was wondering if it was ever going to happen for you. Are you relieved?"

"I don't know."

"Do you remember any of it?"

"Not much."

"We tried to look for you, you know. But we couldn't find you. You're fast. I never knew how fast you were."

I said nothing. The swiftness with which I had run naked through the woods was an unfathomable topic for me.

Polly, observing my reluctance to speak, stopped in the road and turned to face me. In some dim part of my mind, I found myself enthralled by the abrasions on her skin. I could wander free on the landscape of her injuries.

"Hey," she said. "Are you all right? I know it's a big deal. It's scary. I remember my first time."

I remembered her first time as well. She hadn't seemed scared at all. She had seemed proud and gloating.

"Do you remember," she said, smiling, "how you used to say it wouldn't happen to you? I mean, you were so convinced that you were different. I bet that seems silly now, doesn't it? All that worry for nothing."

"I guess so."

"You get used to it. You do. You begin to look forward to it, even. Look, we're young. We're only going to be young for a little while. Then we'll be old forever. We might as well enjoy it, you know?"

A car came, and we stepped out of the road into a snowbank.

"You know," she said, "I kind of envy you that you're just starting. But it'll be better now. We'll be together. It's like you moved away for a while—but you're back now."

The thought that I had traveled so far by accident the night before made me sick.

"It feels wrong, Polly," I said. "It just feels wrong."

"But it's not," she said. She took my shoulders and gave her head a maternal shake to reassure me. "It's not. Don't you see? It's the most natural thing in the world. It's only beautiful. That's the only thing it is."

She shivered, then put her arms around me.

"Come on," she said. "Hug me. It's cold. Let's just forget about everything up till now. The past is dead and buried. That's what the breach is all about, right?"

I put my arms around her. Beneath the perfume of her shampoo, her hair smelled like something else—the fecund tang of earth and rot.

———

MY SECOND VISITOR of the day was Blackhat Roy. I saw him coming from down the street, and I rushed to meet him outside so my father wouldn't see him at the door.

"What are you doing here?" I said.

"Heard the news," he said. "You're out. You're fair game."

"I'm not out." In the daylight you scoff at the shadows you cowered from the night before. I had my mother's blood. I knew I was different. I had faith that I was still not like the others. "I was helping my friend, and I was attacked. I ran."

"Spent all night running away?"

"Go away."

He sniffled from the cold, wiped his nose with the back of his hand.

"I saw you," he said.

"When?"

"Last night. In the woods."

"You didn't. I remember. I ran away from everybody."

"Fuck everybody. It was just me. And you saw me, too."

"No, I didn't."

"The way you looked at me," he went on, ignoring my denials, "I've never seen anything like that before. You didn't just want to tussle—it was like you wanted to rip me to pieces."

He seemed delighted by the fact. The way he said it made it seem lascivious.

"No," I said again. "I was just running. But I'm not doing it again."

"You want to know the truth? I stayed out of your way. I'm not scared of much, but last night I was a little scared of you."

He smiled when he said it, a smile of filth and gloating. So what was that churning I felt in my belly when he winked at me?

"See you on the wild side, girl."

I went back in the house and shut the door on him.

In the kitchen, my father was making ginger tea, which was our favorite.

———

WHAT WAS I?

Defective, for one thing. I had grown wrong somehow. My atoms and molecules were failing to adhere to one another the way they should have. My organs were stunted, dwarflike. My body was one pale refusal.

It didn't matter that everyone else was doing it. Their doing it was native—my doing it was criminal.

Even in this I had failed. Everyone was relieved that I had finally gone breach—they felt that they could talk to me now, that I was one of them, joined together in their wild union. But I wasn't one of them after all. I was still different. They welcomed what I feared. They jumped when I cringed. They howled while I whimpered.

Not that I was looking to be like the others. But to be *between* was too much to bear. To be defined by betweenness is not to be defined at all. It is to live your whole life at dusk, which is neither day nor night and therefore an hour of sad nothing caught between one kind of life and another.

This was my inheritance from my mother.

If I was truly out, as Blackhat Roy had said, why wasn't I glad? And if I hadn't fully gone breach, then what had caused me to blister myself with running?

And that was something else, something my brain burned to think on. If I was still as breachless as my mother's blood had made me, then the night before—when I had stripped myself bare and woken in the melted snow at dawn—who was the girl who had done that? What was she driven by?

What excused her actions if those actions were not to be excused by instinct and biology or the horrible magic of this place?

———

NOT EVERYONE IN our town acquiesced to the breaching so easily. It was difficult, sometimes, for parents to accept that their children could behave in such a way. Sometimes they even tried to delay the breaching or prevent it. There were urban myths about ways to keep your child from breaching. Giving them high doses of thiamine was one. Another was to make them sleep in a fully lighted room throughout their teenage years. For a while, before I was born, I even heard that some parents had begun to believe that if they kept their children shaved, completely hairless, the breaching would not set in. So for a period of five years or so, according to my father, there were a bunch of bald, eyebrowless teenagers walking around.

I was fascinated by the idea. I liked to close my eyes and picture it. And I wondered about these parents. What did they believe? That savagery was something you donned as though it were a pelt?

Other parents believed it was the town itself, our pinprick location under the moon, that was the cause of the breach. Sometimes parents would send their children away for the breach year to live with relatives in safe-sounding places such as Florida or Colorado or Arizona. And moving away did seem to work—insofar as the children did not see fit to run wild over the warm, sandy streets of Scottsdale. Sometimes, if they could afford it, the whole family would relocate and then return when the coast was clear.

So that worked—kind of. Except not really, because when they returned, the breachers seemed different, odd. It wasn't just that they no longer *belonged* to the town—though there was that. It was something else. I remember studying Caroline Neary when she came back after a year of living with her aunt in San Francisco. It was her eyes. She seemed scared. Not of anything outside—but of something else. I think I knew what she was scared of. There was something trapped in her—something grown too big to fit in her body, something stretching her at the seams because it wanted to get out but couldn't. She moved out of our town the minute she graduated from high school—and we all thought she would be better off for it. But then we heard the distressing news, just a few years later, that she had impaled herself on a picket fence by jumping out the second-story window of her pleasant suburban home in the middle of the day on a Saturday.

So I suppose whatever was trapped inside Caroline Neary eventually got out after all.

There were other parents who, when the breach was upon their children and they knew they couldn't escape it, tried to keep it at least *contained,* usually with disastrous results.

When we were in the sixth grade, Polly and I had heard about Lionel Kirkpatrick, whose parents, unwilling yet to see their precious boy go breach, had locked him in the basement to keep him from running wild. Over the course of the night, Lionel had ravaged the space, trying to get out. It cost the Kirkpatricks ten thousand dollars in repairs, including a new water heater, because Lionel had somehow toppled the existing one and flooded the basement. In the morning, they found him asleep, curled on top of a pile of boxes, a castaway on an island in two feet of water.

Another thing, from just the previous year: Amy Litt had gone breach and had come to school one morning with bandages all over her fingers. She, unashamed, explained to us that it was like the Bible story of Noah. Her father had found her sleeping naked in the street one morning after breach. He was a righteous man, and he felt a curse had befallen him for having accidentally seen his own daughter without clothes. So the next night he had shut her in the basement, just as Lionel Kirkpatrick's parents had done to their son. Except Amy Litt's destruction was of a more self-directed variety. All she had wanted was out. When her father had gone down to check on her in the morning, he found the concrete walls smeared with blood and his daughter huddled in the corner, shivering with pain. She had ripped all her fingernails out in trying to claw her way to freedom.

The Kirkpatricks restored their basement, and nine of Amy Litt's nails eventually grew back—so these unfortunate occurrences, like most things, were reversible with time. But they served as admonitions to the parents of our town not to stand in the way of the natural course of events, no matter how ugly or shameful.

I know this now—and I raise my child to understand it as

well. Some parents in our neighborhood do everything they can to keep their children away from violent images. And then, when something terrible happens, like murder or rape or genocide—well, then a conversation has to be had with these young innocents to explain that, yes, goodness is sometimes a fiction, like Santa Claus, and that humanity is, underneath all the cookie baking and song singing, a shameful and secret nastiness. Me, I'm going to raise my son differently. What he will be made to know is that there is violence in everything—even in goodness, if you're passionate about it.

But he already knows that. It's why he pulls hair, why he bites what he loves.

———

BUT THOSE WERE parents who had intervened against the wishes of their children. Their stories were different from mine. I was a half-breed. I wasn't some wild creature. I was good. I was daylight and homework and logical answers. I was no tide to be puppeted by the moon. I had my mother's blood. Maybe the night before had been an aberration. You didn't have to give in to every impulse that stirred your blood. You could be better.

I decided, whatever I had become, not to go outside the next night. I was determined not to yield to whatever disease was growing inside me.

When it got dark, I found my father reading in the living room.

"Good night," I said.

He looked at his watch.

"It's early," he said.

"I know. I'm worn out."

"Good Christmas, Lumen?"

"Good Christmas, Dad. Good Christmas for you?"

"Great Christmas. Among the best."

He was a sweet, oblivious man. He was the kind of man you wanted to be good for. How could you want to damage such a man with the truth of things?

So I had to hide it from him—whatever it was. Up in my room, I shut my door and put my desk chair in front of it. I had seen people do this in movies, though my door didn't seem any more secure for it. Through my window, I could see the moon through the tree branches, low on the horizon.

My skin was itchy all over. I was feeling ragged and burned. There was a fan in my closet that was meant for the hot summer months—but I got it out and plugged it in and sat in front of it with my eyes closed, the air making me feel like I was moving at high speed, on my way to someplace grand and dramatic.

Once, when I was much younger, I had asked my father what my mother had done all those nights when everyone had gone breach around her. He laughed and took me onto his lap, and this is what he said: "Do you want to know what she did? She sewed rag dolls. She was the most amazing seamstress, your mother. The dolls she made, they were exquisite. She became known for them all over town. Children would come by her house and stand beneath her window, and she would throw dolls down to them."

I always loved that story, and it wasn't until I was older that I began to wonder why none of my mother's rag-doll creations were still around. And then, later, my father's story became even stranger to me because of its resemblance to something I read in *Little Women*. Still, I treasured the image of my mother sitting beneath a lamp at night sewing dolls, and I wondered what comparable thing I could do.

I put my headphones on and listened to some music at volume level seventeen—I normally wouldn't allow myself any volume over ten for fear of ruining my eardrums. But there was a bustle in my head that needed drowning out.

On the wall over my bed there was a mismatched seam in the wallpaper, and tonight, for some reason, it bothered me. I picked at it without thinking, digging my fingernails underneath it until I had ripped away a whole flap. My hands wanted something to do. I made myself stop and reaffix the flap with white glue. But then I found myself winding my fingers around strands of hair and tugging them out of my scalp.

To keep my hands occupied, I opened my sketch pad and started to draw a map. It was a map of a place I didn't know. Sometimes those were the best ones. You started with a river and grew a town up around it. You discovered the place as you created it. Sometimes there were surprises.

But tonight, for the first time, I was irritated by my little fictional operettas. The music in my ears seemed mechanical and false. The map emerging under my artless hands seemed flat, predictable. I began to wish I knew how to paint scenes rather than just maps. I wanted to paint like Edward Hopper. I wanted to show the depth of the dark by delivering just a small, broken segment of light. I wanted to look into windows from the outside.

I was hot, and there was nothing the fan could do about it. My skin itched, the kind of itch that made diving into a thorny shrub sound like a delicious dream.

It was only nine o'clock. I went to the window. It was safe, I imagined, just to look. I renewed my resolution not to set even one foot outside. The moon was still low. I could see it superimposed over my reflection on the pane of glass, yet still very far away. I pressed my forehead to the glass and used my hands as a visor in order to see more, to get closer, but my breath quickly fogged the view.

I unlocked the window and slid it upward. It was just something I did. It required no thought or bargaining.

I knew a rhyme that had always seemed powerful to me. If I spoke it aloud, maybe I could still be saved, even with the window open. So I leaned as far as I could out the window into the night and repeated the rhyme over and over.

> *There was a crooked man, and he walked a crooked mile.*
> *He found a crooked sixpence upon a crooked stile.*
> *He bought a crooked cat, which caught a crooked mouse.*
> *And they all lived together in a little crooked house.*

I leaned out the window, and the air sighed upon my itchy skin.

Were these, then, the pathways to damnation—and was this why they were so difficult for people to resist?

There was a crooked man, and he walked a crooked mile.

My window was in a dormer, and I crawled through until half of me was lying on the downward slope of the roof.

But my legs were still inside the house. Inside the little crooked house. No walking a crooked mile tonight—not without those little crooked legs.

You could breathe the night. I never knew that before. The air tasted different when it was uninfused with light. It went deeper in you. You could want it—just that.

And it was cold. There was a high-contrast sharpness to everything. It was a wakeful night—so wakeful that daytime consciousness seemed a blur.

He bought a crooked cat, which caught a crooked mouse.

Yes, the crookedness of things. I could see it now.

You could get sick to death of delicate symmetry. You could want other things, and that wanting could be ambrosial all on its own.

You could even become angry at your own prohibitions — you could begin to suspect the origins of all the tinny moralities that point you in all the directions of your life.

It occurred to me that I would like to feel the moonlight on my bare skin. The thought occurred to me, and I studied it in the cool, rational part of my brain — but while I was studying it, I noticed that my fingers had already begun the process of undoing the buttons on my pajama top. I watched them, curiously, from the rational distance of my brain — I wondered who they thought they were, those fingers that had spent so much time doing my bidding in the past.

Those little crooked fingers, they run their crooked way.

You could sometimes want to run. You could sometimes want to run out your window, off your roof, down the street, deep, deep into the unlit heart of an emptied town.

———

I DARTED FROM yard to yard, looking in windows. Squares of light. Actions playing out in them. Like television screens hung randomly along the street. Sometimes you could see a television screen inside the television screen of the window. Layers of lit life in the distance. And here was I — shrouded behind the curtains of night, lost in the muffled dullness of a noiseless winter. And it was okay. It was better than okay. It was glorious.

I could leap. Fences were nothing to me. Rules were for those small enough to live inside them. I was large.

It was possible, I saw now, to be a grotesque, to be huge and free, to wander the streets in utter freedom despite your atrocity, as long as you did it when everybody else was sealed inside their little lit boxes.

Now it made sense—why monsters came out at night.

CHAPTER 6

I scrubbed myself clean in the morning, coating my skin with lotion that smelled of lemons.

I didn't tell my father. I decided to keep it from him as long as I could. I dreaded being found by him curled naked on the back porch or befouled with mud.

The second night was more lucid than the first. I stayed by myself for a long time. In the distance I could hear the others, roaming the streets in packs. When their voices got louder, I hid. I watched them pass by, tangled around each other and caught up in their passions. I did not want to be joined with them.

In front of the church, I watched from a copse of trees as a group of breachers knocked apart a manger scene left over from Christmas. I waited until they were gone, then I put everything back aright.

As I put the baby Jesus back in his little nest, I stood back and looked at it.

It had nothing to do with God. It was just glowy and sweet, and it spoke of aching desire and a longing for peacefulness.

I wished the scene had been baked in an oven so I could eat it.

—

ATTACK THE NIGHT.

I was hungry for things I didn't know the names of, and the full moon was a strange kind of manna. It emptied you of yourself, and you were relieved.

Such release—you have no idea. Everything absolved. A world where signs meant nothing, where everything was permitted. The claustrophobic restrictions of life falling like clipped fingernails at your feet.

I ran the woods, and I was unstoppable. I thought nothing of school deadlines and frowning fathers. I was entire and alone—blissfully alone. There was nothing outside my skin that mattered—except maybe the odor of tree sap and the brittle ice that depended from tree branches. I wanted to go farther. I wanted to run all the way out of town—through the streets of large cities, leaping from the hood of one taxicab to another, laughing and indifferent.

You could nuzzle your face against the warm world. The undersides of everything. This is how you knew love. There was no ugly. All was beautiful. The bodies, dark or pale, bruised or unspoiled—they were beautiful. The violence was delicious in the way foreign food sometimes is—surprising on the tongue, fresh and sharp. My daytime resentments sloughed away, and I would have gladly merged my life with the lives of others—put my body, all uncovered, against theirs.

Except that I was afraid. Still afraid of myself. And of the others.

Later that second night I watched them from a distance. I ran across them, finally, in the middle of town, and I climbed a dumpster to the rooftop of the Sunshine Diner to observe them. There were so many of them, at least thirty, making loud noises in the square.

They seemed to run in packs, mostly. Like social cliques at school during the daytime. When these packs crossed paths during the full moon, there were fights. Sometimes the fights turned into revelry. Below me I could see some girls, locked into combat on the wide lawn, pulling at each other's hair, biting, choking, shrieking. But they soon grew tired, and their violence became pathetic, little compulsory slaps as their chests heaved with exhaustion. Even kisses.

Elsewhere, near the gazebo in the middle of the square, a pale pink knot of breachers, most of whom I knew, were locked together in various manifestations of sexual congress. Girls, boys, it made no difference. You were skin, and they were skin, and you buried yourself in the skin of others as they buried themselves in yours. Some of them cried, and some of them howled—and whether the crying and howling was pain or pleasure, you couldn't tell, and maybe they couldn't, either. Such are the ambiguities of primal youth.

I could name almost everyone I saw—because I was the kind of girl who knew everybody's name, even though I was allied with none of them. There was Ellie Wilkins, Carl Bodell, Frenchie Lassister, the twins Margot and Marina Anderson, Wally Kemp, Gary Tupper, George Ferris, and also George Dodd. Mildred Gunderson, Marcel Judd, Theo Kaminer. Cameron Mayer, whom most people just called Monkey. Adelaide Warren and Sue Foxworth and Florabel McCarron (who had started breaching so early that she was picked on by the others and had to be hospitalized after her first full moon). John Stonehill, Joel Phelps, Barbara Montgomery. Worth Loomis. Sylvia Hitchcock.

Rose Lincoln was there, too, looking like a matriarch overseeing the soldiery of her empire. She walked among them, her head held high and regal, her pale body indifferent to the bodies around her.

Peter Meechum was there, the king to Rose's queen. He lay atop the gazebo roof, stargazing, while Bessie Laurent nestled against him, her hand moving with a lullaby rhythm between her legs. He paid no attention to her. And that was good, because I was quite sure I loved him—and that I could with very little remorse bite the tongue right out of Bessie Laurent's mouth. That was the kind of clarity you could have on nights like these. All the fine-tuned complications of the day give way to the big absolutes: love, hate, life, death, good, evil, boy, girl, angel, fiend.

Blackhat Roy was there, too. He was relegated to the margins.

I watched them from the safe distance of the diner roof. I watched them, because these were my people. These were the people I had been born to. This was my heritage on true display.

Then, in the distance, there was the sound of a car engine. Headlights on the horizon.

Sometimes people came from the outside. Travelers. We were a long way off the main freeway through the state, so it didn't happen often. But sometimes it did.

Some of the breachers below scattered by instinct. Others stayed. Blackhat Roy stayed, drawn by curiosity nearer the road, to the base of a granite monument in the shape of an obelisk. Peter stayed, raising himself up on his elbows. Rose Lincoln leaned against a tree trunk and crossed her arms, waiting.

The car drove once around the square, its windows rolled

down. We could hear loud, overlapping voices coming from in-side, the voices of teenagers like us.

Unlike us.

"This is it? I don't get it."

"I thought you said we were gonna find a liquor store."

"This place doesn't seem so scary. Why's everybody always warning us about it?"

"Fucking Mayberry."

"Aren't there supposed to be ghosts or vampires or some-thing? What the fuck?"

Then they must have spotted the breachers who had made no effort to hide themselves. The car stopped at the edge of the town square, and one of the boys got out and said, "What the hell is this?" and the others also got out and began to laugh and point. "They're naked!" they said, and, "What are they? Hippies? Is this what we're not supposed to see? Hippie bullshit?"

I watched from my perch on the roof. Blackhat Roy, his body covered in soot, moved closer to them. He cocked his head slightly as if considering the visitors.

It was one thing for the breachers to attack one other. That was accepted. That was the nature of the place. It was our nature. But this was something different. Outsiders, the few we got, were usually left alone. It was a precarious balance that worked out most of the time. On the one hand, breachers nor-mally preferred to roam the dark woods rather than the overly bright downtown streets. On the other hand, most residents from neighboring towns stayed away from us during the full moon out of a superstitious fear of the town's reputation. But sometimes there were exceptions in both cases—the habits of breachers were broken, and the mythologies of the town were forgotten by the outsiders.

I might have warned them. I might have called down to them to get back into their car and drive away. But I didn't. I didn't want to.

The five of them were out of the car, some still pointing, some laughing with gaudy, wide mouths, some revolted. That's when the other breachers emerged from around corners and from the dark of alleyways. They came out, naked all, and surrounded the travelers.

Two of the five were girls, and they didn't like what was happening. They got back into the car and begged the three boys to take them home. But the boys continued to laugh. "A town full of retards," one said.

"Please!" the girls said from inside the car. "Please come on!"

But then something strange happened. From my height, I could see that the breachers, led by Peter Meechum, who had hopped down from the gazebo roof, were closing not around the travelers but around one of their own, Blackhat Roy.

It was a sign of dominance, territoriality. I understood it instinctively. Instead of attacking the interloper, attack one of your own. Put on full display the untamed wildness of your power.

By the time Roy saw what was happening, it was too late to run. I could see, even from my height, the panic in his eyes. His head turned around, wondering from which direction the first attack would come.

"It's gonna hurt, Roy," I could hear Peter saying. "You know it's gonna hurt."

But then something occurred to Blackhat Roy. Instead of defending himself, he turned on the travelers, the boys laughing and pointing from their car.

"What do you fucking know about hurt?" he said to the boys. "You and yours. I'm gonna teach you something about hurt."

Roy advanced on one of the boys, going up close and sniffing his neck as a dog might. Then he said something to him, low in his ear, and I couldn't hear what it was. But the boy wasn't laughing anymore, and he was no longer hypnotized by the naked bodies all around him—he just wanted to get away.

Roy wouldn't let him. He grabbed the boy and flung him to the ground, then seized him by the arm and dragged him into the middle of the park. The crowd of breachers separated to let him through—Roy was giving them something to be hungry for.

"Tear him," Marina Anderson said, breathless, to Blackhat Roy. "Rip him."

"Rip him," the others started to say. "Bleed him."

The other two boys tried to run to their friend's aid, but the breachers fell on them, too, beat them and tore off their clothes and rubbed themselves lewdly against the whimpering boys.

Then they came back to the car for the two tearful and screaming girls.

I watched.

I was stirred.

The breezes blew, and I wondered how much awfulness had to be released from one location before you could smell it on the wind.

The girls had locked themselves in the car, but they didn't have the key to start the engine. I could hear their muffled shrieks as the breachers stalked around the vehicle, trying all the doors, pressing their hungry faces against the glass. Blackhat Roy slapped a bloody handprint on the windshield. It was impossible to know whose blood it was.

"Open your eyes," he called to the girls. "Open your goddamn eyes!"

The breachers rocked the car back and forth, some climbing up the hood and onto the roof. The girls screamed.

Finally someone brought a cinder block from the alley and threw it through the windshield. Then it was just a matter of reaching in and dragging the girls out by their fragile, flailing limbs.

———

IN THE PAST, the infrequent attacks on outsiders hadn't been so bad. They could be explained away, mollified with sympathetic fictions. A troubled local youth gone off his medication. A traumatized girl, escaped from her abusive foster home, taking out on innocents what had been perpetrated on her for years. In the daylight, the breachers could be brought forward to apologize, which they did with all true sincerity. They had not meant it. They were full of regret.

Truth be told, even during the full moon, breachers could sense the difference between themselves and others. In general, there was no joy in preying on those who did not stink of nature and violence. The outsiders usually came away with maybe a bruise or a busted lip. Maybe not even that. Sometimes just the uneasy fright of witnessing a naked figure running across the road in front of your car and howling at you as it passed.

The sheriff from the next town over might visit our mayor. There may have been jolly slaps on the back, amicable chuckling, head shaking with regard to the moral abandon of teenagers these days. What was to be done? Mutual shrugs. It was a brutal time we were living in. Sad nods. But the children would survive and be better for it, as the two men had. Reassured stares skyward.

This time, though, it was different. I had seen it. Had just one breacher been there, or two, they might have made a display of animalistic defiance and run off. But it wasn't just one breacher, it was a whole pack. Violence, I discovered, could be contagious. It fed off itself until it had lost its purpose. The result was five teenagers mauled in our town square on the day after Christmas.

The attacks were just too brutal to be ignored. Two of the boys and one of the girls were hospitalized. One of the boys had had his eye gouged out and would have to wear a glass eye for the rest of his life. One of the girls was a cheerleader and had promised her parents and her pastor that she would remain a virgin until the day she married. Someone had to be held responsible.

So our sheriff questioned some of the breachers. It didn't even take a whole afternoon. All we needed was a scapegoat, and we had one readily at hand. The next day everybody knew that Blackhat Roy had been held responsible for the crime and would be sent away to live in Chicago with his uncle.

I hated him. Still, when I thought about him going far away, part of me ached for him.

On certain days in the spring, in late April, say, it is possible to believe what the animals believe—that horror and beauty are hearty allies, and that when you live in the full roiling of your guts it's impossible to make distinctions between them.

———

LATE THAT AFTERNOON, near sunset, Peter Meechum came to me. He came to the front door, rang the bell, and stood there looking mournful and respectable.

"I came to apologize," he said.

"For what?"

"For everything."

I wondered about his willingness to apologize for everything in the world. It was the marvelous kind of stuff that martyrs are made of. He stood there, sheepish and strong, and his smile was just on the final edge of regret, ready to break through to whatever passionate gesture was next. Maybe I was still weak to the fact that he seemed interested in me when there were so many other girls whose doorsteps he could be standing on—but it was more than that. He was wound up, kinetic, and you felt that you could either go along with him or be left behind—and I wanted to go with him.

I invited him in, but he didn't want to be indoors. Instead we walked, wrapped in our winter coats. I kept my eyes on the shoveled sidewalk, paying close attention to whether or not I stepped on the cracks. I wondered if he would try to take my hand, and I left it dangling just in case—but he seemed morose and inattentive.

"You know where I've been all morning?" he said.

"Where?"

"Church."

"Oh."

"It used to make me feel better," he went on, "but it doesn't anymore. I forgot how to be good."

"You didn't forget."

"All the things I've done. The way I've behaved. Do you ever feel like you're two entirely different people? I mean, there's the person you know you should be, the person you want to be, the person everybody else would like you to be. And you can be that person most of the time. It's work. I mean, it's hard—but you can do it. But then there's this other person who does awful things. The sun goes down, the moon comes up—and suddenly you're watching yourself do ugly things. Like you're complacent, at a distance, just watching the happenings of your body as if you had nothing at all to do with them. Do you ever feel that?"

I was silent for a moment. But he didn't give me a chance to answer before he continued.

"No. You wouldn't know about that."

"Maybe I would," I asserted.

"No, you wouldn't. You don't understand."

"I do. I promise."

His smile was generous, but he didn't believe me. I wanted to be something in his mournful life—a comfort or a remedy. Simple fancies, but my chest ached with them.

"Listen," I said. We stopped, and I got in front of him to look up into his eyes. I put my hand on his chest to reassure him. I wanted him to feel the truth of what I was saying. I wanted to press it directly into his heart as though it were soft clay. I could feel the confession spilling out of me, and there was no stopping it. "Listen," I said again, "sometimes . . . I don't know . . . sometimes I hate myself. Especially lately. I don't know what to do. I don't know who I am anymore—what I am. My dad, he doesn't know I go out at nights. I can't tell him. I'm not a breacher like other people, I don't think. I can't be. I don't want to be. But I don't know. My mom, she used to make dolls—except now I don't know if she really did. I wish I could make dolls. I wish I were the girl who made dolls instead of the girl who—"

He put his arms around me. "Shh," he said. "It's okay."

He held me and stroked my hair for a few moments until I calmed down. Then, when he let me go and looked me in the face, his expression had changed completely. His mood had transformed—he was elated. Had I done that to him? Did I have that kind of power?

"Come on," he said, taking my hand. "I want to show you something."

He pulled me into the middle of the street.

"Wait," I said. "We're going to get run over."

"It doesn't matter."

He let go of my hand, took me by the shoulders, and turned me around so my back was to him. He put his head over my right shoulder, and I could feel his breath on my cheek.

"Look down there," he said, and I looked at the row of houses and the purple sunset beyond.

"What?" I said.

"No," he said. "You have to look harder."

Just then the street lamps came on overhead with a little click and a buzz. Consecutive pools of light appeared in a bracelet of illumination that fronted all the houses, each of which domiciled any number of lives and dramas and passions and catastrophes. There it was, the way the street arrowed on to the horizon, the way the housefronts glowed rich, organic sepia into the night, the way the parceled land shivered with the deep harmonics of order and structure. I looked, and what I saw was the story of the place, the crystalline symmetry of the houses on their identical plots of land, the swooping curve of the curb and the wispy fans of the sprinklers that came on in the summer with timed precision. I saw the bones and the blood of the town, the infrastructure of copper pipes and PVC and electrical conduits and sump pumps and telephone wires suspended in elegant laurels overhead. I saw everything it took to make this one street, and I saw that street multiplied into a neighborhood and that neighborhood multiplied into a town and that town multiplied into a city and a country and a whole world.

I saw it. He made me see it, and I saw it.

"Think about it," he said. "People *built* this. There used to be nothing here, and now there's this. And the people who built it, were they pure? It doesn't matter. Whatever they were, they overcame it to make something bigger than themselves. Look harder. It's beautiful."

It's become popular for people to talk about suburban dread, the cardboard sprawl that cheapens life, reduces life down to lawn ornaments, manicured shrubs, televisions with extra-large screens, quaint and degraded notions of family life. It's easy to say that life should be grander, more meaningful, heartier—like a meat stew.

But what Peter showed me I'll never forget. It was the land brought to life, the earth made conscious. And it was beautiful. It really was.

"What does it mean?" I asked.

"It means that it doesn't matter what it means," he said. "It means that it'll be okay, Lumen."

———

THE THIRD NIGHT I went into the woods because I was finished with other people and their capricious ways. I wanted my freedom to be mine alone. A wind blew through the trees, and the moonlight lit up all the icy branches, and it was like I was surrounded by stars.

The next morning, when I woke, my body was covered in crystals of ice. I was in the backyard of my house, on the lawn, in a little concavity my hot body had made in the snow. Sitting up, I saw a ghost of myself on the ground.

The sun was up, just visible on the horizon. I guessed it must have been five o'clock. My father would still be in bed.

"You sleep nice."

The voice came from behind me. My body, still moon-driven and instinctive, shot rigid into a crouch. Flee or defend.

Blackhat Roy, still naked, too, sat on the stoop of my back porch. He looked haggard and somehow raw. He was raked with dirt, his hair caked with dry, frozen mud. He scratched at himself casually.

"Your eyelids," he said. "They flutter when you're asleep. You remember what you were dreaming about?"

"You're supposed to be going to Chicago."

"Leaving tonight."

"What are you doing here?"

"Now, me," he went on, "I remember all my dreams. I wish I didn't. Good or bad, it doesn't matter. I wake up in the middle of some fucking fantasyland campfire story, and it takes me a while to get my bearings. You know, what's true and what isn't. Where are you really? In the middle of some horror show with smiling dogs, or maybe an orgy of alien women, or maybe just tucked safe away in your bed. It's a goddamn nuisance is what it is. You ever have that problem? Not knowing for sure what's real?" He scratched behind his ear and picked something from his hair — a bug of some kind — then crushed it between his fingers. "Or have you got it all figured out?"

"You shouldn't be here."

"How come?"

"Why are you here? What do you want?"

"You really want to know?"

Suddenly I didn't like being naked around him. It was too personal, too intimate. Now that the sun was rising over the horizon, it was no longer just nature and breaching. Now there was something else involved — the shame of day. I stood and turned sideways, folding my arms over myself as best I could.

He chuckled, and I was embarrassed about my paltry modesty.

"Let me go inside," I said.

"Who's stopping you?"

I was keenly aware that I would have to pass close by him to go up the porch steps into the house. Taking two steps forward, I watched him to see what he would do—but he made no move. His eyes followed me as I got closer, and, as I put my foot on the first step, I thought his arm might shoot out and he might grab me by the ankle. And what then? Where would he drag me? What dirtiness would he scrape onto me? How would it feel on my skin? Would I hate it?

I bolted, running up the rest of the steps until I had my hand on the knob of the back door. Only then did I turn around to find he had not moved at all—he hadn't even turned around. I looked at his back. There were scars all over it, little white and pink indentations highlighted by dirt and grime.

He had not seized me. He had not dragged me off somewhere, and now I didn't know how I felt about that.

"You shouldn't have attacked those people," I said.

"Is that what you think happened?"

"You attacked them. I saw you."

"If you saw it, then you know better. Sometimes you get tired of being the town garbage. And sometimes, when you're tired like that, you realize that the only way to keep from being the prey"—he turned to look at me—"is to put someone else in your place. Besides, the whole town loves a slaughter. How come I don't get to enjoy myself in the same way once in a while?"

I knew what he said was true, but I had no answer for him.

"You should go home," I said.

"Home," he grunted, turning away again. "Right."

"You act like you're separate from it."

"From what?"

"All of it. What everyone's going through. The breaching."

"Pomp and faggotry," he said. "Girl shit."

"But you're doing it, too."

"Nope," he said simply.

I waited for him to say more, and eventually he did. Though he did not turn around, so I still could not see his face.

"What I do, it's personal. I take responsibility for it. It's me. It ain't some hormones or rite of passage or mass hysteria. I don't fucking cry about it in the morning."

———

BY THE TIME the sun went down, Roy was gone.

I was nervous, because it was the fourth night. Usually the breach went three nights—but the jury was still out on what form of sinner I was. So I thought maybe I would go out again. Maybe for me it was an everyday thing for the rest of my life.

But when the sun went down, I didn't feel the urgent tugging in my chest. I was able to keep my bedroom window closed. And so I knew I would be free of it for another month.

When school started up again after the holiday, things were different. People weren't exactly friendlier. They didn't strike up conversations with me in the cafeteria—but sometimes they gave me a cursory nod as they passed. And I noticed something else, too. When I walked down the hallways, people moved out of my way. Before the winter break I had had to be very conscious of where I walked, because if I weren't careful people would simply walk right into me. But now there was an understanding of presence, a mutual shifting of bodies as they moved through space.

It was as though I had become suddenly *visible*.

In the girls' restroom, I encountered Polly and Rose Lincoln. They were brushing their faces with powder and looking at themselves in the mirror. First they sucked their lips in, then they puckered them out.

Polly still looked pretty beat up, but there seemed to be no animosity between the two of them.

"Lumen!" Polly said when she saw me. "How are you?"

"Fine."

"We didn't see you after the first night," said Rose. She didn't look away from the mirror.

"You didn't try to stay in, did you?" said Polly.

"No," I said.

"It's strange the first couple times, I know."

"Are you okay?" I asked.

"What, this?" Polly said, gesturing to the abrasions showing through the powder on her face. "It's nothing. I didn't mean to frighten you the other night. Sometimes things get a little emotional in the moment. But everybody gets busted up sometimes. Life, you know?"

"One thing you can say about Polly," said Rose approvingly. "She knows how to take a beating."

I didn't say anything.

"You should come with us next time," Polly said. "We'll take care of you. Shouldn't she, Rose?"

"Uh-huh," said Rose.

"I don't know," I said.

"Come on," Polly said. "I know you just started, but mine's almost over. Just for once I'd like to run with you. Don't you want to run with me?"

Rose Lincoln closed her powder case with a snap and turned to us.

"She won't come with us. She's too busy praying at manger scenes."

"I wasn't praying," I protested.

"Where were you the night Roy almost killed those people?"

"I was there."

"No, you weren't."

"Yes, I was. I was watching, and it didn't happen that way. It wasn't just Roy."

"Watching!" Rose Lincoln scoffed. "All you ever do is watch. Well, don't pray over me. I don't need it, and I don't want it."

I didn't know what to say.

"But I wasn't praying," I said lamely.

"Never mind," Polly said. "You'll run with me next time, won't you?"

"I guess."

"Do you promise?"

"Yes."

Promises are easy to make. You utter a word or two, and it's done. But those are magic words, too. They speak of a defined future to which you are required to adhere. They commit you beyond the length of your experience.

What they do is they take away possibility.

Promises are the opposite of hope.

MY FATHER SAID, "You look tired. Are you all right?"

"Yes."

"Come here. Let me feel your forehead."

I went to him. He placed his palm on my forehead.

"You feel a little hot. You're sure you're not getting a fever?"

"I'm fine," I said. "You've been cooking. It's probably your hand that's hot."

He looked at me with suspicion.

"Really, I'm okay. Look."

Then I did some dancing twirls, the kind I used to do for him as a girl. He clapped. He was delighted. He was convinced, once again, that everything was just fine.

———

AND THERE WAS something else. Peter started visiting me in the afternoons, as he had earlier in the school year. He looked at me in a new way since I had gone out during the last moon—as though he had never had sex with Rose Lincoln, as though he had never taken me to the woods and been unable to rape me.

One day after school, he showed up on my doorstep with two wooden mallets and a large bag hoisted over his shoulder.

"What's this?" I asked.

"Croquet!" he said. "It's the game of kings."

"Is it?"

So we drove the wickets into the frozen ground of my back-yard, and, bundled in our coats, we hammered our colored wooden balls through them. It felt good—like reclaiming for civilization the very same lawn where I had woken up in shame just a couple weeks before.

Afterward we went up to my room. While I organized my homework into prioritized piles, I could feel his eyes on me.

"I'm something to you now," I said, turning to him.

"You were always something to me," he said. "But for a while you were too much of a something to me. You were all the way up here, and I was all the way down here." He used the full stretch of his arms to make his point.

"So now I'm all the way down there with you?"

"Not quite." He smiled. "But at least you're close enough that I can see you from where I am."

"And where's Blackhat Roy on that scale?"

Peter shook his head. "It's good he's gone. That guy was bad news. Really, Lumen, you don't even know how bad."

He was restless and disinclined to study. While I copied dates from the world history textbook onto note cards, he browsed the books on my shelves. Once, I had to stop him.

"Hey," I said. "Don't open that. Put it back."

He held in his hands a composition notebook he'd plucked from my shelves.

"What is it?" he asked.

"Just notes."

"What kind of notes? School notes?"

"No. Other kinds of notes. Lists and things."

He gave me a teasing smile.

"Like what? What kinds of lists? Give me one example, and I'll put it back."

"I don't know. Like a list of my favorite authors."

"Hm. Interesting."

But he put the notebook back, as he had promised.

For ten minutes he helped me sort note cards into thematic categories. Then, without warning, he leaned over and kissed me. He pushed his chest against mine, and I liked how our breathing became one breathing. With my eyes closed, I could almost forget about everything.

I still held fans of note cards in my hands, and I didn't know what to do with them. When he finally stopped kissing me, I tried to remember where the cards belonged — but my mind was no longer functioning by the logic of categories.

"Is your father at home?" he asked.

"No."

"When will he be home?"

"Six, usually."

Peter looked at his wristwatch.

"That's two hours," he said. He kissed me again, and I dropped the note cards to the floor and wound my arms around his neck. But when he moved against me, we jostled the desk and my purple pencil cup tipped over with a loud clatter that startled me.

"I think we should stop," I said.

"How come?"

"I don't know. It's a big deal."

He backed up and eyed me with a playful smile.

"Okay," he said. "Fair enough. But we're at an impasse, because I think we should keep going."

"You do? How come?"

"The usual reasons, I guess."

"Like what?" I liked this game. "I'm prepared to listen to logic."

He posed himself thoughtfully on the edge of my bed, a prosecutor prepared to make a complex case.

I laughed.

"You know," I said. "I've never done it before."

"Uh-huh," he said. "Acknowledged. And is it your plan never to do it at all, or do you have an intention to one day make love?"

"It's not my plan *never* to do it." I went over to him where he sat on the bed and stood before him. He looked up at me, and I leaned down to kiss him. He put his hands on my waist. Then he backed away for a moment, again with that sly, strategic smile.

"I see," he said. "So it's a matter of situation. Timing, choice of partner, and the like?"

"I guess."

"So in terms of timing—you just started breaching, I understand?"

"Kind of."

"And you know the types of activities breachers participate in?"

"Yes."

"And in terms of choice of partner—would you say that you have a mostly complete sense of the potential romantic partners available to you here in town?"

"Yes."

He grinned—and I grinned, too.

"I don't think I'm being immodest when I say that this is a case that makes itself."

"Maybe," I said. I kissed him again. I wanted badly to be with him, but I didn't know how to say yes to such things. "I just don't think it's a good idea."

"You don't?"

I shook my head.

"Okay," he said, undeterred. "How about a little competition? How about if I can guess the authors on your favorite authors list? How many do you have on the list?"

"Ten."

"Let's say if I can guess three, we'll call it fate. And when fate tells you to do something, you know you better do it."

"What, with unlimited guesses? That bet's stacked in your favor."

"Well, I'd say it's in both of our favors, but okay. How about ten guesses?"

"Three correct out of ten guesses from my list of ten favorite authors?"

"Right."

I narrowed my eyes at him, and he narrowed his at me.

"Okay," I said.

I went to the shelf and took down the composition notebook and flipped to the page that had my list of favorite authors. I inscribe it here for the record:

CHARLES DICKENS

WILLIAM SHAKESPEARE

JUDY BLUME

JACK KEROUAC

EMILY BRONTË

C. S. Lewis URSULA K. LE GUIN

TRUMAN CAPOTE

RUMER GODDEN

James Thurber V. C. ANDREWS

P. G. WODEHOUSE

"Okay," Peter said, leaning eagerly forward. "Let's see. How about Shakespeare?"

"No fair," I said. "That was an easy one."

"Your predictability is not my problem. How about Mark Twain?"

"Huh-uh."

"F. Scott Fitzgerald?"

I shook my head.

"Really?" he said.

"He's probably number eleven."

"So a good guess."

"Yeah, a good guess." I moved toward him and gave him a kiss. "That's for your good guess." Then I backed away again.

"All right, all right." He rubbed his palms together and stared at the ceiling. After a while he said, "Dickens."

"Because of *David Copperfield*," I said. "Not for *Tale of Two Cities*."

"So I'm right? Two out of four. That leaves me six guesses for the last one. How do you like my odds?"

"I don't like them at all."

"Remember: fate."

"I remember."

"Okay, let's see." He glanced over at my bookshelves.

"Hey, no unfair advantages."

"Sorry."

He covered his face with his hands.

"Ernest Hemingway," he said eventually.

I gave him a look.

"Okay, no critiques on the wrong guesses, please. Oh, I know. Who's that guy who wrote the Buddha book?"

"Hermann Hesse?"

"Yeah."

"No."

"Sylvia Plath?"

I shook my head.

"Kurt Vonnegut?"

"No."

"Oh, wait, I know—*Lord of the Flies.*"

"That's not an author."

"What was his name?"

"William Golding. And no."

"Damn it. How many guesses is that?"

"You have one more."

He was quiet for a long time, his face buried in his hands, and I liked how his sandy hair hung tousled over his fingers.

Suddenly he sat up, looking pleased with himself. He reached out for me and pulled me to him so we were sitting next to each other on the bed. Then he leaned in close. I could smell his skin.

"I got it," he said. "Do you believe I've got it?"

"No," I said, my voice almost a whisper.

"Well, I do. I've got it. Are you ready?"

"I'm ready."

He said it slowly, each syllable a victory:

"J. D. Salinger."

I looked at him for a long time, that pristine boy with his acrobatic teetering between glory and shame. Our faces were impossibly close. We shared the heated air—what he breathed out, I breathed in.

"Well?" he said. "That's it, isn't it? I got it, didn't I?"

And I said, "You got it."

We live our lives by measures of weeks, months, years, but the creatures we truly are, those are exposed in fractions of moments.

It was nothing. Three words. Two of them were even plosives, or stop syllables. *You got it.* Nothing at all. It was a flake of a moment, a fingernail of time—but it was there in that narrow margin between one thing and another that I saw who I really was.

He placed his hands lightly on my chest as though to encase my lack of breasts and protect them from harm. Just as you do with newly planted saplings.

The look on his face, beneath features scarred by moonlit nights in the wild, was awfully earnest—and I didn't think that anything Peter Meechum wanted to do could be very bad. It was a legitimate, daylight thing—it was something done all over the world all the time. It had nothing to do with that ugly, lecherous, queasy feeling in my stomach during the three nights of the full moon. This was something else entirely.

As an act, it was cool, somber, polite.

He removed his clothes, and he told me I should remove mine as well. After that, I lay down, and he scooted his body over mine. His chest against me was bony and raw.

"Are you okay?" he asked.

"Yes."

"Are you ready?"

"Uh-huh. Yes."

I didn't know what to expect. There was a pinch, a slight off feeling, as of something being lodged where it shouldn't be. Like a piece of spinach between your teeth. It hurt a little, but not so much. Peter was very careful and considerate.

"Okay?" he said.

"Okay," I said. "You don't have to keep asking."

So he closed his eyes and went about his business. I watched him, a little firebrand of industry, chugging away at his given chore. It made me think of those chain gangs from movies, the prisoners all shackled together, swinging their pickaxes in unison. The idea made me smile, but I didn't want him to think I was laughing at him, so I turned my head and hid my face in the pillow.

His face grew a deep red color, and then I knew he was done, because he fell off me to the side and made sounds that suggested pride and relief.

I felt something leaking out of me, so I went to the bathroom. I took some of the stuff on my fingers to examine it, because it was new to me. It was slippery and a little sticky, and it smelled like pancake batter. I thought about all the invisible, microbial creatures swimming around in it, and it made me a little nauseated, so I washed my hands. But I wished them all well, his little sperms, as I sent them down the drain.

I wasn't on the pill, but I was pretty sure you couldn't get pregnant when you were amenorrheic.

I was suddenly shy again, so I wrapped a towel around myself before I went back to the bedroom. Peter was still collapsed on the bed, all used up.

"You have to get dressed," I said. "Before my father gets home."

"Okay, but kiss me first. Come here."

He held his arms out, so I went to him. He wanted a long kiss, one of those drawn-out ones from before—but it seemed to me that our sex had changed the kind of kisses called for. So I gave him a quick peck and an amiable pat on the bare shoulder. His skin was flushed and clammy.

He stepped into his underwear and his pants.

"Are you getting dressed, too?" he said.

"Yes."

"What are you waiting for?"

"I don't know. I don't want you to see me."

"You are aware we just had sex, right?"

"I know, but still."

"Tell you what," he said, turning to face the closet door. "I promise not to peek. Let me know when you're decent again."

Which I thought was, after all, a very nice thing.

———

AND ALSO: I'M still waiting. With everything that happened after that day—all the things I have done.

When will I be decent again?

CHAPTER 7

My husband closes the door of his office and turns to look out the window while he eats the lunch I packed for him in the morning. He rotates his head in a small circle, meditatively, as though working out some stiffness in his neck. When he takes a bite of his sandwich, he leans forward, then leans back again to chew it, his eyes squinting at the sunlight coming through the window. With his empty left hand, he taps his fingertips together in sequence — which makes it look as though he's counting something, but I don't think he is. Sometimes, between bites, it's almost as though he has forgotten entirely what he's doing. He just sits, his eyes gone far out over the land, his whole body very, very still, until he remembers to take another bite.

I lean back behind the trunk of my tree so that he cannot see me. There's a sandwich of my own tucked in my purse, and I take it out and eat it along with my husband, taking in the same view he sees. I imagine what it must be like to have an office, a desk, a computer to keep track of your appointments, and people visiting you all day, asking you questions and getting you to put your signature on documents.

A man who works for the school walks by with a rake. He waves at me. I smile at him but make no gesture. It is what a ladybug would do, I imagine, smiling indifferently at the world and continuing on her way.

I peek around the tree trunk, and when it is safe, I continue watching Jack. There's one young woman who visits him frequently—she looks like a teacher. During dinner, he usually recounts his day to me in some detail, but he has never told me about her. She wears her hair in a ponytail and speaks in a very animated fashion and does a funny thing where she sits on his desk while she talks. I wonder if they have had sex, locked in his office after hours or suddenly, fervently, in her car in the deserted parking lot under the buzzing lamplight. She is very pretty, and she laughs easily.

Later, when I go to pick my son up at school, the children are all running to and fro on the playground. My son is being chased—or he is chasing, it's impossible to tell—and as I watch, he trips and falls and begins to cry. He sits up and raises his scraped palms to the air. I can see that they are streaked sooty black and pocked with gravel, and they are bleeding a little. Hands are things that never stay undamaged for very long. They go everywhere, and they feel the suffering of all the tactile world. That's why people use fingerprints to identify you—the scarred record of everything you have touched.

My boy cries, as children do when they are in pain.

His teacher, Miss Lily, is suddenly beside me.

"Mrs. Borden," she says.

"Yes?"

"Marcus," she says, pointing. "Your son."

"Oh, yes," I say and go to fetch Marcus and tend to his bloody hands. We wash them in cool water, and I tell him about mountain streams and all the animals that cool their paws in them.

He asks me have I ever been to a mountain stream, and I tell him I have.

He asks me have I ever had my hands scraped like his. I tell him I have, indeed, had that—and much, much worse.

———

WE ALL PREPARE faces to go outside. The world at large does not see us for who we really are, does not see the version of ourselves that's exposed maybe only in front of mirrors in our tiny bedrooms. So we look out our windows, and we dress ourselves for the day, and we put on our masks, and we become the performance of an hour or two—before we can find a place to be alone and breathe again, just for a moment.

Somewhere along the line, we are taught to restrict ourselves for the benefit of the outside world and to be only truly free behind closed doors. Somehow the outside and the inside reverse themselves.

But what if it didn't have to be this way? What if upon stepping outside we shed everything that was not ourselves? We might feel our skin pressed up against all other skins. Discover how meager are the boundaries between our flesh and the flesh of others, the pulpy flesh of trees, the gritty flesh of soil, the tarry flesh of tarmac cooling after collecting a day's worth of sunlight. What if we clambered roughshod over the surface of the earth? Wouldn't the world be our true home?

———

I BECAME, AFTER that first moon, a creature drawn to dark, enclosed spaces. The maps I drew were now heavy with ink, cut through with narrow paths of white. After school, I would sometimes sit in the very back row of the darkened auditorium, watching Mr. Hunter and the drama club rehearse for the school play. I didn't know what the play was — something about union workers in the oil fields.

Mr. Hunter paced back and forth below the stage, trying to explain the significance of the oil. He spoke of the blood of the land — faces gone black with crude, raised to the grimy rain of the stuff. He urged them to think about their own connection to the land, those reveled-in, mucky parts of themselves.

He always seemed to know I was there. He would come to the back and sit next to me, and we would watch the actors declaiming.

"They don't get it, do they?" he said to me. "How can they not get it?"

"They might be a lot of different things," I said, "but they can only be one thing at a time."

He gazed at me with eyes that were accustomed to the dark, and I looked away, embarrassed.

I found myself returning to the quarry — the place where, two years before, Hondy Pilt was chased from the mouth of the mine by a possum. I liked the definition of the place, the artful ridges, the geometrical clefts, the shaved planes of earth — like God's precise fingerprint. I bundled myself up against the cold and lay flat on the frozen earth at its very lowest point.

Once I heard the approach of others and fled to the mouth of the mine, where I watched in darkness a boy and a girl kissing each other on the berm, creating little landslides of pebbled stone. It was an hour before they were through. To keep myself occupied, I felt my way deeper into the mine, one hand flat against the wall, one directly in front of me so I wouldn't run into anything in the pitch black, my feet moving an inch at a time so I wouldn't tumble into an unseen shaft.

I liked it in there. The closeness. The dark. The feeling of being inside out.

What I did was I started mapping the mine.

In our garage, I found an old lantern, which I revived by cleaning the contacts and loading it with fresh D batteries. This was preferable to a regular flashlight for exploring the mine shafts because its light shone in all directions at once. I also carried a penlight in my pocket and held it in my teeth when I paused to inscribe some new part of the map in my notebook. I drew the map as I went. If I reached the edge of a notebook page, I continued on another page and coded both pages with letters and numbers that identified the sequence. I measured distances by my paces and noted those as well on long, straight passages. I drew in features of the mine as place markers. I knew to go left at the overturned mine cart because right was a dead end. I drew a picture of a collapsed wooden frame that looked like a crucifix because it marked the passage to a three-way split in the tunnels. For places where there were no natural markers, I brought along a hammer and nailed ribbons into the ground. The different colors of ribbon meant different things, and I wrote codes on them in marker that referred to the codes in my map notebook.

I carried a baggie of trail mix, too, for when I got hungry. And a stick to scare away possums and rats.

It was cold underground, and damp. The walls were wet with icy water, as though the thaw of spring had not penetrated to this stratum of the earth. I wore a plastic slicker, because sometimes the caverns rained on me, the water droplets echoing loudly in the confines of stone.

I was frightened each time I went—and I thought that I might die. People did die all the time in old mines. There were wide vertical shafts of pure black that seemed bottomless when I listened for the sound of the stones I dropped in them. But it was also peaceful there. And living and dying were not everything to me then.

It was clear that no one had gone deep into the mine in a very long time. The ground up to the first intersection was cluttered with empty bottles, flattened potato chip bags, torn sweaters, tin cans that had been shot through with holes or fashioned into marijuana-smoking devices, even a rotted teddy bear half buried in the packed dirt. But beyond that first intersection the atmosphere was thick with dust, and with my stick I had to brush away spiderwebs that quivered to and fro in the currents of stale air. Once I accidentally dislodged a rock and found a swarm of white spiders that ran off every which way and hid themselves in other fissures of stone.

What was I looking for? What did I seek?

I fantasized about finding some ancient miner who had lost his way in the caverns and never found his way out. He would have set up house somewhere deep underground, a pretty little cave of a living room lit by torches, a patchwork area rug made of discarded miner's clothing.

He would greet me, knowing me on sight, of course, as a fellow dweller of the substrata. We would speak in the secret language that I knew must exist between travelers in the dark.

Sometimes I hummed as I went, and my voice in those caverns was like the sound of my voice in my own head when I closed the flaps of my ears.

I was accustomed to being alone.

I had been spelunking empty caverns my whole life. What I sought were the tunnels that led back underneath the town, the ones that would disclose all the buried truths of the place. There might be whole cities under the surface of the earth, populated by wise men who could see in the dark and who knew, better than I or anyone, how the secret gears of the world worked. And I could speak with them. And they would love me and call me their little light from above, and they would take me in as one of their own.

I had grown sick with questions—and what I searched for was a kingdom of answers.

———

ROUTINE IS IMPORTANT for people like me. It keeps us anchored in reality. It's how we keep from spinning off into the ether.

After I went breach, I did my best to establish a new set of routines to accommodate the disturbances my life became subject to—to diminish their significance by making them normal. Every morning before I brushed my teeth, I examined the sheets of my bed. I knew I would find no blood, but the checking itself became the point. I made my demon disappointment into a simple pattern and so exorcised it. That's how you keep things safe.

Peter started coming over regularly after school, three afternoons a week—three because that is a fairy-tale number and because I liked putting symbols on those days in my calendar to anticipate and memorialize them.

We had sex on those three afternoons every week. We never said much—never said a thing afterward. The act was bigger than words. I was illiterate in the language of bodies, so I abandoned myself to it, and it was lovely not to think so much—simply to feel the firecracker spark of nerves starting in my toes and skittering up my legs.

When it was done, we were diligent about our homework.

I was frequently embarrassed. I knew what we were doing was natural—but not all nature was the same. The stars didn't care about sweat and kisses and panting. They glistened prettily way up there in their heavens. They beatified the sky with their cool, gemlike indifference.

So why shouldn't I?

JANUARY'S BRITTLE MOON came.

I didn't want to see anyone else, so I didn't go to the woods. Instead I ran in the other direction, to the center of town. In a parking lot, I found a woman still out after dark. I stood watching her, naked, unashamed. I felt as though I could hurt her. The town, it was mine. The parking lot was mine. She saw me in the distance. What I must have looked like—the tiny, pale-skinned naked girl with her little fists clenched! The woman ran. When she saw me, she ran to her car, fumbled her keys, dropped them to the ground, picked them up again, finally got the car door open, launched herself inside, and closed herself in.

I twitched for wanting to claw at her face. I wondered when was the last time her skin was opened up.

Two thoughts occurred to me simultaneously:

Why was this woman afraid of me?

Why wasn't she more afraid of me?

I went to the town square, where there was a clock tower, a

monument to the soldiers of some war, a gazebo surrounded by grass and trees and shrubbery. It was the place where, last month, the breachers had attacked the girls and boys from the next town.

I trampled over the grass, the frost crystals tickling my toes. The storefronts were all lit up by buzzing street lamps. In the far distance I could hear the low, tidal hiss of the freeway that carried traffic past our little town. But there were no cars going by on the streets around me. No one drove on the three nights of the full moon. Adults lived in dread of running over the wild breachers bounding across dark streets.

Also, they didn't want to see. Once, out of curiosity, I crept up on a house down the block from where I lived. The lights were on in the front room, and I could see someone in there, sleeping on a recliner in front of the television. I put my face against the pane of glass and even tasted it with the tip of my tongue. It was metallic, cold. Then, as though he could sense me there watching him, the man woke suddenly and turned to the window. Our eyes met. I recognized him. We'd never spoken, but I knew him from the neighborhood. He wore a straw hat when he watered his lawn and always smiled at me when I passed by on the way home from school.

Now, seeing me, he looked at his watch and clambered up from the recliner. For a moment he seemed undecided about what to do. I was surprised, standing naked before his window, that I wasn't more self-conscious. But I wanted to see him for what he truly was. I wanted to watch. Finally he came to the window. We looked at each other again, but then his eyes dropped, as if in shame or modesty—and then, very slowly, so as not to incite me, perhaps, he drew the curtains closed.

The nighttime shame of our town. It's what curtains were made for.

Now, in the town square, I reflected on the man's shame.

I decided I wanted to be on top of the gazebo, the way Peter had been when he had looked so kingly during the last moon, so I stalked around it until I found a way up by overturning a trash can and climbing onto the sloped roof. I scraped my belly to pieces hoisting myself over the lip of the roof, but once on top, I lay back and luxuriated in the sting of my cuts.

It was quiet there in the dead center of things. So quiet. I could hear the insistent insect buzz of the street lamps. I could hear the creak of the hanging sign suspended over the barbershop, swinging back and forth in the breeze. I could hear the low mechanical click of the stoplights as they turned from green to amber to red—signs without meaning, because there was no one around to be directed by them.

It was a time to take stock of things, but I couldn't think straight. I wanted to put it all in order, to line it all up. I wanted to go through the list of the people I knew and assess where they fit in my life. I wanted to draw a map and put them all on it. But my thoughts were all bloody or obscene, and it made me want to cry. And I did cry. My mind did weep while my body raged—and there must be something of the mind in the gutters of the body, because I could feel the tickle of real tears creeping down the sides of my cheeks and into the folds of my ears.

I must have slept, because when I opened my eyes again I could hear someone in the gazebo beneath me. It was still deep night, still no one in any direction I could see. I crawled to the sloping edge of the gazebo roof and lowered my head to look.

Hondy Pilt was there, staring right at me, as though he knew that's where I would appear from.

———

"HELLO," I SAID.

"Hello," he said. He never said much, Hondy, but when he did his words were serene and wise-sounding. Even a simple hello.

I swung myself down off the roof of the gazebo, and I sat with my knees to my chest on the bench across from Hondy. For a full minute, we stalked each other with our eyes, as was our habit in those days. Because we were so keenly aware that any human interaction could end in passion or violence, it was important to determine, with muscles rigid and teeth clenched, the direction of the exchange as much as possible before you began it.

He sat pharaohlike, with his palms flat on his thighs, almost completely hairless except for the top of his head and the curls around his lumpy genitals. His skin looked pink in the light of the street lamps, ruddy and young. His stomach bulged a little, and there was a roundness to all the parts of his body. He was a large boy—but my instincts told me I didn't have to defend myself from him, so I relaxed and breathed more deeply.

"How come you're not with the others?" I said.

He smiled up at the serene stars.

"Let me ask you a question," I said. "How long've you been breaching? It's got to be over a year now, right? Are you ever going to stop?"

The street lamps buzzed their electrical buzz.

"Yeah," I said, as though he'd actually answered. I glanced around to make sure no one else was in the vicinity. "You want to know something? I'm not a real breacher. At least, I'm not the same kind as other people."

I watched for his response. Perhaps he would look at me with shock and horror. Perhaps he would march off to unite with the common heart that was not mine.

His gaze came down from the sky long enough to look me in the face.

But the pale gentleness of his eyes did not change. My secret shame, the starry sky, a leaf of newspaper blown down the middle of an empty street—to Hondy they were all of a kind. The progress of the slowly turning earth. We turned with it.

And I suddenly wanted to tell him more, to tell him everything.

"My mother, she never breached. That's how I know. See, I have her blood. So I can't be a real breacher. I'm something else. Something worse, probably—because for me it's not about nature. You understand? It's not natural for me. Even this—being here like this—it's a lie. And my father, he doesn't know. He's been alone for a long time. He misses my mother more than anything. Sometimes that's all he is, the leftovers of my mom. And sometimes I do things with Peter Meechum, who used to be called Petey, and I don't know why he wants to be around me, really, he could have any girl—but there was also Roy Ruggle, who everyone calls Blackhat, and he's gone now, and everyone's happy about it except me, and I don't know why I feel bad for him but I do, and Rose Lincoln used to be called Rosebush, and everybody seems to have a new name except me—I'm just Lumen, which means light, but I think there's something gone rotten in me, Hondy—"

I stopped short. It seemed that the night might crack apart.

"I've gone rotten somehow," I said. "I used to be good. I used to know things. People used to give me prizes for what I knew. Now I don't know anything, and I don't even know what good looks like anymore. Remember we used to send valentines to everyone in class? They had hearts and flowers and shy girls in dresses and boys with straw hats? That's what good looks like to me now. That's how far away. And I don't know what it means, except that I'm rotting out from the inside."

Hondy Pilt shook his head.

"No," he said quietly.

"What?"

"No."

"What do you mean?"

I went over and sat next to him. He looked at the stars.

I wanted to smell his skin, and I did, putting my nose at the place where his arm met his torso. He smelled of powder.

Then my lips were on his chest, but it wasn't like kissing—instead, they were parted slightly, and I brushed them over his skin as though I were reading some truth in the textures of him.

He looked at the stars.

He was so much bigger than I was. I leaned into him, pressed my little body against his. From my memory, a phrase throbbed into my brain like a heartbeat—"more than the sum of our parts"—and I liked it. I wondered what was made in the meeting of our skins. Something large but invisible.

I'd confessed to him.

I reached over and put my hand on his genitals. They were soft and warm. They felt strangely loose, unincorporated.

I wanted to stay there all night, but Hondy Pilt pushed me away. With one hand on my shoulder, he pushed me back as though I were a blanket somebody had thrown over him on a hot night. There was no malice in the act, the same way you don't blame a door for being open or being shut.

Was I an open door or a shut one?

He stood, his attention suddenly caught by something I couldn't see down the street. Some vagary of the night, I supposed—there were so many things I did not see.

———

MY FATHER GOT the map I made him for Christmas framed and hung it in his office, where he could look at it all the time.

Peter Meechum continued making love to me in the afternoons. He said it made him very happy. One time he wondered aloud why I only had sex with him between full moons—which made me the exact opposite of some other girls. He wasn't really asking, so I didn't feel the need to answer him.

And it turned out that January's Brittle Moon was the last breach for Polly. When February's moon came, Polly remained indoors.

"Only eleven months," she said. "I was cheated."

"Maybe you just mature faster than other people," I said to reassure her.

"You're right. Maybe that's what it is."

She smiled, satisfied. She seemed to take it to heart. Suddenly she had no more patience for childish things. Her first order of business was to redecorate her bedroom. She told her parents she could no longer tolerate the pinks and purples. What she required, she told them, were what she called "tasteful blues and creams."

The weeks went on. I hid my full-moon activities from my father, but I think he must have known. Once, there was a long scratch on my neck. He didn't ask about it, but I know he saw.

We all have our fictions. It's not for other people to expose them. And yet I wondered more and more about my mother. I wondered what fictions she might have had. What did she do indoors during the full moons? How did she occupy herself? What stories did she tell herself, all on her own, while the whole town went crazy around her?

—

IN FEBRUARY EVERYTHING was crystals. There were icicles on every eave. I, too, was a brittle stalactite. It seemed that I might not ever grow up, that I might not ever be fully alive. Wandering the mine shafts, I had buried myself. I had shrouded myself with death. I was a premature ghost.

That was also the month that Mr. Hunter asked me to tell him stories.

It was in the middle of a *Hamlet* test. The only sounds in the classroom were the hiss of pens on paper and the occasional creak of a desk as we repositioned ourselves in our seats. I was in the middle of an essay question on the significance of Ophelia's suicide when he startled me by leaning down and whispering in my ear.

"I'm pressing you into service," he said. "Meet me in the auditorium after school."

I couldn't tell you how I finished that test, my stomach tight, my face gone flush, my pen clutched too tight in my fist. I had always been wary of the man, and I was not the kind of girl who received whispered invitations. But I went because I did what I was told to do. Agreeableness was my secret pride.

The auditorium looked empty when I got there, with a high, echoey stillness like that of a church between services. I let the door close softly behind me and waited for my eyes to adjust to the dimness.

"Lumen," he said, and I could make out his form sitting on the edge of the stage. "Come in."

"It's dark."

"I don't want to be bothered."

I walked slowly down the sloping aisle between the empty

187

seats, which always made me feel like a bride, and when I got to the stage he told me to sit, so I sat on the stage near him, but I kept my distance, my legs dangling over the edge, as his were.

He smiled a strange smile at me, and I didn't know what it meant, and I waited for what would happen next.

"I want you to tell me about it," he said. "The breaching."

"Tell you?"

"Tell me what it's like. You know I didn't grow up here. I didn't experience it myself."

It felt like such a personal thing for him to be asking in such a direct and unapologetic fashion.

"I want to know," he said simply.

"Why me?"

"Lots of reasons," he said. "The main one is that you want to tell it."

I didn't enjoy being fathomed like that.

"I better go," I said.

I stood and started to walk back up the aisle. I wondered what he would do. If he would demand for me to halt or seize me from behind. But he did nothing at all.

I was halfway up the aisle when I stopped and turned and saw him still sitting, unmoved, with a bemused look on his face.

"Where are you from?" I asked from my safe distance.

"East Saint Louis."

"What's Missouri like?"

"Actually, it's Illinois—it's across the river from Saint Louis."

"Oh."

"The mighty Mississippi. It runs brown with mud."

"Oh." Each word I said sounded smaller in the dark.

"Normal."

"What?"

"You asked what Missouri's like. It's normal. Illinois, normal. Saint Louis, normal. East Saint Louis, normal. Partridge Street, with its kids riding bicycles before dinnertime—normal. So much normal you could choke on it."

There was a roughness to him always, as though he were constantly chewing on some bitter root. He was someone who seemed to have little tolerance for things. His demeanor suggested I could stay or go as I pleased. So I stayed.

"It's like a highway," I said, feeling for a moment like I was standing alone, speaking to myself. "The breaching. It's like a long highway in the desert, and you can't see the end of it, and you can see everything for miles in every direction, and there's nothing but you—and maybe that's a good thing, or maybe that's a bad thing, or maybe it's both. But it's just you and your guts in the middle of a desert."

I waited for him to respond, but he said nothing at all. He just leaned forward a little and waited for me to continue.

And that's how it started between him and me.

———

SOMETIMES I TELL myself stories still. During the days, when my husband is at work and my son is at school, I walk through the house tidying things and listening to the tales my voice has to tell.

"There once was a man, just like you and me," I say, "except that at night he liked to remove his head from his shoulders and keep it in a wicker basket beside his bed."

I straighten the pile of coasters on the coffee table and am gone out far in my imagination.

Lola King, who has let herself in by my kitchen door, startles me.

"Who are you talking to, sweetie?"

"Oh," I say. "No one. Just doing some cleaning."

"You're losing it," she says. "Let's us girls have a couple Bloody Marys and go put dirty magazines in Marcie's mailbox. What do you say?"

Lola is lawless. She sees me as the innocent she delights in corrupting. I wonder what she might look like running wild in the woods, naked under the moonlight, tearing at life with her painted fingernails.

She tells me stories about her life before she came here—in New Jersey, where her husband was acquainted with some bad men who sometimes cleaned their guns at her kitchen table. She means to appall me, so I widen my eyes and shake my head slowly back and forth.

We all have stories to tell. Our demons are sunk deep under the skin, and maybe we use stories to exorcise them—or at least know them truly.

———

BEGGAR'S MOON CAME at the end of February. I went into town—but different parts of the town, the places where the others never went. I ran until I was out of breath, my burning lungs heaving for air while I stood naked and alone in the middle of an empty supermarket parking lot. There was an unearthly luminescent glow coming from the supermarket, and I walked toward it until I stood on the sidewalk in front of the massive plate-glass windows. Next to me was a recycling bin filled with empty beer bottles. It gave off an acrid smell that I found comforting. The rear of the store was dark, but they had left the overhead lights on in the front. I pressed my palms to the glass, wanting to feel

190

the nighttime haunt of a place that the daylight had seen all populous.

Surely spirits lingered. Surely they moved slower than bodies, always half a day behind their corporeal counterparts. I knew this to be true, because I felt my own spirit still alive somewhere in the daylight, left behind in the comfort of my bedroom, reading a book or calculating trigonometry. My spirit was graceful and true—something to make my father proud.

I felt it alive somewhere. Somewhere else.

There was a sound behind me, and I turned. It was Roddy Ewell. We knew each other from school. He was in the grade below me, and he was small, too. I had wondered, the previous year, if he might ever consider being my boyfriend. Though it had been a long time since he had crossed my mind at all.

He casted a splay of shadows beneath the humming lamps of the parking lot—as though his own spirit were manifold and on the escape.

"I followed you," he said.

"Why?"

"How come you don't run with everyone else? It's not natural."

I turned my back to him and gazed through the plate glass into the empty store. There was a delicate magic to empty places. I wished myself inside and wondered what it would take to break the window with my head.

"Never mind," he said behind me. "I like you. Can we do it?"

"What?" I said, not looking at him. "What did you say?"

"I said, can we do it?"

"Do what?"

"You know."

"Oh, that. No."

"But the moon." He pointed at the sky, though there was no moon to be seen because it was hidden behind clouds.

"No."

"Why not?"

This is what I had learned about breachers—you were either weak or you were strong. How you presented yourself determined what happened to you. Roddy Ewell did not bother to attack, because he assumed I presented no threat. He thought, between the two of us, that I was the weak one.

He should not have thought that.

When I didn't answer, he came up behind me and wrapped his arms around my body. I could feel his penis, erect, against my bottom. I turned myself out of his grasp and shoved him backward.

"Stop it," I said. "You're pathetic."

He cringed, surprised. "What?" he said. This was not going as he had imagined it. My defiance had caught him off guard.

I hated his weakness. I wanted to kill his weakness. I could feel the violence in me twitching all up and down the nerves of my body.

"You're different," he said. "You didn't used to be like this."

For reasons I did not care to explore, this was unacceptable to me. I reached for one of the empty bottles from the bin next to me, and I threw it at him. He flinched, and the bottle hit him in the shoulder then fell and smashed on the concrete.

"Ouch," he said.

"Don't say ouch."

I took another bottle and threw it at him. He knocked it away, but it made a gash on his forearm, and there was blood.

"Ouch," he said. "Stop it."

"Don't say it. I told you not to say it. You don't come to me unafraid. Don't you dare. You think I don't know how to make pain?"

I attacked. I leaped at him, this meager boy, even though I was smaller than he, smaller than everyone. I threw myself at him, and we tumbled to the tarmac of the parking lot, the grit digging into our skin. He held his arms up to defend himself, but it made no difference. I clawed haphazardly, my fingernails digging bloody troughs in the flesh of his arms, his chest, his shoulders.

"Stop!" He sobbed. "Please, please stop it!"

I couldn't hear for all the horror happening in my head. I didn't think. I couldn't tell what was happening. All I knew was ravenous hunger. I wanted to eat that little-boy soul. I wanted to chew it up and swallow it so that maybe he could be a little stronger, or so that maybe the world could.

I could hear my own voice, like a mongrel dog's, grunting and gurgling, and I was surprised. I was blank. The world was white skin and red blood.

I tore at him until he wriggled out from under me. We were both bloodied and raw.

He ran into the darkness, the soles of his feet slapping wetly against the pavement.

I remember nothing else. My mind was truly lost.

I woke the next morning weeping, huddled in a tight ball against the front door of my house. My body shook with the pain of its injuries and the suffocating strength of my sobs. For a long time, I could not stop, and I put my fist in my mouth to hush my cries.

After a while, I had calmed myself enough to go inside.

That was the end of Beggar's Moon.

—

BETWEEN MOONS, I went back to the mine. And I discovered something new in my exploration—a large, hollowed-out chamber, an echoing cistern. Even though its entrance was near the mouth of the mine, I had never noticed it before because it required that I pry loose a collapse of stones and crawl my way through a narrow aperture.

It was a majestic place, a sacramental place. The cave was circular, the dripping walls rising high like a dome in a church. At the very top of the dome was an opening, the size of our kitchen tabletop at home, through which I could see the dusky pink of the late afternoon sky, the overhanging bristles of tree branches.

The floor of the cave was mostly flat, but in the middle was the mouth of a wide shaft, roughly the same size as the opening above, that descended down into pure abyss. I wondered if the shaft and the opening had shared some kind of purpose in the old days of the mine, so symmetrical and aligned did they seem—as though God had poked a gigantic needle into the pincushion of the world. I crept close to the edge of the chasm and felt my stomach do vertiginous tumbles. I stared down into the void so long that I lost track of myself. I hugged a nearby outcropping of stone because I didn't trust myself to stay sane exposed to such nullities. If I leaped in, I might fall forever. I wondered if I would die of fright before I hit the bottom so that my landing might be a curious ghostly bliss.

I thought maybe that's where my previous self had gone, down there in the depthless black, and I spoke to her.

"Lumen Ann Fowler," I said, trusting that my meager voice would carry down the well in the absence of any material to impede it. "Lumen Ann Fowler, Lumen Ann Fowler."

I knew that repetitions of three had power to them. And if you could summon Bloody Mary by uttering her name three times in a mirror, then I reckoned you could summon a lost girl in a similar way.

"It's me, Lumen," I said. "I came looking for you."

I waited, listening to my own breathing in that silent place.

"I know who you are. I remember you. Do you want me to prove it? Your mother wore orchid gloves at her wedding."

I swallowed, and there was grit in my throat. I leaned my head against the outcropping of stone and gripped it tighter.

"It's all right," I said. "You don't have to say anything. We can just be quiet for a while."

It was a home. It was a chapel. A shaft of light shone down at an angle through the opening and lit up all sparkly the grains of dust afloat on the air. This was a chamber of echoes that might as well have been the clattering ossuary of my own mind, and I decided it would be a place of pilgrimage for me.

When the light through the opening above dimmed with impending night, I crawled back out into the mine shaft proper and piled a few stones in front of the entrance to my private citadel so that it would not be stumbled upon by strangers.

Once outside the mine I tried to locate the place in the ground where the cistern opened to the sky, but I never could find it.

As though the avenues of inside and outside used different maps altogether.

CHAPTER 8

Worm Moon was wet with rainfall. You listened to the showers against your windowpanes. You imagined what it must be like to luxuriate in such a torrent, naked, and you thrilled with anticipation. Blackhat Roy came back.

I went to bed early, listening to the thunder, and I fell asleep. But my body jolted itself awake an hour after I lay down. I lurched to the window and opened it and leaped out. It was all very simple when the moon came out. All the considerations and doubts and rationalizations of the daytime were sloughed away. I wanted to be outside, and so I went outside.

It is sometimes a joy to be rained on. The chill of it against your scalp, the tickle of it down the inside of your thighs.

I ran down to the lake to see the ripples on the water and to watch the lightning fork down from the clouds. The others were already there. Some were swimming in the black water, others lay on the muddy earth. I liked looking at the bodies from the shadows of the trees. To look at someone's naked body in the moonlight is to know that person in a new way. Lumpy humanity laid bare. A person stripped of all masks. For surely, I realized, that is what we do. We start with one pure and concentrated version of ourselves, then we modify and mold, we layer defense over pretense over convention. By the time we're done getting dressed in the morning, there is little left of who we really are. It's all just art. Twee and ineffectual art. Cartoon figures drawn in crayon on a paper place mat in a family-friendly Italian restaurant.

Hondy Pilt was there, gazing monklike into the downpour. Sue Foxworth was there. And Adelaide Warren. Rose Lincoln came, too, emerging from the trees with Peter Meechum behind her. Rose's breach had gone on longer than a year. Each full moon was supposed to be her last. But here she was again.

I wondered if she and Peter had been having sex in the rain, and I thought I might enjoy killing her. But such instincts in me seemed to go straight to the brain, where violence takes seed and grows larger over time rather than permitting itself release in the moment. I would say nothing.

Idabel McCarron came up to me and pressed her slippery body to mine. I allowed it, because the sensation was new to me—and, besides, we were all a little rain-drunk.

"Did you hear?" she whispered in my ear. "He's back."

"Who?"

"Look."

She pointed, and just at that moment, emerging from the lake like some mammalian vestige of prehistory, was Blackhat Roy.

He was different—I saw it immediately. He seemed larger, for one thing, a bigger, more solidified version of himself—though after just three months, I don't know if that was possible.

Peter was also seeing him for the first time. He left Rose Lincoln's side and approached Roy. The two stood face-to-face on the lakeshore in the rain. When they were together like that, I could see that Roy still had to angle his head up to meet Peter's eyes. But he was bigger. I swear it. Somehow he commanded more space.

"I thought you were in Chicago," Peter said quietly.

"I'm back."

"Why?"

"You want to hear the whole story? It might cause you grief."

He was different. In my mind, I tried to telegraph to Peter to be careful, because Blackhat Roy was different.

Thunder quaked in the distance. The rain unfurled sideways, like a sheet pinned to a clothesline in the wind. We didn't shield ourselves from it.

"You shouldn't have come back," Peter said. "You don't belong here."

"Really? I would have thought this is exactly where I belonged."

"You terrorized those people."

It seemed that Peter, along with everyone else, had convinced himself of certain fictions about that night.

"Terrorized!" Roy laughed. Then he said the word again, as though he didn't think much of it. "Terrorized."

That's when Peter struck him, his closed fist cutting across Roy's jaw. But Roy didn't move. He put his hand up to his face—as though curious about the pain he found there. Then he raised his voice, because he wasn't just talking to Peter—he was talking to all of us.

"Nobody cares about your noble faggotry. You want dominance? This is how you get it."

And he grabbed Peter's shoulders and kneed him in the crotch. Peter went down, and Roy was on top of him. For several minutes we watched as the two grappled together on the wet earth, the lightning capturing them in gaudy white tableaux, their blood, as they clawed and bit at each other, streaming together with the rain.

Peter stood no chance. There was no fairness in the way Roy fought, no reason, no daylight. He fought as though the choice were pain or death and he had made his decision years before. Peter curled himself into a ball on the shore, but Roy kept after him, crouching over him, biting through the skin of his neck, licking the blood from his lips while Peter whimpered beneath him.

A great foulness, and we all stood and watched. Some, boys and girls alike, rubbed their hands unconsciously between their legs as they observed. We had appetites back then. We knew what we felt.

———

THE RAIN STOPPED. The tree branches overhead continued to drip for a while, but they finally stopped, too.

Once he was through with Peter, Roy walked away. I kneeled over Peter, trying to clean him up, but he hit my hands away.

"I'll kill him," he hissed. "Kill him."

"You're bleeding."

"He's filth."

"Put your hand on your neck. Otherwise you'll get dizzy."

He would not let me touch him, but I tended to him as best I could and made sure he got home in the morning.

Me, I snuck back into my house and was in bed before my father woke. As my bedroom turned pink with early light, I fell asleep and dreamed of boy-skin made slick with blood.

———

THE NEXT DAY I went to Peter's house, but his mother told me he didn't want to see anyone. I asked if I could write him a letter, and she gave me a pad of notepaper and a ballpoint pen.

I wrote:

Peter—

I'm sorry about what happened to you. It doesn't mean anything. Sometimes it's a hideous world. Please call me if you need anything.

Love, Lumen

That night I went back to the lake. It seemed to me that things had changed, and I wanted to see how.

Peter was not there. Instead there was Blackhat Roy. Just like that. And so masters and slaves are nothing but the turn of a card.

It was Blackhat Roy, pulling along, as if on a leash, Poppy Bishop, a girl I knew who herself had just started breaching. She was his. She had regressed to infancy, as some do under the influence of the full moon. Her violence was an infant's violence, as was her sensuality. She trailed along behind Roy, sucking her thumb and using her other hand to tug on her earlobe. When she had a tantrum, she became hysterical, striking out this way and that with a toddler's murderous rage. Afterward, when she settled down, you might find her curled up, her head in Roy's lap, nursing at Roy's indifferent penis as though it were a binky.

And there were two other new breachers, too. A boy and a girl I recognized from school—from the grade below mine. They held hands like Hansel and Gretel finding their way through the wilderness of mythology, and they were frightened.

I didn't like to look at Blackhat Roy—who seemed to have contempt for everyone around him—and I thought about running off on my own. But I wanted to stay and look at the new members of the brood.

The skin of the two new ones—their names were Ben MacClusky and Mandy Cavell—shimmered pale against the trees. They seemed somehow brighter than the rest of us. As though we all started out luminescent and then faded over time. As though we were all just waiting for our lights to gutter out.

Mandy Cavell was not entirely naked. She wore a pair of white cotton underpants.

Blackhat Roy left Poppy Bishop sucking her thumb atop a rock and approached Mandy Cavell. He said nothing for a moment, instead just walking a slow circle around her while she stood there breathing hard. Then he stopped in front of her.

She would not meet his eyes. Her own gaze had been cast demurely downward, and then Blackhat Roy positioned himself in such a way that his genitals must have been directly in her line of sight.

"Hey," he said. And he had to say it again before the girl looked up at him. "Hey."

"I'm sorry," she said.

"For what?"

She had no answer to this.

"Don't you want to take those off?" Roy said to her.

She shook her head.

"I think you do," he insisted.

She looked at him. Then she looked at the boy next to her, but he was no help. His eyes snapped back and forth between the trees and all the naked girl bodies around him.

"You want to take them off," Roy said again. "But you don't do it. Why not? What's the point of fighting against yourself?"

"It's not nice."

Roy laughed.

"Not nice," he said. "That's true. Nice is one thing it's not."

Mandy Cavell looked around helplessly. I felt for her. She reminded me of some lost version of myself.

"Stop it," I said to Blackhat Roy.

I emerged from the shadows, and everyone looked at me. I didn't like all those eyes on me, but I was feeling hard, and it was a feeling new to me—and I wanted to own it for myself. Somehow Peter's beating the night before had made me romantic for suffering.

"Leave her alone," I said.

Blackhat Roy did leave the girl alone. Instead he came and stood in front of me. I didn't feel like quailing, so I didn't.

"Leave her alone why?" he asked me.

"What do you care if she wants to leave her underwear on?"

"Do you see anybody else out here with diapers?"

"Isn't she supposed to be able to do what she wants? Isn't that what this is all about? Or are you just replacing one kind of conformity for another?"

He looked down at me, and his eyes wanted to gnaw on my bones.

"No," he said. "I'm just showing concern. When the moon's out, you should be able to piss where you want."

Then, without moving, Blackhat Roy let go a stream of urine that splashed against my thigh and ran down my leg. It tickled as it

202

streamed over my ankle and between my toes and made a muddy puddle around my foot. The smell was sharp, and the heat of it in the cold night made a steam that rose between us as our eyes locked.

I made no move. But this wasn't a refusal—not at all. It was an engagement. I stood still, allowing his urine to soak my leg. It went on for an absurdly long time. At first the others laughed. They brayed at this new spectacle. But then, when I refused to run or even look away from his gaze, they got silent again. They recognized that something was happening. They saw that this was not the end of something or a punch line, but really just the beginning.

When he was done, we continued to look at each other. I wondered what his eyes were telling me, then I thought it must be an invitation to violence.

Part of me wanted just to turn and leave—part of me knew that would be the true victory. The animal is no more diminished than when you turn your back on it.

But there was another part of me, and it was hungering to rip and tear. It was wanting to sunder the whole beautiful and ugly world, to play in the exposed guts of all that beauty and ugliness.

It was a desire to kill, and it was ecstatic.

My right arm shot up, my hand like a claw, and it tore across Blackhat Roy's face. Three irregular lines of blood appeared on his cheek where my fingernails had torn him. As we faced each other, saying nothing, the blood began to seep from the cuts, trickling over the ledge of his chin and down his neck.

Everyone was quiet. Tiny waves broke against the lakeshore.

Still, he made no move. A smile spread slowly across his face, and his eyes narrowed.

"Okay," he whispered. "Good."

Then he raised a hand, and that's when I flinched for the first time. But he didn't strike me. Instead he put his hand to his own cheek to wet his fingers with his blood. Then he reached out and drew a bloody fingertip down my chest, making a vertical stripe of his blood between my nipples—like the longitudinal line where they cut you open for an autopsy.

———

HE HAD MADE his point. He returned to his girl, Poppy Bishop, who clung to him.

I left them then. I wasn't in the mood to defend two new breachers—both of whom were bigger than me—from the ravages of the natural world.

I was feeling barbarous, and I hated myself a little.

I found a quiet length of the lake edge and walked into the water to cleanse myself of Blackhat Roy's humors—his blood and his urine. But I had been marked, I knew, deeper than the skin.

I floated on my back. I let myself drift. The night sky was cloudless. So many stars on a night like this. The heavens were crowded. No one bothered to look at the happenings of one small town on one meager landmass on one satellite of one middle-aged star. Maybe no one cared about the moral transgressions of a girl floating on a lake under the moon. Sometimes it was comforting to be nothing at all.

I wanted to run. I needed to run—run like I did on that first night. My muscles ached for it.

But I clenched my teeth and my fists, and I floated. I would hold myself together—I would keep myself contained. Otherwise my body could burst to pieces. It could all break apart. There were shivering hairline fractures everywhere.

———

WHEN I COULDN'T be still anymore, I swam to shore.

Blackhat Roy was there waiting for me. He was alone. He sat on the sandy verge. The claw marks on his cheek had stopped bleeding. They were black in the moonlight.

He watched me emerge from the water but said nothing. He leaned back casually, his palms on the sand. I hated him, but I knew why people followed him. There was some of the follower in me, too.

"Don't touch me," I said.

"Why not?"

"I'll run."

"I'll catch you. You know I'll catch you, right? Are you one of those girls who runs just so you can be caught?"

I went to walk past him up the shore to the woods—but he reached out and caught my ankle. His fist made a shackle, the grip so tight I thought it would snap my bones.

"Let go," I said.

I looked down. His penis was rigid. There was a snarl on his face.

"Let go," I said again, "or I'll hurt you."

But he didn't let go. Instead, he said:

"A hurt is just a different kind of kiss. You want to bite me? Then bite me. Let's make each other bleed."

That's when I attacked. With both my hands made into claws, I swiped at his face below me. I shrieked, primal, pure in a different way, like a banshee, like the true spirit of human pith. There was nothing left of the world beside muscle and blood and bone and thirst.

He pulled my ankle hard, and I fell to the sand. My fingers were wet with his blood and sweat, but I kept striking.

I wanted to hurt. I wanted to hurt everything. I wanted to cause pain.

I thought this must be what evil feels like for those who perpetrate it. Desperate thirst. A craving beyond voices. A will to action that has nothing to do with brains or spirits or codes.

I'd never been so aware of my bones, of my tendons, of how they fit together and stretched—of what a body is really for.

So maybe goodness is a thing of the mind while badness is a thing of the body.

I tore at him, and it felt awful and the awfulness felt good, and the goodness of the awful feeling made me crazy.

He did not move to block me or attack me back. Instead, the skin of Blackhat Roy became the territory of my violence. And he smiled. He did smile. The moonlight showed his teeth, all exposed in a grin.

I struck at him until I was out of breath, until the muscles in my arms ached, until my fingers were bloody and bruised. I found that I knelt over him, that I had climbed on top of him, lemurlike. He lay back, and I straddled his lower belly. If I leaned back, I could feel the tip of his penis against the base of my spine.

I breathed. I sniffled and discovered that I had been crying. When I wiped my forearm across my face, it came away with smeared blood and tears.

Then Blackhat Roy spoke.

He said, "I'm giving you a count of five. If you run now, I won't chase you. If you don't run, something is going to happen. Do you understand?"

I watched the blood trickle down his cheeks. One red rivulet collected in the whorl of his ear. Like a beautiful shell found on the beach—consecrated or defiled by the runoff of savagery.

"Do you understand?" he said. "Nod if you understand."

My head nodded. My neck was sore, the muscles rigid, my skin jittery with popping clusters of nerves.

"Five," he said. "Four."

Yes, something would happen. And my body was unclothed against his. And the night was impossibly loud with the chatter of crickets. The blackest kinds of things were exposing themselves. And, far from turning away, I nuzzled against them. Evil was a body thing. A blanket stinking with sweat.

"Three, two," he said.

I looked to the woods. I could run, but I wasn't running.

Something would happen. And it might be a thing of horror, for I knew that horrors did happen to those who welcomed them.

If you do not flee from the altar, that's when you become wed to the devil.

"One."

I leaped up and ran as hard as I could through the trees. Behind me, I could hear his laughter grow distant and mocking.

———

I HAD MADE a map of our small town, and on the map I had put tiny symbols to mark the houses of all the people I knew so I could see how we stood in relation to each other. I knew where everyone lived. I could have gone anywhere.

But where I ended up was Mr. Hunter's house.

I just wanted to look. It was still before dawn, and all the streets were empty. People were asleep in their beds. And there I was, standing naked and unashamed in the middle of the street under a halo of lamplight, my body dirty and rent from my tangle with Blackhat Roy. I just stood and looked.

His house was so nice. It was a split-level, like so many in our neighborhood, with the bedroom up over the garage. His was painted white with green shutters. There were tall trees all around the sides and back of it. I knew he wasn't married, and I wondered how all the various rooms in the house were outfitted. I imagined walls covered with bookshelves, broken-spined volumes piled to reckless heights. I imagined a little Formica table in the kitchen where he drank his black coffee in the morning.

I stood for a long time just looking at the house, until the black sky began to grow pink at its rim. All of a sudden the street lamps shut off on their automatic timers, and when the reflection of the lights was gone from the glass panes, I could see a figure standing there in a window on the second story, leaning against the frame, gazing down at me. It was Mr. Hunter. He stood still, his head crooked gently to the side, his hands in his pockets. He had not been asleep at all. How long had he been looking out the window—all night?—before I came along and wandered into his view?

I did not run. Aware as I was of my nakedness, I did not make any move to hide myself. Every one of us is a little calamity. That's what I felt at that moment.

He must have known that I could see him now, because as I watched, he raised his left hand and placed his fingertips against the inside of the windowpane.

And me, I responded in kind. I raised my hand in a simple, meager salute. We were both travelers, and our destinations were—both of them—very far away.

———

IT WAS THE opening of garage doors down the block that made me suddenly aware of the time. The sun had risen. My father would be up soon.

I ran. I fled down the streets, feeling the tarmac cold and gristly under the soles of my feet. I leaped over fences and trotted through backyards, never minding the whip and cut of tree branches against my skin. I ran until my lungs burned.

And this was not the gallop of the free absconded from all chains — it was the panicked herding of the damned.

———

I WAS NOT in time.

When I came through the front door, my father was there. He saw me, and he was ashamed. There was no hiding my nakedness.

He looked down at the floor, pretending to have been walking from one room to another when I came in.

"Oh," he said. "I was just — um. Making breakfast. How about waffles? Would you like waffles? Uh — right. Good morning."

Without looking at me, he went to the door of the den and then remembered he was supposed to be going to the kitchen, so he backed out and fled down the hall.

Later, when I came downstairs dressed in the most modest outfit I could find, he was standing over the waffle maker. He stared intently at the steam.

"Ready for waffles?"

I could see him take a testing glance in my direction out of the corner of his eye, to make sure it was okay to look. Then he smiled widely at me — but he had trouble meeting my eyes.

"I was, um, going to use bananas," he said, "but they're still too green."

"I don't mind a green banana," I said, trying to be helpful.

"No, neither do I. But for pancakes and waffles, riper is better. That's a good rule of thumb."

"Okay."

"What kind of syrup? Maple or boysenberry?"

"Boysenberry," I said. It's the kind I preferred when I was little.

He always heated the syrup bottle in a saucepan of water. It was not right, he said, dousing a hot waffle with cold syrup.

He had rules for everything, my father, and the life he lived as a result was just a bit more vibrant, more true.

After we ate, I washed the dishes.

Behind me, I could hear him clearing his throat.

Then he said, "Are you okay?"

I didn't look up from the sink. I scrubbed the plates until every last remnant of impurity was erased.

"I'm fine."

"You know, you could—you could tell me if you weren't."

"I know."

"Do you, um, need anything? A prescription or something?"

"No. I can take care of it."

"Okay. All right."

I thought he would tell me he loved me, but I hadn't heard that from him in a long time. When I was a little girl, he would say it routinely. He seemed compelled to say it. But the declaration had gone the way of tall tale and myth.

As though the love between a father and daughter were only a childish thing. As though womanhood made obscene that which had previously been precious and perfect.

And so did we all fall—and in such a way were a million Edens lost.

I WENT TO Peter's house again, and this time he met me at the door. There was a thick wad of white bandage taped to his neck.

"Stitches," he said. "Fourteen of them. Thanks for the note. I didn't really want to see anyone."

In his bedroom, I sat on the edge of his bed, and he swiveled his desk chair to face me.

"Did you go out last night?" I asked.

He chuckled a little. "Did you ever try not to?" he said.

"Where did you go?"

"Down to the railroad tracks. Watched trains go by. Thought about hopping one of them."

"What stopped you?"

"I'm not afraid of running away," he said. "But I won't run away from *him*."

I said nothing.

"And," he continued, "also you."

"Oh."

He looked at me hard, and I blushed.

I put my hand to my neck, a mirror image of the place where he had his wound.

"Does it hurt?" I asked.

"Aches, mostly."

"Can I see?"

"Do you really want to?"

I nodded.

He got up from the chair, took off his shirt, and knelt before me. The bandage was right at the base of his neck, where his shoulder began.

"You do it," he said.

With my finger I tugged at the edges of the tape until they came free, then I folded the bandage back.

The skin was purpled and raw, the laces used to stitch him up blackened with blood and so tight that they pooched the skin up into bumpy ridges. I ran my fingertips over the raised script of his damage to see what might be read there. I had never really thought about stitches as being the same kind of stitches as in sewing—but they were. I thought that flesh must be a pliable and rude sort of fabric, difficult to work with. I pictured an old woman with a thimble pushing a long needle through his worsted, pinched-up skin. Our bodies are craftwork.

I put the bandage back and pressed the tape back into place.

He looked up into my eyes, and I thought he was going to say something, but he didn't. Instead he just leaned forward and pressed his head to my chest. I put my arms around him and stroked his hair.

———

BACK AT HOME, I shut the door of my bedroom, leaned against it, listened to the silence of the house, and felt myself jaundiced, yellowed by life. Strangely, I was relieved to be away from Peter Meechum, whom I loved.

In school the following day, Polly wanted to talk to me about her new adult preoccupations. I found excuses to escape her.

Funny: now that all these people were talking to me, I wanted nothing to do with them. Was it possible, I wondered, to be out of sync with everyone else for your entire life? I felt walled up behind bricks. Like holy people, who are also out of sync. It was called immurement—the practice of walling people up—a fact I had discovered when I had done my research on saints and anchorites.

Even Rose Lincoln seemed more interested in me since I had stood up to Blackhat Roy.

"Did you do all the rest to him, too?" she asked, her dark eyes bright. "It's like a devil got at him."

I was a devil now. It was no surprise. And the worst kind of devil is the kind that believes itself to be holy. Like Satan—the morning light, the angel. One's taste for corruption, it seems, has everything to do with one's memory of goodness. The inversions braid around each other, and it is too hard not to fall.

———

IT WAS THAT same week that Miss Simons, my physics teacher, offered to give me a ride home. She pulled up in her car beside the bike cage. Her hair was still done up, and she still wore her fashionable lipstick.

"Lumen, would you like a ride?"

I told her no, thank you. She had never offered to give me a ride before, and I thought it might have to do with her hearing about me going breach. When you were raised by a single father, sometimes women felt the philanthropic need to step in and have surrogate maternal chats with you.

"Come on. I'd enjoy it. There's something I've been wanting to talk to you about."

"But my bike."

"I'll help you put it in the back."

A previous version of me would have been concerned about being seen getting into a teacher's car. I mused on that while she and I hoisted my bike into the back and I climbed into the passenger seat.

"Do you want to know a secret?" Miss Simons said as we pulled out of the parking lot. "I was married once."

She paused and glanced over at me to make sure I appreciated the gravity of that revelation. I didn't know what response would satisfy her, so I said the most innocuous thing I could think of.

"You were?"

"That's right. It was a long time ago, and I was very young. It didn't last long. Fifteen months total. Almost immediately we both knew it was a mistake."

She talked for a little while about her ex-husband, about how he was now an important person on Wall Street, about how she begrudged him nothing, about how she had been single for a long while because she was determined not to make the same mistakes she had made before.

I listened patiently, wondering why I was chosen for these privileged glimpses into the woman's past, until finally, while the car idled at a stoplight, she turned to me with great earnestness.

"The reason I'm telling you all this, Lumen, is that—see, I'm fond of your father. Very fond of him, actually."

Oh. So she had a crush on my father. She was asking my advice about how to approach him. Maybe even asking my permission. I was touched by her deference while at the same time determined never to trust her again as long as I lived.

The red light turned to green, and the car glided forward again. We were just around the corner from my house.

"Do you think . . ." Miss Simons began. But she didn't seem to know how to phrase the next part.

I wanted to put her out of her misery. It made me anxious to see adults flounder like that.

"The thing is," I said, "he's still in love with my mother. I've told him he should try to move on, but he just thinks about her all the time."

"No one could ever replace your mother, and that's not what I'm trying to do here."

"I know."

Now I was beginning to be confused by the conversation. But we were pulling up in front of my house, and it seemed important to finish things.

"Anyway," I said. "You're very nice, but I don't think he'd be interested in dating right now."

She looked at me, and she seemed confused. Then something occurred to her.

"Oh," she said. "I'm afraid I've messed this all up. I just wanted to do right by you."

Just then the door of the house opened, and my father emerged. It was a strange thing, because he was not usually home at this time of the afternoon. Also, he did not seem surprised to see me sitting in my physics teacher's car, nor did he come down the path to meet me.

"I asked him," Miss Simons said, "your father. I asked him if I could be the one to talk to you about it."

I felt sick to my stomach in the way that you sometimes do at those moments when you realize the world has been playing tricks on you.

Miss Simons had not been asking my permission to see my father—she was telling me that they had already been seeing each other behind my back. She was not the petitioner but the executioner.

I opened the car door and pushed myself up and out.

As I passed him on the way into the house, my father called after me in a voice that expected no response:

"Lumen. Lumen."

I walked out of his voice. That's what it felt like. I opened the door in the room of my father's voice, stepped outside, and shut the door behind me.

———

THEY HAD BEEN seeing each other since the fall—but I was only told about it after the fact, perhaps as a punishment for my having succumbed to the corruptions of adulthood. Everyone was dirty now. We might as well bare it all. It soon became a habit for Margot Simons to spend evenings with my father and me at our house.

She was maybe ten years younger than my father and very pretty in an angular way. Her lipstick always looked like it had been recently applied, and her brunette hair was trimmed perfectly along her jawline. Her purse rattled with tubes of mascara and clamshells of powder and tortoiseshell combs and an assortment of clips and fasteners to hold her comeliness in place. She wore jeans when she came to our house, and the first thing she did when she arrived was take off her shoes to expose whatever playful color her toenails were painted that day. Her feet were bony, and she folded them up under her when she joined my father and me on the couch for our regular Saturday evening viewings of black-and-white movies.

She would yawn and rest her head on my father's shoulder, and I hated her.

Her attempts at befriending me did not help. She promised she would take me shopping at the mall the next county over. When she said it, my father chuckled uncomfortably and shook his head. He knew I was not a typical teenage girl, one who

216

gets giddy about shopping for dresses at the mall. I glared at him.

One night, after she had left, I confronted him in the kitchen.

"Do you love her?" I asked.

"I don't know. I think I could."

"Will you marry her?"

"Lumen." He leaned forward and touched my hair with his hand, as though trying to incant some long-lost version of himself and me. "I used to hold you on a pillow in my lap. Look at you now."

But when I gave him nothing but a cold look in return, he drew back his hand as though it had been bitten. He looked poisoned, miserable.

"Look," he said, and now there was nothing delicate about his voice. He had rarely in his life used this tone with me, and it had always made me feel criminal. He was explaining something, for better or worse, and whether I liked it or not was beside the point. I shrank back. "I didn't tell you before because I didn't want to hurt you. No one can replace your mother."

"No one's talking about her. Who brought her up?" I was irritated at the way everyone was forecasting the damage I would suffer as a result of my loyalty to my mother. I didn't like being second-guessed.

"I'm just saying I was being careful. But now, now that you're . . . growing up . . ."

And that was it. It was his euphemism for breaching. We are always told that honesty and truth are the shining ideals. But sometimes the truth could be used as a punishment. That's what I learned on that day.

"Go away," I told him.

I wanted to hurt them. I wanted to hurt them all. My father and Margot Simons. Blackhat Roy and Rose Lincoln. Boring, bland Polly. Peter Meechum, who seemed ennobled by hurt. Even my mother, who left me early on rather than staying by my father's side and being the one single love of his life—even my mother, the imaginary doll whose enfabulation seemed to grow more and more childish with each passing day. I wanted to hurt her, too, for not being real.

———

THE KIND OF geologist my father was was an engineering geologist—which meant that he studied how characteristics of the natural landscape might affect the man-made structures that are built on top of it. He was a person who knew how to harmonize man and nature. He created elaborate three-dimensional simulations on his computer that spun freely in space. When I was a young girl, I admired them, wishing to be able to create such pretty artifacts of my own. He also had a whole set of magnifying lenses that I liked to observe the world through.

Now, though, I tried not to go into my father's office at all. A border, a line had been drawn between us. Also, I didn't like to catch sight of the map I had made him, framed and hanging on the wall. All his creations were so pure and crystalline. Everything I made was corrupt.

I was different now. And he was different, too, though he put on a show that suggested otherwise.

We were all going on with our lives as though the world had not been burned to the ground, as though we had not all become grotesques in a pathetic and disgusting circus. Everybody pretended that everything was just as it had been before.

But I, for one, was made sick by reminders of what the world used to be.

I cleared my room of all its stuffed animals. I boxed them up and put them in the very back of my closet. Harmless animals with big baby eyes and soft, cuddly fur. It seemed like a cruel joke that I was only now beginning to understand.

I sat in the middle of my empty bed then, my knees to my chest and my chin pressed into my knees, and I tried to think of my home as one of my father's computer models—all straight lines and pure white planes. So clean, and everything calculated, accounted for. I could spin it in my mind, floating and free, with nobody but me inside.

———

SOMETIMES YOU WERE impatient for the full moon. Because you were just looking for a reason to run.

I was growing sour to the appurtenances of civilization—the clerks at the stores, the way they smiled politely and bestowed pleasantries on you. The progressive roar of lawn mowers, the tittering of sprinklers.

I went to the mine. It was between moons.

I went to my holy place, the cistern, and I prayed my prayers down into the pit. There were two songs that my father used to sing to me when I was a little girl, and I sang them both down into the void. They echoed and disappeared.

Nothing was the same as it had been.

One day you were one thing, and the next day you were another.

———

EVEN NOW.

I bake snickerdoodles for the meeting of the community league at Marcie Klapper-Witt's house. I pile them high on a cut-crystal platter. Marcie puts them on a long table with other snacks brought by other upstanding members of the community. Fancy, Marcie's daughter, walks up and down the side of the table, sampling the food. She borrows a brownie, takes one bite, and puts the remainder back on the tray. Same thing with the thumbprint cookies, then the cucumber sandwiches. No one watches her.

There is a planter in the shape of a dachshund, and while the girl stands on tiptoes to reach a platter of truffles on the back of the table I take the planter and place it on the ground just to her right. When she moves to continue down the length of the table, Fancy Klapper-Witt stumbles over the dachshund and falls, the tiara tumbling from her head. She begins to cry, sitting there like a pale pork, her hands raised in supplication.

Her mother rushes over, grabs the girl up in her arms, asks her why she moved the doggie planter.

And me? I retrieve the tiara from the floor and deliver it back onto the feathery blond head of the little girl.

Her mother smiles at me gratefully.

My husband, Jack, does not attend these meetings—but I am surprised to see there a woman I recognize. It's Jack's colleague from school—the one who sits on his desk. Her name is Helena, I learn, and she teaches art. Her hands are speckled with dried paint, her fingernails short and scuffed. I don't speak with her, but I put myself in position to overhear her conversations. She has a very melodious voice, and she is absolutely positive about the world. She just recently moved into the neighborhood from California, of all places. She misses the weather there, but she finds the people here delightful.

I follow her from room to room, remaining unobserved. Helena is attentive and careful, much like me. Once, she goes into the kitchen, and I peek at her from around the corner. I see her rinse her glass in the sink—and then, thinking she's alone, she picks something from between her teeth with her fingernail and flicks it into the sink.

I like a woman who pays attention to her teeth.

When the meeting itself gets under way, we all sit around in a big circle in the living room. I stay toward the back, leaning on a windowsill, directly to the right of Helena. She has marvelous ideas about the restoration of the local park. When she is lost in thought, I notice, her lips part slightly and she breathes out of her mouth.

Only once do our eyes meet, and she gives me a small, indistinct smile, as though we were casual compatriots. I wonder if we are.

———

IT WAS THE middle of March, between moons, and our town had its first spell of spring. Afternoons, I would open the window of my bedroom and let the breeze curl the pages of my homework as I finished it. Then, thinking to avoid my father and Margot Simons, I returned to the mapping of the mines. There were too many people aboveground, too many rivalries, too many betrayals, too many suffocating passions—so I went below and found absolution in the pitch black of those lonely passages.

Underground, the air was tight, and the empty spaces felt like a persistent ache—those crumbled walls, those low overhanging beams that were so soft they sometimes turned to wood dust in your grip. I did not mind stumbling upon dead ends, because it meant I could call an end to whatever tunnel it was on my map. I marked cul-de-sacs with special skull symbols. Pretty soon my map was filled with skulls. You could travel in many directions, but there was only one destination.

That was why, one night, I went deeper into the tunnels than I ever had before. I was reckless with voids made out of possibilities.

Getting lost was not a problem anymore. I'd developed a distinct understanding of the dark, a natural sense of how the tunnels were built and which direction they were going. I could feel, in my bones, the elevation of the earth. I could sniff my way north, south, east, and west. I knew the way the breezes blew through those ancient causeways.

But a human body was something I never imagined stumbling upon. Perhaps I was foolish. I don't know.

Still, in the middle of a running life, you sometimes discover death sitting peacefully, just around corners. Waiting for you.

It was the body of a girl.

Where I found her was a dead end, but this was unlike the other dead ends I had found. It wasn't a collapse, it was simply a terminus. The tunnel widened slightly, like a little bulb-shaped room, and then it just abrupted—a round stone room.

I could tell it was a blind tunnel because I knew that the dust hung heavier in the air in caverns that had no outlet. I could feel the end of things in my lungs. I had stopped, leaning one hand against the cold stone and bending double to cough the dust out of me. That's when the dim glow of my penlight fell on her.

Her hair was like wheat. Like dried hay in a barn. Her hair was like that. Like an empty barn on a day when you walk alone down the hill to discover the world for yourself.

Her hair was like hay, and her skin was brittle and dry, like papier-mâché. Her skin was gray—and it was stretched and dried up and petrified by age. It did not give under my touch. When I put my cheek to her cheek, it felt like nothing human. It was the cheek of an old doll. Her skin, her hair—they were kindling for a fire that would burn down the world.

The eyes were closed, the lids glued together by time. The lids were flat and sunken because, no doubt, the eyeballs underneath were shriveled grapes. They did not stare. There was no staring.

Her mouth was the worst thing. And it did not speak.

The skin of her face had dried and shrunk over the bone. Her lips pulled back, exposing two rows of white teeth. Her teeth were dusty. With my finger, I polished them, and they were perfect underneath the dust—rows of pearls. But they looked too big, her grin too wide. And no grin at all, not really. The dead don't laugh. Their mouths are not expressive, they are just hungry. Her jaw hung open, her gaping maw stretched wide, as though she would swallow you. It looked as though she might be calling to me, as though she had something to say. But there was nothing. There were no words. She was dumb as bones.

Hair like hay and her skin like paper. But her mouth was the worst part. It was the start of a dry passageway that went all the way down into the dry sack of her belly. The girl was her own abandoned mine shaft.

She wore no clothes, but her body was half covered by a burlap sack. The burlap was stuck to her. It and her skin and the earth had all melted together and frozen. She leaned, half sideways, against the cave wall. It was an awkward eternity.

She must have been cold. I tried to pull the burlap up to warm her, but it turned to dry shreds in my hands.

———

I HAD NEVER seen death so up close. She was dried like a mummy in a museum, and I wondered who she had been in life. She was small—young, like me. I wondered if she had had friends like mine or enemies like mine. I wondered if she came here to be alone, as I did. I wondered if this meant that I was now friends with death itself.

The other thing it meant was that I was no longer just a girl. It was the beginning of awful discoveries.

It was the start of everything that came after.

———

I TOLD MR. HUNTER that I was mapping the mines, but I didn't tell him about the dead girl. When I told him, I watched him closely—expecting that he might scold me or try to persuade me to talk to my father about my self-destructive habits. But he didn't. He leaned forward, in the dark of the auditorium, and he said, "Is it beautiful there?"

"That's not the right word," I said, because it was something other than pretty.

I liked to tell him things, because he seemed to comprehend what things meant even before I tried to explain them. I felt no need to apologize for myself to him. I told him my stories, and his eyes went distant—as though he were recalling some long-ago memory. Sometimes his eyes even glazed over, and he would turn his head away. Sometimes his breath smelled of alcohol.

At dinner one night, I asked Margot Simons about Mr. Hunter.

"What's he like?" I said.

"How come?" she asked. "Have you got a crush on him?"

I held my knife in a grip that whitened my knuckles. I imagined driving the blade between her ribs.

After giving my father a playful glance, she responded to my question.

"We don't see each other that much," she said. "Mostly he doesn't hang around with the other teachers. But I like him. There's something about him. Did you know he didn't grow up here?"

"I know," I said, eager to show off the priority of my alliance with him. "He's from East Saint Louis."

"But," she went on, "he doesn't seem entirely like an outsider. Does that make sense?"

It made perfect sense. But I didn't like that her evaluation of him was so parallel to my own.

"Miss Simons," I said, changing the topic. "Did you know that my mother never went breach?"

"Yes," she said, making her voice hard like a wall. "I knew that."

"So my father told you? He told you she was unique? Isn't it interesting that she was unlike everyone else?"

"Yes, it is," she said again. She did not know the right way to respond. She looked helplessly at my father.

"I thought I might be unique, too," I went on. "I thought it might be in my blood. Do you think things travel that way? From generation to generation? Through the blood?"

My father's fork clattered down on his plate.

"Lumen," he said, "that's enough."

"Sometimes," I said, "sometimes the world isn't as honest a place as you would like it to be."

And then dinner was over all of a sudden. My father asked me to leave the table, and I did. There was a quiver in his voice when he said it, and Margot Simons wore a hard scowl that I knew later would melt into miserableness, and I felt tremendously sorry for her. Her lipstick was smudged at the corners.

I should have been kinder. To my father, to Margot Simons, to Peter Meechum, to everyone.

In English class, Mr. Hunter taught us *Wuthering Heights.* Violent Heathcliff. The smoky moors. Child Cathy tapping at the window, wanting to come in.

He evoked that scene for us. He said, simply, "There is a difference between being inside and being outside," and we knew what he meant. We all nodded our heads, and our eyes grew unfocused.

When you are at a certain in-between age, you believe that adulthood is all about exclusion. You believe that what makes adults adults is that they are legitimized in their suspicions and hatreds. You exercise your own condemnations, and you believe this is the key to growing older.

And what do I believe now—me, a mother and wife, a woman who keeps her past concealed from her adoring husband? Is there something of that mine-dwelling girl left in me, who stalks her husband from makeshift blinds? Or has that girl grown into someone else altogether, naked to hurt, diminished by love?

CHAPTER 9

When my husband goes to work in the morning, I leave our son at the neighbor's and drive to our family doctor. There is nothing wrong with me, but Jack insists that we have regular checkups. So I sit in a cold room wearing a paper smock and smile up at the doctor and the nurses, and I try my best to do exactly what they ask of me. I breathe when they tell me to breathe. I lie back. I answer their questions.

Sometimes I wonder if they will find something awful in me. I imagine the doctor taking me into his office, closing the door, sighing heavily, and diagnosing me with evil growing behind my sternum.

I would assure him that no, it's not growing, it's always been there. The same exact size, the same exact shape. In fact I've learned to live with it, my evil. There is nothing to be afraid of. I am a loving wife and mother, a perfectly normal person.

To the doctors, you are a body tainted by imperfection. The only question they ask is how far you have strayed from the ideal. That's why white and red are the colors of the medical world. White is the pure self, and red is the damage. That is medicine.

But I am declared perfectly healthy.

My doctor says, "You get an A plus for today."

I grin with pride.

Afterward, I pick my son up. He rushes to greet me, clutching at my leg as though I were the only thing standing between him and rude death. I put my palm on the top of his head.

"Mommy," he says to me in his little voice.

He is white and I am red. But one day he will be red, too.

I take him to our neighborhood park, where he likes to fling himself treacherously around the monkey bars. I sit on a bench and look at the cloudy sky through the tree branches overhead.

People like to run around the perimeter of the park, and one of those runners collapses on the bench next to me. Breathing hard, she removes the cap from a bottle of water and upturns it to her lips. The plastic bottle crinkles. I keep my gaze focused on the sky.

"I know you," she says.

Only then do I realize it's Helena, the art teacher who recently moved from California and likes to sit on my husband's desk.

"You were at the community league meeting," she says. She wears tight leggings with a stripe down the side, and I can smell her sweat, sweet and pungent. "You know what? Somebody told me I work with your husband. It's Jack—right?"

"That's right."

"How funny! I teach art."

"No school today?" I ask.

"Part-time," she says. "So what are you doing here?"

"I'm with my son."

"Oh," she says, looking around. "Which one is he?"

"He's over there somewhere."

She laughs. Her teeth are amazing. Her hair is tied up in a ponytail. Her skin is healthy and brown.

"I do ten circuits three times a week," she says. "Trying to get in shape. I'm getting married in August. My fiancé—he's why we moved out here, for his job."

"Congratulations."

"Anyway, your husband, Jack, he's so great with the kids."

"Is he?"

"Such a sweetheart. They all love him. I mean, there are some awful ones, obviously. Like that Nat girl. Im*poss*ible. You don't even know. The nastiest little thing you ever saw. I'm surprised they haven't expelled her yet. Did you know she left a used tampon in one of the teacher's desks? I mean, who does that? Re-volting."

"Maybe she's looking for someone to beat her up a little," I offer.

Helena leans back and looks at me for a moment, then she laughs again with all those white teeth of hers.

"I like you," she says. "You're funny."

I smile graciously.

"I better get back to it," she says. "Gotta keep up the stride. But promise me we'll talk again."

"Okay," I say.

And then she's off, running loops around our little park. I watch her without looking like I'm watching her. I wonder what she eats. Probably oats and grains, radishes and kale. I imagine she has many recipes for quinoa. I pick at my fingernails. I sup-pose if you cut her, her blood would shimmer a bright, healthy color.

———

IT WAS SPRING. The world had thawed, melted, and dried out. Summer was ahead of me, followed by two more years of high school—followed by what? It was impossible to speculate. They said I was destined for so much.

I returned to the mine—I did—to visit my friend Death, who had brittle wheat for hair. I wondered, briefly, if I should report her to the authorities. Then I decided not to. Half buried in the earth, her skin dried to papery thinness, she had been there for many, many years. Whoever might have been looking for her once was looking for her no longer.

I wondered also who she was and if there were some way I could find out. But there was no one I could ask without disclosing what I'd found. And I didn't want to do that.

She belonged to me.

I went to the public library and searched archived newspapers for any clues about who the dead girl used to be. But I had no idea how long she had been there or what she had looked like before she had died. I couldn't even really tell how old she had been.

What I did learn was that girls disappear all the time. They just vanish. I wanted to cut out all the newspaper photos of those lost girls and make a collage of them on my wall. But how much of a memorial did my life have to be?

———

IN MAY PETER began to talk of getting back at Blackhat Roy. "He can't just come back here like that," he said. "He can't just grab whatever he wants. He hasn't earned it," he said. "I'm going to stop him," he said.

In the afternoons we had sex. I closed my eyes and liked the feeling of the sunlight from the window on my skin. Afterward I felt warm and blanketed, and I pressed myself into his arms. He compared me, in abstract terms, to the world at large. "You're the best, truest thing I know. You're not part of all the nonsense. You're above it."

In school, Blackhat Roy seemed to want to tear down to dust all the things that people like Peter spent so much elaborate energy erecting. I began to think of his viciousness and Peter's benevolence as two tides of the same shifting movement.

"You know what?" Roy said. "I've been watching you. Mostly everyone else looks right past you—like you're nothing to worry about. Your smallness, they think that's all you are. But I know different. I've tasted you. You've got some meanness in you, Lumen Fowler, just waiting to get banged out."

He grabbed my arm up near my shoulder, and he squeezed it hard, as though he would drag me to the ground right there in the hall of the school. But then he smiled and let go and walked away. My breath returned, trembling, and for the rest of the day I found my mind was unable to focus.

And yes, it wasn't like Peter Meechum at all—not like him, with his concentrated and generous adoration. Roy was something else. Brutal. Unapologetic but also unwaveringly true. You needn't have worried about social convention around Blackhat Roy. You could drop it all—and sometimes you could almost get the impression, when speaking to him, that you were seeing the world as it actually was.

And there I was, in the emptying hallway of my school, my chest burning—as though Blackhat Roy had persuaded me to open my mouth and swallow a burning ember, as though he had talked me into it somehow.

And now I could feel it, the searing in my lungs and my stomach and other places, too.

———

I WALKED INTO the woods. First I went to the lakeshore, where the sun was low on the horizon and dappled the surface. Then I walked to the quarry, where everything was still but the little rivulet running into the mine. It was wider now, with the season and the melt from the mountains above. There was no one around.

The light grew richer, more full of gold. The sun would set soon. I walked farther, but it was between moons, and I got lost. If I wasn't nosing my way by instinct through the landscape of the moonlit night, then it seemed I was just wandering.

For a long time I went around and around, the sun getting closer to setting, until I climbed to the top of a very high ridge to get a better view. But on the other side of that ridge, I discovered an industrial park—low glass-and-metal office buildings with trapezoidal parking lots between them. I had somehow stumbled upon a back route into civilization. What's more, I recognized the office park. It was in one of those buildings that my father worked.

This was clearly a sign, and I clambered down the opposite side of the ridge and went in search of the meaning of things.

When I found my father's building, I realized the sun was just at the right angle in the sky to show me the insides of the place. I could see him there in his office, bent over his desk, examining some complex paper chart against a spreadsheet on his computer screen. The last time I had visited his office was many years ago when I was too sick to go to school. I must have been eight years old, and he had sat me in the break room with coloring books, and everyone was very nice and seemed to want to talk to me all day.

It would be different now, I thought. His colleagues, they would not know what to say to me now that I had grown into a young woman. People fear those curious interstitial creatures who are neither children nor adults.

So I did not go inside. Instead I sat on the low curb, feeling the coldness of concrete, and watched my father work. I felt alien in that place, watching as the sun went down and the workers began looking at me as they came out of the offices and climbed into their cars. I could smell the oily exhaust of their engines coming alive. I could hear the lonely sound of tires poppling against the surface of the parking lot.

Finally my father came out and saw me. He asked me what I was doing there, and I told him I was waiting for him. He asked how long I had been there, and I told him an hour. He asked what I had been doing—just sitting and watching? Sitting and watching, I replied.

"Sometimes, Daughter," he said, "you are unfathomable."

I liked it when he called me Daughter, and he put his arm over my shoulder, and we walked together toward his car, and for a sliver of a moment I remembered what it was like before things went bad, and I wondered if it would ever be like that again.

———

THAT WAS THE same time that Blackhat Roy Ruggle began parking in front of our house. He had a car now, an old Camaro, once red but now a faded, patchy orange, and it was sitting silent near the woods across the street when I was going to bed that night. I stopped cold when I saw it from my bedroom. I could see the silhouette of Roy's head, backlit by the street lamps, through the rear window. Cigarette smoke rose from the driver's window, and as I watched, his arm reached out and flicked ashes onto the tarmac.

This was the first time. There were others. I meant to confront him, to march out to his car and tell him he did not scare me—but whenever I approached, the Camaro growled to life and sped away.

Sometimes in the morning I found a collection of cigarette butts on the street or a smashed soda cup, the plastic straw twisted into anxious knots. Sometimes I could hear the distinctive sound of his engine pass by without stopping, a high-pitched rumble while approaching and a lower-pitched one departing. I knew this was called the Doppler effect, and in my imagination, I pictured explaining the phenomenon to him, sitting in the passenger seat of the Camaro, maybe drawing a diagram in ballpoint pen on the back of a paper fast-food bag, and him—the all-at-once light in his eyes as he understood—smiling. Sometimes I turned off the light in my bedroom and watched him through a slit in the curtains. He could not have seen me, but he seemed to be looking right at me.

There was nothing I could tell from his dark form.

Maybe he was angry and plotting revenge over something I had done.

Maybe he was sad, like the rest of us.

———

MY FATHER WONDERED where I was going those afternoons and evenings. He did not ask about it directly. It was not his way. Instead he said things like, "Boy, you've been keeping late hours," or "Do you think you'll be home for dinner?"

The house was quieter in those days. We were too aware of each other—like two guarded animals circling each other on a solitary hill. We had sniffed out all the shifts that had occurred in both our lives, and we were keen to them. It wasn't anger or discomfort or fear—just a heightened sensitivity to certain silent currents that seemed to ebb and flow through the house.

We didn't avoid each other. In fact, more frequently than I had in the past, I did my homework downstairs, spread out on the floor, while my father read the newspaper and drank Earl Grey tea. But I was distracted. I couldn't help but be watchful, listening for the fluttering sound of the newspaper pages turning, the sound of his teacup clattering against the saucer as he lifted it and set it down, the sound of his hand running across the scruffy line of his chin while he read.

Sometimes I would listen at the door to his office when he went in there to talk to Margot Simons on the telephone. I couldn't hear particular words, but I didn't need them—I was listening for cadences, certain lilts and tones that might speak to who he really was when I wasn't around to discomfort him.

—

THERE'S SOMETHING ELSE I remember—from a long time before that. When I close my eyes, I can see it still.

My father, he looks the same as ever in my mind, no variations. That magisterial jawline, that long face, those rough hands.

In my memory, he sits on the edge of the couch, and I am caught between his knees. I have a splinter in my finger, and he has fetched the tweezers from the medicine cabinet. He has a monocular magnifying glass wedged magically in his eye—I don't know how he does it. I can't get it to stay in my eye when I try. He switches back and forth between two instruments: the tweezers and the blade of his pocketknife.

I writhe in panic, but his knees tighten around me. They hold my little body still. I am pressed between the muscly levers of his legs, and I am safe.

"Don't worry," he says. "It won't hurt at all. You won't feel a thing. I promise."

He pinches my finger tight.

"Ow," I say.

"Oh, come on," he says. "That doesn't hurt."

He tells me it doesn't hurt, and I believe him, and so it doesn't hurt. He instructs my body on what to feel. And I am relieved, because I relish instruction. How does one know what to make of the world if one is not told?

The vise of his legs, crushing with absolute control my wild little body.

He unpinches my fingers. He tells me the splinter is out. It does not hurt.

His legs release me, and I feel suddenly light—too light, as though I might spin off into the sky like a rogue balloon lost to the thinness of ether.

———

MY HUSBAND IS a good father. When our son gets hurt, Jack is the person he runs to by instinct. I watch the two of them—the way Jack puts his two big hands on the boy's shoulders, creating pacts among males.

When Marcus's teacher calls home to talk about his biting

problem, Jack takes the call. He expresses grave concern. He is apologetic and thankful for the opportunity for social correction. When he gets off the phone, he turns to me, reproaching.

"She says she's spoken with you about Marcus's problems in school?"

"I guess she did," I say. "I don't remember."

"You don't remember? Ann . . ."

He shakes his head and walks out. He has a talk with Marcus later, sitting the boy next to him on the couch. They discuss acceptable modes of expression, ways for Marcus to communicate what's inside of him without hurting others. After it's over, Jack lifts the boy and hugs him tight. I watch from the dining room.

I am concerned that Jack is making our boy too soft. So later that night, after everyone is asleep, I creep into the boy's bedroom and speak rhymes from my own childhood over his slumbering form.

Mary's gone a-breaching,
ho-la-lay, ho-la-la.
Mary's gone a-breaching,
ho-la-lay, ho-la-la.
Mary's gone, and she lost her head.
What might she do with her body instead?
They scored her flesh, and they broke her bones.
Now who will she be if she makes it back home?
Mary's gone a-breaching,
ho-la-lay, ho-la-la.

My husband would not like it if he heard, so I have no choice but to sing my songs to my boy in his sleep. I see his eyes shifting wildly under his lids, and I wonder what animal dreams he's having.

When I go back to bed, Jack wakes briefly.

"Everything all right?" he asks, half asleep.

"You're a good father," I say.

He throws an arm over me and gives me a squeeze. Soon he is asleep again, and I gaze at the stars through the bedroom window.

———

I DREAMED OF the restless dead. Everyone I knew, walking down the street as if in a trance. I ran among them, trying to get their attention, but their eyes were lost to some unknown distance. I tried to speak to them, but they did not respond. I screamed in their ears—my voice was hoarse. Everything was so quiet. I was even deaf to the shuffle of their feet. The only sound was the trickle of water over stone. I looked around to find the source of the sound, but there was nothing to be seen. I closed my eyes and listened harder, trying to recognize it because it sounded so familiar. And then I knew. It was the rivulet that led into the abandoned mine, miles away in the woods. Standing there among the silent zombies of everyone I knew, I could hear it. I could hear the sound of that tiny waterfall, the baby stream of melted ice. What does it mean for something to be inside your skull and miles distant at the same time? I didn't like it. I swallowed, and there was dread in my throat.

When I woke, light was flickering against the wall of my bedroom. I rose and went to the window and saw that the street lamp outside was dying. It stuttered on and off, strobing the street with black and shadowed light.

Parked beneath the street lamp was the faded Camaro, and inside it I could see Blackhat Roy staring right at me, as though he had expected me to come to the window at that very moment.

I froze in place.

While I watched, he brought a hand up in front of his face, opened his mouth, and sank his teeth into the meaty heel of his palm. His head lashed back and forth as though he were a coyote trying to tear away a piece of flesh from its fallen prey—and I could see his face go red from the effort. Finally he stopped and held his hand before his tearing eyes. Then he extended his arm out the car window and held it up for me to see. He had bitten through the skin, and blood ran from the wounds down his wrist and dripped onto the street. In the flickering light, the blood looked black as crude leaked from the earth.

There we were, insomniacs on a moonless night, a pestilent little Rapunzel in her cotton nightdress and her barbarous prince, calling to her with his blood.

———

WE WERE IN the living room watching a Glenn Ford movie, *Blackboard Jungle,* when Margot Simons inadvertently revealed to me a great secret.

She was huddled against my father, and even though there was room for me on the couch with them, I sat cross-legged in the easy chair. The movie is about a rough urban high school, and Margot Simons kept making sly, joking comments to me through the whole thing—about how this school wasn't nearly as wild as our own. I smiled politely in response.

Then, at the end of the film, when the credits rolled, she said, "Huh, that's funny."

Joshua Gaylord

"What?" asked my father.

She pointed at the name of the writer whose book the movie was based upon: Evan Hunter.

"Mr. Hunter from school," she said. "His first name is Evan, too."

I thought about all the possible meanings of this connection. I didn't much believe in coincidence. In my experience, harmonies existed everywhere if you were willing to hear them.

You sometimes want answers, and you sometimes go looking for them.

The next day I went to the auditorium after school, even though I knew it was a play rehearsal day. I sat in the back row and watched.

Peter found me there and tried to get me to leave with him, but I wouldn't.

"What do you want to stay here for?" he said. "You're not even in the play. You've got nothing to do with it."

Mr. Hunter could see me talking with Peter, and our eyes met while he directed the students on stage and I shooed Peter away.

"Go on," I told Peter. "I'll talk to you later."

The auditorium emptied out, the students hopping down from the stage, walking past me up the aisles, chatting and ignoring me. I shifted against the hard back of the seat, my skin feeling itchy, as I heard their laughter die out behind the closing doors until all sound had been drained from the auditorium and a great deafness took over. The air was dead still, and I felt flushed. Mr. Hunter stood on the stage at the opposite end of the empty hall, but I didn't make a move toward him. Instead I waited for him to come to the back row, where I sat. Eventually he did.

"Lumen?" he said.

"Everybody lies," I said. "That's what you told me."

240

"Lumen, are you all right?"

"I think I found out something," I said.

"What did you find out?"

"Are you really—your name, is it really Evan Hunter?" I asked.

He looked confused.

"Evan Hunter," I said. "Born in 1926. He wrote *Blackboard Jungle*. You know what else? He changed his name, too, to write cop books."

"Lumen, there are lots of people with the name—"

"Liar." My hand jumped to my mouth. I had surprised myself with my impudence.

Then he laughed, but it was a terminal kind of laugh, a laugh that meant the end of something.

"Okay," he said and started walking back down the aisle toward the stage. "Come on."

"Where are we going?"

"Come on if you're coming."

He led me behind the stage to the drama office, a little closet of a room with exposed pipes overhead and tall, gray metal cabinets with a fine coating of dust on the tops of them. He sat at the desk and pulled a bottle from a drawer and poured some into a plastic cup. It smelled strong.

"You want?" he said.

I shook my head. Then he downed it in one gulp and poured himself another, then capped the bottle.

"All right," he said with a heavy breath. "You want to talk about the truth of things? Is that what we're doing?"

I said nothing. An awful moment passed, and then another. Finally he shifted and took out his wallet, removed something from it, and slapped it on the desk in front of me. It was a faded photograph showing a skinny teenage boy standing outside the doors of a school. The school I recognized—it was my own.

"Who is it?" I asked.

"Philip Anderson," he said. "Me."

I looked closer at the picture and could see some resemblance in the eyes to the man sitting in front of me. But I realized then that Mr. Hunter must color his hair, because the boy in the picture was blond.

"You're from here?" I said.

He nodded. "Born and raised. When I left for college, I thought I would never come back. I was ready for the real world, you know?" He shrugged. "I managed to stay away for nine years."

"Why did you come back?"

"I don't know," he said, leaning back, his eyes narrowed in thought at the pipes suspended from the ceiling. "I don't think I quite know how to be anywhere else."

"But your name," I said. "How come you changed it?"

He looked down at me, his eyes weighty with meaning. "Sometimes you don't like the person you've become. Sometimes you'd like to try being someone else for a while. You wouldn't understand."

It was quiet then, and he drank and I smelled the spirits.

"Then you breached?"

"I did," he nodded. "When I was your age, I used to breach. Now I do this instead." He grinned and raised his cup.

"You knew my father?"

He nodded. "I was nothing to him. A kid. I've seen him since I've been back. We've talked. He has no idea who I am. Your parents, they were ahead of me in school. They were seniors when I was, I don't know, maybe in seventh grade."

"Wait," I said, my breath catching. At the suggestion of my mother, something inside me fell from a shelf and smashed. "You knew her? My mother?"

The springs in his desk chair creaked. His face seemed to change. He rubbed it, then rubbed hard at his eyes.

"We ran together. Sometimes," he said. "Felicia," and his eyes were now pink, holding on to tears.

"You're lying," I said. "She never breached. You're still lying."

He was sick, this man. And me, I was young and foolish and unkind.

"You look just like her, you know. She had skin like yours. And your eyes."

"She didn't breach," I said again, shaking my head. "Stop lying."

"The moonlight. Sometimes it makes it so you can see right through people's skin. Your mother, her veins are something I remember. Nobody was ever as beautiful. I miss her. We all do."

"Stop it."

"You look just like her," he repeated, and his hand reached out to touch my face.

I recoiled, standing quickly and knocking my chair over.

"You're a liar," I said, my eyes burning. "You fucking liar."

He shook his head.

"Darling," he said, kindly, as I rushed out.

———

BECAUSE THERE WAS nothing to be done, because there was nowhere to go, because there was no one to interrogate or confess to, I ran to the mine. I allowed myself to cry.

People were never what you thought they were. I was ugly and alone, and the world was ugly, too, uglier every day, and there was death in everything, because it didn't matter how many maps you drew, because everywhere was the same place, and you could be fanciful about it but what was the point, especially right there interred in the earth, where it was quiet and where there was nothing to keep your mind from burning itself with running, with hating itself and loving itself, too, because that's what it is to be a teenager, after all, when your little sluglike body aches for things it doesn't understand, glows in its very pores from the effort to explode itself over the world . . .

So I cried because I could not explode myself, because we are too tiny altogether, too weak and malleable, because our bodies are not even the fingernails on God's hands.

I cried until I howled, my voice a tinny echo in an empty cave. I howled like a beast—I howled like a dying thing—I howled like a little girl. I howled until my throat was dry, and then I blubbered, and it was nothing magical at all. I cried until my tears were useless, until I was numb to all my little tragedies.

III

CHAPTER 10

As a result of that tumorous instinct that grows in some boys, Blackhat Roy treated many of his defeated enemies with the basest kind of contempt in school. In math class, to the mocking delight of a group of jackal boys, he bit Rose Lincoln's pencils in half so that she had to write with one half and erase with the other. He targeted, especially, anyone associated with Peter Meechum. He would have his revenge.

His new girl, Poppy Bishop, continued to trail behind him, because sometimes she liked the way he, upon her request, would attack those she didn't like. But his attentions to her were capricious at best, and sometimes he would turn on her. She took tap dancing lessons, and once, he told her to get up on top of the table during lunch in the cafeteria and dance.

"I don't think I should," she said.

"Do it," he said.

She climbed slowly to the top of the table and shuffled her feet a little. Everyone watched her quietly. Her face went empty.

"That's not dancing," said Blackhat Roy. "Faster. Here, you

need more space?" And he used his arm to clear a wide space on the tabletop, sending people's lunch trays to the floor. "Faster!"

She danced faster, trying to make taps with her sneakers.

"It doesn't sound right," he said. He looked around to the others. "It's usually better. She's not at her best today. You might not know it, but she's got a good body under there. Cute little oval birthmark on her left tit. Poppy, show 'em your birthmark."

She stopped dancing and stood frozen. She crossed her arms over her chest.

Since nobody else would do it, I crossed the cafeteria and made myself as tall as I could in front of Blackhat Roy.

"Stop it," I said. "Leave her alone."

"We're just having some fun. What've you got against fun?"

"Stop torturing people."

"What do you care? You don't even like these people."

It was not the response I was expecting, and I wondered if what he said was true.

One of his friends, Gary Tupper, took me by the arm, saying, "Come on, pocket size, I'll give you a ride to class. Hop on my shoulder."

"Don't touch her," Roy said to him.

"How come?"

In response, Roy punched him in the solar plexus.

It took a minute for Gary to catch his breath and get himself upright again.

"Jesus," he said. "I was just..."

But by then it was over. Poppy Bishop had climbed down from the table, everyone in the cafeteria had resumed eating, and Blackhat Roy was long gone.

And still he came to my house sometimes at night. I spotted his old Camaro in different places on my block—not always just in front of my house. One night, approaching a full moon, I went outside to talk to him. I walked down the street to the place where his car was parked—at the corner, under a street lamp. I'd tried before, and he had just driven off when I approached—but not this time. He was waiting for me. I wondered what he would do when I accused him of stalking me. He was rough and humorless, but there was also a fragility in him that fascinated me. Many times in school he looked away from my gaze, and I wondered if he might be ashamed. I was not another Poppy Bishop to him. He did not make me dance or call me names. I wondered what I amounted to in his world.

I approached his car from behind and noticed that the driver's-side window was down. I would demand that he leave me alone, and if he attacked, I prepared myself to fight. Blood could be spilled—we needed no moon to give us permission.

My heart beat hard in my chest, and I leaned down into his window to confront him—but he wasn't there. He wasn't in the car at all. He had just left his scent behind—dry leather and cigarettes and sweat.

I stood suddenly and looked around me. The street was quiet. The night breeze rustled the leaves of the trees. A dog barked in the distance.

He could have been anywhere—hidden behind the trunk of any tree, around the corner of any of these peaceful houses.

I shivered, and I could feel his eyes—as though they had gotten under my clothes somehow and were skittering around on my skin.

I was being hunted.

———

I GOT A D on my geometry test. Mr. Ludlow took me aside. He was a little round man with dandruff on the shoulders of his jacket. His voice was high and gentle, and he frequently spoke of trips he took with his wife to quaint towns with antique stores and tours of houses that belonged to historical figures. Even though he orbited my life only at a great distance, I liked him.

When he spoke to me, he was kindly and solicitous, saying he didn't believe that this grade reflected who I really was as a student. He knew I was better than a D. He asked me whether I was having any problems at home. I wondered if he knew his colleague Miss Simons was eating dinner at my house twice a week. I said no, that I was just tired. I explained that I deserved the grade and didn't blame him for it—because he seemed sad that he had had to write the letter D on my exam. I told him he was a very good teacher and that I would try to do better next time.

He said, "I'll make you a deal. You don't tell anyone, and I'll let you take a makeup next week. I don't want your grade to suffer because of some aberrant exam. What do you say?"

I told him thank you.

"Trust me," he said. "I know exactly the kind of kid you are. You're the kind of kid who doesn't get Ds on exams."

They wouldn't allow me to fall. I plunged downward hard and fast, and they swooped down and fetched me back up before I hit the ground.

Mr. Ludlow said he knew who I was. He would not let me be anyone else.

———

IT WAS LATER that same day that Mr. Hunter wanted to talk to me as well. He let class out twenty minutes early and asked me to stay behind. I did not move from my desk, and when the room was empty he came and stood over me.

He had been distracted since our last conversation. I could smell his breath again. He was just a drunk with odd notions — that was all.

"Lumen," he said, "I want to apologize."

I was stubborn and did not meet his eyes.

"My father's not a liar," I said.

"No, he's not."

"She never went breach."

"No, she didn't."

I accused him with my eyes.

"Then why did you say it?"

At that moment, he looked away again, which made me not trust him. And instead of answering my question, he said this:

"You know something? I knew you a long time ago. When you were just born. I mean, I didn't know you — I knew *of* you. When your mother — when she died, everybody in town brought your father gifts for you. I did, too. I remember I brought you a giraffe. It was purple."

He smiled in memory.

"I have to go," I said and stood.

"I didn't mean to hurt you," he said as I moved toward the door. "I would never —"

But I didn't want to hear it. None of it made any sense to me, and I trusted no one. But here was one thing: I still had that purple giraffe, its fur pale and ratted, its plastic eyes scuffed dull, packed away in a box in my closet because I had thought that I was finished with my childhood.

—

THAT AFTERNOON, ON my bedroom floor, Peter wanted to move me to the bed so we could have sex.

I shook my head.

"We can stay here if you want," I said.

"Here? On the floor?"

And during, I said, "Make me hush."

"What? What do you mean?"

"Put your hand here," and I gestured at my neck.

He caressed my neck with his hand. But he didn't get it. He was too gentle.

"Harder," I said. But he was embarrassed, and the whole thing became awkward.

"I don't want to hurt you," he said.

"I know," I said. "You're nice."

And that night, after I had said good night to my father and climbed the stairs and opened the door to my bedroom, I found Blackhat Roy standing there.

I came close to screaming, but I stopped myself, doubling over and swaying instinctively back from the doorway. But my father was shutting off the lights downstairs, so I lurched into the room and shut myself in there with Roy.

My stomach felt like I had swallowed needles. What was he there for? To kill me, maybe, or rape me, or cut me with a knife? He was an atrocity in this place, where all the safest parts of my identity were hidden.

But he didn't even turn when I came in. He leaned against one of my bookcases, a book open in his hands.

"How did you get in here?"

"Window," he said casually.

"It's the second floor."

He just shrugged.

I saw the book in his hand was my old paperback copy of *The Heart Is a Lonely Hunter*. "Did you read all these?" he asked.

"Get out!" I hissed, trying to keep my voice low. I had backed myself up against the wall, and I was feeling vulnerable there in my pajamas with cats on them. "Get out now!"

That's when he finally deigned to look at me, and his eyes went up and down my whole body.

"Cute outfit," he said.

"Get out."

"I'm going," he said, tossing the book on the desk instead of putting it back on the shelf. "Don't worry. I ain't here to buy. Today I'm just looking."

He moved toward the window to leave, then he turned around once more.

"Nice room," he said. "You could sleep good in here. Cozy. Forget all your worries."

Before he left, I found myself saying, "You can take it if you want."

"Take what?"

"The book. The Carson McCullers. You can take it."

And that's when he flinched as though I had struck him. He crossed the room in two long strides and slammed me against the wall, grabbing my head and holding it in the vise of his two palms. He looked like he wanted to kill me and spoke through gritted teeth.

"Bullshit," he said. "Intellectual clusterfucking bullshit. People cleaning their glasses and discussing themes. Don't fucking mistake me. I ain't here for your classroom handouts."

I stood all hot, unable to breathe, until his anger subsided. Then he let go of me and left. But on his way out the window I saw him look once more at the bookshelves, and I recognized in his expression the ardent pining of a grown man banished from a religion that as a young boy he thought he might be able to truly love.

———

I THOUGHT IF I remembered what it was like to be a good girl, these things would stop happening to me.

The next night, at dinner with my father and Margot Simons, I ate two servings of everything. With great politesse, I passed the dishes to and fro, across the table. I said please and thank you, and I complimented Margot Simons on the corn casserole she had brought in a foil-covered dish.

"Somebody's in a good mood," said my father, and I simply smiled blankly in response. They were pleased, I could tell, though I also caught them giving me suspicious gazes when I wasn't looking.

I helped clean up after the meal. As my father washed the dishes, I dried them and put them in the cupboards where they belonged, arranging them neatly in stacks, making cheerful conversation and chuckling at the stories they told that were supposed to be funny—as if nothing in the world mattered outside these walls, as if there were not grown men speaking drunkenly of my dead mother, as if no pestilent boys were breaking into my bedroom, as if things were not about to change for good.

Afterward I went to the mine. I found my way to the cistern and confessed myself to the inky black of the chasm. I spoke to my mother, because I thought her soul might be down there somewhere in the airy echo of the night, floating free and buoyed on the drafts. I could hear my voice being carried somewhere, and I thought it might be to her.

I told her of many things. Of my two boyfriends, the dark one and the light one, and how they hated each other but both coveted me for some reason. Of my wee body and how I knew it contained some force larger than itself, and how it hadn't yet bled, though maybe that was because it needed that blood for the strange and frightening power it possessed. Of the man who said he knew her, who had gone away and changed his name and then come back just to gaze at me with endlessly suffering eyes. Of my father and his goodness, though not of Margot Simons.

I spoke of many things, and it relieved me. And then I fell asleep, cuddled against a stone outcropping over that depthless shaft.

I guess I knew then why some people speak to God.

———

AND THIS, TOO, is chattering down a well—telling stories to myself in the dark.

My husband and child are upstairs, and they are dreaming of colorful things. But I don't sleep well. I rise from the marriage bed like the ghost of a wife. I creep downstairs, haunted. I pour myself a glass of milk and squeeze chocolate syrup into it. I stir it with a spoon that goes tink, tink, tink on the insides of the glass.

And then I fetch my pages from their hiding place on the top shelf of the pantry, behind the stacked boxes of spaghetti that are no longer used since my husband has become fearful of carbohydrates. I set the stack of pages on the kitchen table, and I add to it, one page at a time. I never knew I had so many words in me. I dust them up, the words, like a good housewife, collect them where they gray the white paper.

But who am I writing to? To Jack? To myself? Who are you?

You are not my mother, who wore orchid gloves on her wedding day. You are not my son, to whom one day, as an acknowledgment of his blossomed manhood, I might bequeath his mother's lineage. No, not that. You are not the world at large, from whom I seek forgiveness or solace. Never that. You are not even some version of Lumen herself, not future or former or alternative or lost.

You are no one. And you expect nothing. And your eyes fail you, your head nods in drowsiness. I hope you are happy there in whatever empty, lightless caverns you roam and call home.

Earlier today, this afternoon, there was a commotion at the park. My son runs to the monkey bars, and I notice all the neighborhood mothers constellated in excited chatter at the edge of the playground.

Lola is there, too, sitting apart on one of the benches, stretched out and smoking.

"Did you hear?" she says to me. "The coven caught a bad man."

"Who?"

"I don't know. Some guy. Apparently he was sitting on a bench near the playground, but he didn't have any kids with him. Oh, also he was listening to music on his headphones, and he wore sunglasses. So we called the cops and had him escorted away. Now we are rejoicing."

She flicks the ashes from the end of her cigarette.

Then Marcie Klapper-Witt spots me and comes over.

"Ann," she says, "I'm sure Lola has filled you in on the situation, but I just wanted to let you know that we've taken care of the problem. And we're forming a neighborhood watch to keep an eye on things from now on if you'd like to volunteer. I can order vests—as many as we need."

"But what is he said to have done?" I ask.

"Who?"

"The man."

She shakes her head.

"Ann," she says, "what was he doing in a playground? He didn't have any kids with him. It doesn't take a genius to spot a pervert. You don't know—my husband's cousin is a police officer. The world's not as nice as you think. Jennifer's putting together a petition—and I think it's a good idea that we all sign it—saying that we don't want any adults without children within a thousand feet of the playground."

"A thousand feet," I say dreamily. "That's a lot of feet." Then I say, "Your daughter, she's about to fall."

It is true. Fancy Klapper-Witt hangs upside down by one bended leg from a domed metal latticework. Her frilly blue dress spills over her face, and her polka-dot cotton underpants are exposed.

Marcie Klapper-Witt runs and catches her daughter in the holy safety of her arms.

Later in the evening, after our boy has been safely enveloped between the sheets of his bed, I tell Jack about Marcie and her neighborhood watch and the man in the park.

"Well," he says, "I think a neighborhood watch is a good idea. I'm glad they got him."

"You are?" I am surprised.

"Ann, what's a guy with no kids doing hanging around a playground?"

"That's what Marcie said."

He comes up behind me and puts his arms around me. We are in our nightclothes, preparing for bed, but the gesture is unsexual. His penis, flaccid in his pajama pants, is pressed soft and benign against my bottom.

"It's how you're supposed to feel," he explains, "about your family. I never want anything bad to happen." I can feel his sincere breath on my neck and ear. It tickles, and I writhe out of his grip.

"Nothing's going to happen," I assure him. It isn't a lie. I am quite sure of it. Every day I am quite sure of it.

Nothing is going to happen.

The world will keep spinning within its margins.

He cuddles against me, curled up like a baby in a bassinet, until he falls asleep. I listen to his breathing for a while, so placid and secure, in no way fearful—and then I come downstairs.

I sit at the kitchen table. I drink my chocolate milk. Soon the sun will rise, and the man who delivers papers will toss one from the window of his car onto our front walk. I will fetch it barefoot so I can feel the dew on the soles of my feet.

And in my ankles, and all up and down my calves and thighs, there will be the long-suppressed instinct to run.

CHAPTER 11

Cordial Moon came at the end of May, and I had been waiting for it. The first night, I sat at my window and kept myself from climbing out as long as I could. I wanted to feel the force of it, and I wanted that force to be excruciating. Sometimes these are the games we play with our own minds. I gripped the window jambs, and the tips of my fingers turned white. The smell in the air—I became desperately afraid that I would miss it. It was impossible that that spring nighttime should exist without me in the middle of it. I clamped my jaw on the skin of my upper arm—I bit down hard. I stopped short of breaking the skin—because I wanted the dull ache of compression rather than the sharp sting of pain. I chewed at my skin until it was slobbery wet and bruised purple.

And then, when it was all too much to bear, I flung myself out the window into the night.

Earlier in the day, my father had approached me. Did I need anything? Would I be careful when I went out? Did I want pancakes for breakfast when I returned in the morning? The questions embarrassed both of us. Finally he gave them up and went to read the newspaper in the living room with a mug of coffee. When next we spoke, he was jolly and amiable, everything having been tamped down neatly into place between us.

And now such exchanges seemed all the more ridiculous to me. There was nothing to talk about. There were only wildernesses to breach.

———

DO YOU KNOW what it is to run wild? To lie naked on ordinary ground? To feel against the bare soles of your feet the force of the sunlit day disseminating from the concrete sidewalk? To be neither cold nor ashamed but rather luxuriant in empty space? It is a membership in something greater than yourself, a merging with the populace of insomniacs. There are two worlds, you realize, and you might leap between them and find yourself at home in both.

We are many things all at once. We mistake self-denial for character—or else why not join yourself to every and all custom?

Boys, too. A menagerie of different species, and yet you could love them all. There were the kind boys, like Peter Meechum, who did not peek at you while you dressed, who were pretty and noble, who made love to abstract futures. You could follow them and build skyscrapers on horizons of goodness and truth. And there were awful boys, like Blackhat Roy, who did not fear filth, even the filth you sometimes thought you were, who seemed to see darker truths and did not shrink from them. You could follow them and be on the thrilling, shivery edge of wrong until you died.

Truly was I inexplicable. I wanted others to tell me who I was so I could write it down and know myself true and inscribed. But words were not their medium, so I tried to read their appraisal of me in the bruises on my neck and wrists. My scars would be the palimpsest of my life.

When the moon was out, you could be aware of all the pieces of night — you could see all the things you didn't see during the day, all the subtle little fragments that the world uses to join its wholes. The ladybugs hidden behind the bark of trees, the breath of the daffodils over the dew of a cut lawn, the hum of a power box on a traffic-light post, the gritty taste of rust from old patio furniture, a fawn standing still on a deserted highway. You could see it all — the patterns the lake made and the lightning in the clouds, the patient settlements of dust and the groaning fissures of the earth, the slumber of a whole town and its heartful waiting for dawn. You could fall in love with it all — and you could want, finally and truly, to set a match to it.

I ran to the mine, to the tunnels that twisted this way and that, and I felt my way through them, liking the cool unknown of the inky dark. Maybe I would get lost — I grew out of breath thinking that I could lose myself in those caverns and stay there forever. I could starve to death, pressed tight between worlds, living out my days in darkness, with nothing, with no one.

I could burn the whole world down, because there was some honor in destruction, which was why the Vikings immolated their noble dead.

Then I doubled back to my cistern and uttered no words of prayer or remorse or wishfulness as I watched the sky grow pink with morning through the opening at the top of the cave.

It was not a night for the decencies of language.

———

THAT WAS WHEN everything came apart.

First, it was during the Cordial Moon that Hondy Pilt stopped breaching. So many fallen. So many rescued. He would become, in time, the same person he had been before the breaching. He would fade back into obscurity—no longer a noble leader of wildings under the moonlight, just a lonely explorer in the vast, unpopulated cell of his own mind. And so are we all, I suppose.

I had always wanted more from him. We all did. Maybe we mistook his deep, abiding interest in the universe for an interest in us.

There are times in your life when you project yourself against the sky—you see yourself everywhere, even in the configurations of stars, and you think, "How could anyone fail to notice me there, all my desires and haunted dreams in the nightly patterns of God, who loves me and knows me to be special?"

Me, too. I was guilty of such things.

I was a runner of caverns. I skittered and leaped my way through abandoned mine shafts. I knew where the floor opened up onto bottomless depths. I knew where to duck under the collapsed ceilings. I saw nothing. I moved by feel.

The other thing that happened was that Blackhat Roy followed me into the tunnels. Nobody else would dare. Even in their most primitive states, they feared the dark, the dangers they could not see. Breachers were made for moonlight—they relied on sight, to look and be looked at. Me, I disappeared into the darkness, and they snarled after me. When I emerged again, they crouched and gazed at me through the sides of their eyes. They did not trust me. They did not like outliers. But they did not attack. They knew me to be creatured to some darkness different from their own. I was littler than all of them, but they were afraid.

And Roy followed me all the same. He followed me just to the place where it was lightless and the air was musty with age. I could hear him, breathing hard in the dark, groaning after me, stumbling around. He was an echo in my caverns, an echo in my brain. So I stopped and turned and waited for him. When he caught up, his fingertips reached out tentatively and touched me. I let them rest there on my skin for a few moments, and we held our breath. Then I withdrew, and he was lost again. My bones ached.

He followed me, but it didn't feel like hate. It felt like desperation. It felt like I was large in his mind. That I could ruin him. Ruin myself.

Poor boy! He was tortured by the abstract. Love and peace and relief came from places as far away as Tibet. Maybe he would see them one day, if he became a traveler. How did others locate such things so easily? How did Peter Meechum produce love the same way a magician would draw out an endless handkerchief?

Roy said, in the dark, "I don't know where I am."

So I took him by the hand and led him back outside, where the moon caught him up in its spectral light.

They were out there, the others. They paced back and forth, and their eyes glowed.

———

PETER MEECHUM WAS waiting in my front yard when I came home from school the next day.

"I saw you," he said. He looked angry. He had been pacing back and forth before my gate when I rode up on my bike.

When I did not respond, he came and stood close to me—so close I had to crane my neck to look up at him. His eyes were raw, and his breath was hot. I felt sorry for him—all that fury and nowhere to put it. I thought it must be difficult for him, for boys. They get temperamental when they can't shape the world into what they want it to be. It's easier for girls. Girls are raised knowing that the world is unshapable. So they know better than to fuss.

"I saw you with Blackhat Roy," he said. "What did he do to you?"

"What do you mean?"

"Stop it, Lumen. At the quarry. The mine. I saw you come out with him. He hurt you."

"Everybody hurts everybody."

"No."

He said no, but I wondered how could he not see that.

Cruelty is the natural order of things. Through algorithms of brutality does mankind build its greatest monuments. It's when people begin to see violence as personal that they struggle. It had nothing to do with Peter Meechum. For that matter, it had nothing to do with Blackhat Roy. Goodness and badness had nothing to do with anything.

But Peter let it get to him. He was a believer in the meanings of things. If I was hurt at the hands of Blackhat Roy, well, according to Peter, that was different from my being crushed by a toppled tree. I realized that I once used to think that way, too.

"I'm sorry, Peter." But, in truth, I wondered what I was sorry for. Maybe for him and the conception of the world he carried in his honorable brain.

"But I love you," he said.

"I know," I said. "But why?"

"You know why. Because you're better. You're better than everybody."

I wondered where he had gotten that notion. I wondered, for the first time, if that was the impression I gave — if somehow that was one of the things that kept me separate from others.

"That's just something to say," I told him. "It doesn't mean anything."

"No — it's true," he insisted. "You are better."

"No, I'm not. I'm worse. Your love, it's beautiful — but it isn't true."

He looked appalled.

"But he's a monster," he said.

"I know."

He waited for me to say more, but there was really nothing left to say.

"I'm going in," I said and stepped around him.

But he called after me.

"How can you be that way? You didn't used to be that way."

I had gotten to the front door, had my hand on the knob, but I turned back to him. He looked small there on my lawn. I wished for a moment that I could see him as I had seen him in grade school. I wished to have once more so simple and pure a longing.

I shrugged.

"I used to picture us getting married one day," I said. "You and me. I mean, when I was little. I wrote my name over and over as Lumen Meechum. But it doesn't sound right, does it?"

I looked at him sadly.

"Lumen," he said, and there was a reaching in his voice.

But I didn't reach back. I went inside and shut the door behind me.

Joshua Gaylord

———

I WAS LOSING friends, of course. Voids opened up everywhere around me.

Polly and I no longer had much reason to speak to each other. Her disapproval was polite and absolute. I didn't know what, exactly, she disapproved of in my behavior—I didn't know what stories she had been told or whether they were true. But it didn't matter. Her disapproval was right and proper—the common way for two friends to grow apart. It was not for me to get in the way of a natural progression of events.

Peter Meechum was through with talking, but he still watched me from a distance. He was afraid of me, but some part of him must have believed I could still be his. Boys are the most romantic of creatures—their faith is as pure as it is ridiculous.

Rose Lincoln, on the other hand, became increasingly aggressive toward me in school, doing a lispy, babyish impression of the way I speak and throwing old bras at me in the locker room during gym. She didn't like it that I had become the focus of so much boy attention.

I felt for her. I really did. The smallness of her spite was growing pathetic and tiresome to those around her, and there was no other version of Rose Lincoln to fall back on. What happened when your whole identity went out of style? What happened when the boys you used to fascinate were now more interested in some awkward polyp of a girl who had done nothing to invite their affections while you felt yourself growing indistinct against the dusty backdrop of the world? What did you do then?

For one thing, I suppose, you went on the attack.

It happened during gym class on the field, where the girls

were playing softball now that the weather was getting warm. We wore brown shorts and yellow shirts, the school colors. The shorts were tight on some of the girls, who stuck out their behinds with proud vulgarity. On me, the shorts hung like a loose sail in the doldrums, the twiggy masts of my legs pale and meatless.

My team put me in right field, which was okay. It was peaceful out there. Nothing happened, really. You could look at the clouds and listen to the clamor happening elsewhere. You were a placeholder, and nothing was required of you.

If the ball was ever actually hit to me, no one expected me to catch it. My teammates shrugged their shoulders. It was a vagary of the game, a blind spot in the field. Nothing could be done.

But I hated being at bat, hated the moment when our team ran in from the field and I was given a number in the batting order. I couldn't hit. I swung too soon or too late. I had an agile mind, but not a speedy one—not a mind that worked in harmony with my limbs. And if I were lucky enough to hit the ball, it was a strengthless strike, the softball inevitably making a few bounces to the pitcher, who tossed it easily to first base long before I could ever make it there.

On this particular day, Rose Lincoln was on the other team, and she played catcher when my turn at bat came.

I picked up the aluminum bat from the ground, which was muddy from the rain the night before. I stood sideways at home plate and lifted the bat into the air as I had observed the other girls do. But I must have been doing it wrong.

"I guess you can't lean into it," Rose Lincoln said in a voice that only I could hear. "The weight of the bat'll topple you. Don't worry—one day you'll fill out. Maybe by menopause."

The ball came at me. I closed my eyes and swung. The weight

of the bat twisted my little body around, and I had to do a dance to stay upright on my feet. I hadn't come anywhere near the ball.

Somebody called the first strike, and Rose Lincoln threw the ball back to the pitcher.

"Seriously," she said. "How old are you?" Then she called behind her to the other girls on my team. "Should we bring out the T-ball thing?" The girls laughed. "It seems only fair."

"Be quiet," I said to Rose Lincoln.

"Sorry—am I breaking your concentration? Let's try a slow one!" she shouted to the pitcher. "Right down the middle."

I gripped the handle of the bat, liking the heft of it, liking the way it made my palms gristly with dirt. When the ball came, I pictured Rose Lincoln's laughing face and swung hard.

Not even close. Strike two. Behind me, I could hear the moans of my teammates. "Come on," they said to the universe, as though I were a small bit of lucklessness they had stumbled upon by pure happenstance.

"I've never seen anything like it," Rose Lincoln said and tossed the ball back to the pitcher. "How do you carry anything with those arms? How do you open jars? How do you brush your teeth? Do you have to take breaks?"

"Be quiet," I said, gritting my teeth.

"What was that?"

"I said be quiet."

"Sorry—you need to speak up. Use your big-girl voice."

"You're pathetic," I said, turning to her. "Pa-the-tic. Did you understand that?"

Her face changed. This was the confrontation she had been nurturing like a seedling between us. Now her fury had a purpose, a mission. She savored her own delicious rage.

I turned my back to her and raised the bat for the final pitch.

Behind me, in a whispery rage, she said, "I'm gonna get you. You're done. Just wait till the full moon. Just—"

At that moment something was decided in me, like a door slammed shut by a wind.

"I'm not waiting," I said.

"What?" she said, a quiver in her voice.

"I said . . ."

But I didn't repeat it. Instead I turned full around and swung the aluminum bat as hard as I ever had.

She was quick, and it's a good thing she was, because if she hadn't gotten an arm up to block the blow, I would have smashed her head in. Instead the bat caught her in the forearm, and I felt a satisfying, liquid crack vibrate through the hollow instrument.

She screeched and fell to the ground.

I raised the bat over my head, prepared to bring it down again—but she shuffled backward, one arm limp and useless, until she was huddled against the chain-link fence.

I advanced and stood over her. She blubbered, and her face was wet with tears. Maybe she believed she would die there.

I dropped the bat, which made an empty-pipe sound, and I advanced until I stood over her.

She turned her face away from me, raised her good arm to ward me off.

Leaning down, I whispered in her ear.

"Does it hurt?"

"Yes."

"I'm sorry."

She gurgled an animal howl of pain.

"Do you want to know how to get through it?" I asked.

She nodded.

"You have to deserve the hurt, Rosebush. Like love."

When I reached out to her, she cringed her eyes closed, as though my touch were death, but I put my hand gently on her head and smoothed her hair.

Suffering is sometimes a boon. All the creatures of the world hold hands in pain.

So I touched her head, and I felt we were both alive together, both girls wriggling, hapless, in the rich loam of girlhood. You can be happy at the strangest moments.

Then the world around us, which had been holding its breath for a number of seconds, exhaled into commotion. The other girls rushed to Rose Lincoln's aid. Mrs. McCandless, the gym teacher, was there. And Mr. Lloyd, the boys' gym teacher. He's the one who took me by the arm so that I could only walk trippingly, and he tripped me to the office, where my father was called and I was suspended from school for one week.

This was fair.

All things are fair.

The world is pretty, and it finds its own balance.

—

MY FATHER DID not know how to express his disappointment in me. His daughter having become a mystery he was afraid to solve, he narrated what had happened rather than ask me about it.

"She provoked you," he said. "The other girls heard. That's why it's just suspension—that and your good standing at the school. The girl's parents aren't bringing charges. I'm helping with the medical bills. You'll apologize, in writing."

So I wrote her a note of apology, which went like this:

Dear Rose,

I'm sorry for hitting you with the baseball bat and breaking your arm.

I remember when you were called Rosebush, and I thought I would like to have a name as pretty as a flower instead of something so scientific and technical as Lumen. I thought you were lucky. My whole life, really, I thought you were lucky. It seemed like you could touch things and make them your way.

Is that true? Can you touch things and make them your way? It wouldn't surprise me. Do you know the story of King Midas? If you don't, I'll tell it to you sometime.

Somewhere while we were growing up, things got strange. I stopped being able to recognize things for what they were, because the closer I looked the more things changed into something else. Do you ever feel this way, or is it just me?

I remember in the third grade you could draw perfect pictures of fashion-plate girls in all kinds of different outfits, and they all looked beautiful, like runway models. I was jealous, because the only thing I could draw were maps, and they weren't pretty at all—just practical and informational.

Also, I miss my mother, even though I never knew her. I wonder what kind of girl I would have been if she had been here. Maybe the kind of girl who wouldn't have ever broken your arm. Maybe the kind of girl who would have been your best friend and brought you flowers and cupcakes when some other girl took to fury and broke your arm with a baseball bat. I could picture that. I can picture lots of things.

So I'm very sorry. Sorry for this and for so much else, stuff *that doesn't even have to do with you. There aren't enough sorries in the world for how I am.*

Yours truly,
Lumen

I enclosed the letter in a white envelope and put a red tulip sticker, which was the closest sticker I had to a rose, over the back flap.

I wondered if during the next full moon there would be some retaliation for my assault on Rose. But as it turned out, Rose's body had finished its breaching. When June's full moon came, she was not among those who ran. All of a sudden, she had grown up.

I wondered, in my most dreamy states, if I had had something to do with her being weaned from the breach. Had I clobbered her into adulthood? The body had its own magic after all.

The other thing I wondered was this: Would I ever grow up like Rose and like Polly and like all the others before me? Or, having never been a real breacher, would I never fully graduate from breaching?

There were so many beautiful, dark, and lonely ways in the sunken corridors of adolescence—how did everyone else manage to make it through without a map? Were they not tempted, as I was, to linger?

———

HAVING DISCLOSED MYSELF to Rose Lincoln, I found there were things I wanted to say to Blackhat Roy as well. I had spent

too much of my life reacting to people. Now I might be the one
other people reacted to. I was ready to be someone who did
things.

I rode my bicycle to his home—a place everybody knew
about but where nobody went. It was an old house on a dirt road
down near the bottling plant. I stood for a long time outside,
holding onto the handlebars of my bike, just looking at the place.
There was a wraparound porch on the house, but it was filled
with rusted sewing machines, stacks of sun-bleached magazines
tied together with string, old fishing rods leaning in a huddle
against the house, a plastic kiddie car collecting dead leaves, rain-
water, and mosquitoes in its seat, chipped wooden frames with
no pictures in them, planters spilling over with withered creep-
ers. There was a wooden swing suspended from the porch roof,
but seated on it was a stuffed and mounted black boar, its fur
coated with dust, its tusks yellowed with age.

I couldn't stop looking into the glass eyes of that snarling boar,
even when the screen door slammed open and Roy appeared in
the doorway.

"The fuck are you doing here?" he said.

I looked at him, but I found I could say nothing. It was a good
question. What was I doing there?

"This is my goddamn home," he said.

Again I said nothing. I gripped the handlebars tighter and
gazed at him, at this place. I could not muster a response.

Then his demeanor seemed to relent a little. His body shifted
sideways.

"Well," he said in a lower voice, "come on if you're coming."

So I let my bike drop to the ground and followed him inside.

The interior of the house was like the porch—the same dis-
array of aged artifacts—but what was most remarkable was

Roy's comfort with it all, the way he moved through it with a strange kind of ease, as though he were on intimate terms with all the lonely jetsam of the world. He performed a kind of ballet through crusted plates of old food and teetering pyramids of empty beer cans. Where I twitched and fumbled, he shifted. Saying nothing, he led me back to his bedroom, where, pushed up awkwardly against one wall, was a simple iron-frame bed, the mattress, without sheets, skewed a little off the box spring. There was an unzipped plaid sleeping bag bunched up like a quilt on top of it.

On the wall was a framed photograph, crooked, of a man. I wondered who the man was, if it was Roy's father, but when I reached out to straighten it, Roy growled, "Stop. Don't touch anything. You shouldn't've come here."

I turned to him, reminded of my purpose.

"I brought you something," I said. I dug into my bag and pulled out the book. It was *The Heart Is a Lonely Hunter*. I held it out to him.

"Jesus Christ," he hissed. "The fuck do you think you're doing?" His eyes dropped to the book, and I thought I saw something open in them for just a second—but then disdain smeared his features. "What are you doing here, anyway? You come here to make me into a better person? You want to save me? From all this shit? You gonna lift me up? All your fucking decency."

He struck the book out of my hand and sent it flying across the room.

And that's when I did something. I took a step forward and stood in front of him, craning my neck to snarl upward at him.

"What are you doing?" he said, and his voice was different now—surprised—as though he were speaking to a different person entirely.

I dared him. I would dare him.

"It's not full moon," he said.

My hand reached up and slapped him. He did nothing. My hand slapped him again, harder. It would numb itself on his face. It would draw out the taint, but not for me to cure. I wasn't there for purity.

My hand drew back again, but it didn't have time to strike. He grabbed my arm, way up by the shoulder, gripping it with one thick hand, which encircled it completely. He pulled my face to his, but we did not kiss. This was not about kisses. We breathed each other's air, hot and salty.

Then he took me down to the gritty braided rug that covered the wooden floor of his room, still gripping my arm. My choice was to go with him or have my frail limb pulled from its socket. There would be bruises.

He surveyed my body as though he hadn't seen it before. It wasn't the same as before. The full moon had made things different. Now there was clarity in his eyes, and disgust, and worship.

Something swelled in me, in my chest and stomach. Something awful grew there, I knew. I could feel the tears coming. Using all my strength, I turned him over, climbed on top of him, and bit at his neck and arms. He tried to push me off, but I bit harder, digging my fingers into his clothes and skin. I would not release. He must've known I would not release.

"Stop," he said.

But I did not stop. The room stank.

He tried to fling me away, but he only succeeded in rolling over on top of me again. I felt the buttons and zippers of his clothes chafing against my skin. He seized one of my wrists and then another, got them both in his left hand, and held my struggling hands down against the floor above my head.

He had me pinned, and then I felt I could breathe for the first time. I breathed. I licked my lips.

"What are you doing?" he said.

I grunted.

"What?"

"Stop it," I said.

"I'm not doing anything."

"Me. I want you to stop me." And then there were tears. I could feel them on my cheeks. My body shook with fury. I craned my neck to bite his face. I would have gnawed off the skin of his face had I gotten it between my teeth.

With his free hand, he grabbed me by the neck and forced my head back down. For a moment, I couldn't breathe at all—and that felt all right, too. Then he let up.

"*You* stop you," he said.

"I can't. Hurt it."

"Hurt what?"

"The thing that's wrong, inside me. Hurt it. I hate it, and I want it to hurt."

Then maybe he understood. Because he was using one hand to unzip his pants, while I writhed there on the ground, my body convulsed in a furious paroxysm. Like an epileptic, I arched my back and bit at the air with my jaw.

And I couldn't move at all, because his weight was like a sack of iron ingots, pressing me down, and my arms were pinned, and my legs were growing numb, and I said, "Do it, do it," and it was safe because my body was leashed, finally leashed, and I could even feel beautiful and pure and light again because he was beating away all the ugliness in me, hammering it down into a safe little knot that couldn't hurt anyone, and none of it was my fault, it couldn't be my fault, because I had grown wrong and I would pay for it, I would pay for it happily, I would pay for it and breathe again because you had to control wrong things, you had to choke them until they were still and everything was quiet, make me still, make me quiet, make me be still.

And Blackhat Roy pushed himself inside me, deep, to the core of it all, and I thought I must be depthless. He battered my body with his. It hurt between my legs, hurt in a way I could relish in the dark, secret parts of my mind.

Because there was a voice in the room, the low, sickly whine of an animal in pain or in thrall, the throaty mewl of gross instinct, and I heard the voice filling the place and oozing down the walls. It was my voice, I realized. It was a voice to curl all the pages of my books.

This had nothing to do with love or faith or play. It was ugly and selfish. It burned.

And I wept. I knew because I could feel the wetness in my ears. I cried and wailed. I moaned there in the dusty afternoon, and outside the woods went silent and all the tree toads and the crickets muted their song out of dumb respect for me. I was an animal of pain, and the forest listens for such things.

And then he hushed me. I remember it, even now. It's a thing beyond forgetting. He clamped a palm down tight over my mouth, but the sound still came from the organ of my throat, and he didn't know what to do. So with his other hand, he covered my eyes. He blinded me.

And then did I hush truly. Like a horse blindfolded to keep it from spooking, and, too, my breathing, like a horse's, huffing rapidly through my nose, the smell of Roy's sour hand on my wet mouth.

You can only noise yourself for so long. And I felt small again, blissfully, tranquilly small, the ember of my mind cultivated true in the silence and darkness of my bound body. Mute and blind and immobile, the ache of my stubborn muscles, the searing of my bare skin—it was all far, far away, and I was at peace somewhere deep in the lost or abandoned corners of my brain. I was lost and gone, fallen down the deepest of wells, singing myself to sleep while my body burned itself to cinder and ash.

Roy shuddered silently against me.

His breathing slowed. His hands went away, first the one on my mouth, then the one on my eyes. His body rolled to the side. Cool air blew over me, and my skin tingled with the shock of it. I did not open my eyes.

But I was at peace. I was hushed everywhere inside.

———

BECAUSE LUMEN IS also vagina. It refers to anatomy as well as light. The last time I went to the gynecologist, I saw my name on a map of the alien landscape of a woman's insides. The poor woman was only a middle—all splayed open and colorful, with words dangling by black lines from all her secret features.

"There's my name," I exclaimed to the doctor when he came in to examine me.

"Is it?" he said, as though he were speaking to a child. He is a doctor. He doesn't listen to the things I say, so focused is he on the language of bodies.

After I saw my name on the woman map, I went home and did my research, as I used to do as a straight-A student, as my father's good daughter, all those years ago, when encyclopedias were holy magic.

Lumen is just one name for vagina. There are others, many of them crude, which I would not utter but which pulse in my brain and have their own linguistic heartbeats. But Lumen is the best of them all. It makes you think of moons and astronomy and the comforting light of science.

Actually, a lumen is just a tube. It refers to any number of tubes in your body. Your throat is a lumen. And your ears and nose. Your arteries and veins. Your lungs are filled with branching lumens like the roots of a tree growing in your chest. You are made of tubes, and through your body of tubes pass fluids and gases and ephemeral magics that can't be named or quantified.

Our bodies are factories. Food is put in at one end of a tube, it is processed over time, and it is ejected at the other end of the same tube. When it comes out it is something else. Also, the vaginal lumen. A boy puts himself in you. Your body accepts that offering and performs magic on it. Nine months later, out of the same lumen, a miniature human is disgorged.

My name is a processing function.

No. More to the point, a lumen is not the tube itself but rather the space within the tube. That's important. Don't you see how important that is?

That space is the lumen.

So I am Lumen. I am light, and I am space. I am emptiness. I am all the holes of the world. I am hallways and passageways. I am open doors. I am deep, dank wells. Maybe even gaps in time. Maybe I am the empty hiatus between day and night, the held breath of dusk. Or the excruciating nonmoment between an action and its consequence. I am the hiccup on the telephone line when someone delivers tragic news.

I am empty space, and I am the light that illuminates that space.

I am that furious lacuna between prolonged girlhood and the

womanhood that refuses to come—when your breasts don't bud and your limbs stay bony and your blood won't come.

I sometimes grow tired of myself. I grow hateful.

I have been in love with punishable things.

———

I MUST HAVE slept, but I don't know for how long. The sun was low on the horizon when I woke. Blackhat Roy sat in the corner. He was looking intently at the cover of the book I brought him, but when he noticed I was awake he tossed it aside.

He said nothing, just watched me while I shifted my clothes back into place. My skin was pinched, my joints aching, my body on humiliating display. All I wanted was to get out of there as quickly as I could, but when I was about to leave, he came over and stood before me.

"Hey," he said.

"What?"

"Just..."

He reached out, and at first I thought he was going to seize me again—but this was something new, something gentle. He moved himself against me, and it was a full moment before I realized he was embracing me.

Feeling bitten, I recoiled and pushed him away.

"Don't," I said.

"Lumen, I—" And he moved forward again.

"Don't you dare," I said and backed away. "Don't touch me."

He looked at me, confused, then down at his own hands as if to discover some unintentional threat there.

I didn't want to explain. I was revolted by tenderness. I simply didn't want to be loved by Blackhat Roy. The idea was unacceptable to me.

He came toward me again, and I clenched up.

"No," I said. "Don't."

"Goddamn it, Lumen," he said, exasperated, "I'm just trying to—is it this?" He gestured all around him, at his broken-down house, his meager life. "I'm just trying—"

He came at me again, more forcefully this time, trying to bind me in his arms. I fought against him, but the more I struggled, the tighter his hold got.

"Stop it," he said. "Lumen, just stop—I'm not doing anything wrong."

And when I finally wrenched myself free of him, my body swung backward, spiraling out of control, my face catching the edge of a plywood shelf, and I fell to the ground.

At first I was numb, dizzy, and then my hand went up to the sudden searing pain on my cheek and came back covered in blood.

"Lumen," Roy said. "I'm sorry. I—"

"Shut up," I said. "Just be quiet for a minute."

I looked at myself in a mirror hanging on his wall, and I was surprised. There was a girl, a long gash on the side of her face, bleeding fluently, something unfocused in her eyes. That was me.

"Goddamn it," Roy was saying behind me, and when I turned I found he wasn't speaking to me at all. He was pacing the floor, his fists pressed tight against his eyes. "Goddamn it," he said again. "I don't know how. I don't know how." He took one of his fists and rapped his knuckles hard against his skull. "She shouldn't be here," he said. "I hurt her. I broke her."

And there was nothing pretty about it, nothing dramatic. This had nothing to do with the rituals of our little town, nothing to do with breaching or the cycles of the moon. This was something different, horrible in its plainness. His rage, my bloodied face, his fists, my shame. These were not the primal forces of the earth working through our polluted souls, not the bright clamor of youth in the stark urban fields of the modern age. It was just small and ugly and wrong.

The hospital was closer than my house, so I rode there, my bicycle serpentining across the road in my dizziness. I wasn't sure if I would make it. By the time I got there, the front of my shirt was soaked and sticky with blood. I told them I fell. They treated me immediately, calling my father, giving me six stitches. A plastic surgeon was called in, since the wound was on my face. Everyone was very concerned.

The hospital was tidy and clean. It reminded me of civilized places. Places I didn't belong. Places I was too ashamed to go back to.

———

AFTER THE STITCHES, I asked the nurse if I could use the bathroom. I felt funny, and in the bathroom I discovered blood on the insides of my thighs. At first I thought that maybe Roy had injured me—but then I realized what it was. I wasn't amenorrheic anymore.

It hadn't been a very long time since I had incanted magic words to romance my blood into flowing. But now it seemed like I had traveled a great distance from those fancies. I had grown accustomed to blood of all kinds. This was just a period.

———

I HAVE A treasure. Do you want to know what it is? I could draw you a map to it. First you need to find the place where I live now, in a city in the northwestern quarter of our fair country. In the room where I sleep, there is a dark varnished maple dresser whose origins are unknown to me. On top of that dresser, you will find a jewelry box with many small drawers and hinged doors, like a magician's cabinet. The very bottom drawer pulls out a long way, and you will need to pull it out almost completely in order to discover a packet of white tissue paper tied with a string. Undo the string, unfold the wrapping paper, and there you will find my treasure.

It's a necklace, if you really want to know. It was given to me by my father. I don't wear it anymore—because time has made it into a treasure, and you don't dangle treasures from your neck. Not real ones.

It's not the locket he gave me for Christmas. This he gave me that June, that same June that everything was happening. It was for me to wear at the prom. Ours was a small school, so everyone, even sophomores, went to the prom.

When he gave it to me, it was wrapped in the very same tissue and string (such consistencies are important)—except it was also in a gold foil box with a little bow on top. The box is lost now. You can't save everything. You can't save every little thing.

We were sitting at the kitchen table, and it was just before bedtime, so there were very few lights left on downstairs. We sat in a comfortable pool of kitchen light, surrounded by dark doorways, and we felt safe.

"I just thought you should have something nice," he said. "For the dance."

He was embarrassed, and he stirred more sugar into his mug of coffee for something to do with his hands.

I unwrapped it and held it up to admire it. It was a simple gold chain with a pendant in the shape of a dragonfly. Its wings had little bitty rubies in them, and the whole thing sparkled. It was the most beautiful thing I had ever been given.

"It's perfect," I said, because I wanted him to know he had done a good job of making me happy. He smiled and nodded and sipped his coffee, more pleased than he let on. That was our way, then. He and I, we were timid about the common practices of life now that I'd gotten older. But we helped each other along, and we stumbled through. We knew the quiet codes that stood in place of more overt, gangly expressions of love—and we got by all right.

I remember wondering for a few aching moments if maybe this had been a piece of my mother's jewelry. I pictured her as a girl who would like dragonflies. A wisp of a creature with a name that pointed to darker things.

But then he rose from the table and rinsed his mug in the sink.

"I'm glad you like it," he said. "Miss Simons—Margot—she, uh, she helped me pick it out. You might want to thank her, too."

"Oh," I said. I forced a smile, but he wasn't looking at me anyway. "Yes. Yes, I will."

He came up behind me, leaned down, and kissed me on the top of my head.

"Good night, Lumen," he said. And then I heard the stairs creak with his footsteps as he went up to bed.

———

I DIDN'T WEAR the dragonfly to the prom. That was my statement. I wore a party dress that was a few years old but still fit decently, and I wore the Christmas locket my father had given me—the one with pictures of him and my mother in it. My father and I never exchanged words about it. I saw him glance once at my neck, and that was enough. He distracted himself by taking pictures of me in my dress in front of the living room bookshelves.

If Miss Simons noticed I wasn't wearing the dragonfly, she didn't let it show even a little bit. In fact she stood with me before the mirror in my bathroom and helped me hide with makeup, as much as possible, the sewn-up part of my face. When she was done, I looked like a different Lumen entirely—some future version of Lumen, maybe, the woman I might become.

We both looked at my reflection in the mirror. I thought she was going to tell me how pretty I looked, but instead what she said was, "You're tough, Lumen. Tougher than anyone I know. Don't let them tell you otherwise."

After all, I realized, she wasn't a bad woman. I wanted to give her something in return.

"Thank you," I said.

"You're welcome."

"I mean," I said, "for everything. For the necklace."

She didn't say anything, but she smiled at me in the mirror, a true smile, and she knew.

My father didn't ask if someone was taking me to the dance, because he would not pry so far into my personal life—and the answer would only lead to discomfort whether it was yes or no. Instead he simply asked if I needed a ride to the school, and I told him yes.

When he pulled up in front of the school, I could tell there was something on his mind, so I didn't get out of the car immediately. I waited, and together we watched people arrive, walking through the double doors of the big building, linked arm in arm in their finery.

"Margot and I are going to a dinner party tonight," he said.

"Okay."

"Friends of hers."

"Okay."

"I'll be home by midnight. You'll—you'll be home by then?"

It occurred me that we were talking about a curfew. We hadn't had a conversation about a curfew in years—there had been no need for one. Where was I going to go? I had been a good girl, impervious to trouble. But now things were different.

"I mean," he went on, "there's no moon tonight."

I was embarrassed. We both were. I looked down at my hands.

"I'll be home."

"You'll be home," he said. He did not look at me but nodded to himself, as though confirming a truth that he was ashamed to have questioned in the first place.

"I promise."

I lingered. Suddenly I didn't want to be away from him. We waited and watched the others arrive. He shifted in his seat. I could smell his cologne. I can smell it still.

"Did I ever tell you," he said, a thin smile forming in his beard, "how the coal hole got its name?"

What he referred to was a hollowed space in the wall of our house, under one of the eaves. When the house was originally built, a hidden panel was installed in the wall so that the space could be used for storage. When I was a little girl, I liked hiding myself away in there. I felt safe in that cramped triangle of space, which seemed like it fit me but no other human on earth. When my father saw I liked it, he cleared out the boxes of old photographs he had stored in there and set it up as a hiding place for me, with a light and a tiny bookshelf and an assortment of throw pillows I could arrange however I liked. I would stay in there for hours at a time, and he would bring me crackers and cheese. We called it the coal hole, and it had never occurred to me to wonder why.

"It's from *Silas Marner*," he said.

"I never read it," I said.

"I know. It's about a grumpy old man who has to raise a little girl all on his own. He doesn't know what he's doing. He doesn't know the first thing about children. He's all on his own."

My father paused. He looked away from me and was quiet for a while. I wished I could see his eyes, but I was also afraid of what I'd find in them.

"Anyway," he went on, taking a deep breath, "when she starts to act out, he doesn't know what to do. So to punish her, he shuts her in the coal hole of his house all by herself. Except here's the thing. This girl, she's not like other children. She's got a spirit in her—brilliant, mischievous. And it turns out she *likes* the coal hole. It's no punishment at all to her. Once she discovers it, she climbs in there all the time."

"So . . ." I said, though there was a catch in my throat. "So what does Silas Marner do?"

My father smiled.

"What else is there to do with a girl like that?" he said. "He lets her do what she wants. And he sits back and watches her grow up. And he is amazed."

I leaned over and embraced him, my head against his chest, and I felt small and safe with him as I have never felt with anyone else in my life. He kissed the top of my head and stroked my hair.

"But sometimes a father worries," he said.

"I know," I said, and I did not like to think of what I was doing to him by becoming the person I was.

"I know," I said again. "I'll be there when you get home. I promise."

I PROMISE.

I don't like to think about it. I don't like to write it. Outside, our neighbor's sprinklers just switched on by automatic timer. It must be nearing dawn. He has told us that early morning is the best time to water your lawn. There is no other sound to be heard. I have been listening to silence for so long.

I promise.

I would erase it if I could. They say you can't hide from truth. But you can't hide from lies, either. You can't hide from anything, really.

So why do we keep trying?

HELENA, MY HUSBAND'S pretty colleague who jogs around the park, discovers me behind the school, where I watch Jack through his office window.

"Ann? What are you doing here?"

"Oh," I say and smile too widely in deference to her. "I just came to drop something off with Jack."

"Ugh. I know," she says. "Everybody's been so preoccupied preparing for the parent night tonight. Isn't this a nice place just to sit and contemplate? I like it, but nobody ever comes out here."

"It's very nice."

"Say, what do you think about that woman, Marcie Klapper-Witt, and her brownshirts cleaning up the neighborhood? I'll tell you something—I'm not sure I like it. When people get zealous, I keep my distance. That's my policy. Oh—but you're not close with her, are you?"

"My son bit her daughter," I say, shy and proud.

Helena laughs and touches my arm.

"Ann, I'm making a prediction—you and I are going to be best friends. Mark my words."

I would like to be best friends with Helena, but I'm afraid I don't know how. I don't know if I've ever been best friends with anyone—especially someone like her, who is so merry about life, whom people enjoying being around. I worry that I don't possess the spirit required to uphold the friendship of someone so vigorous. What manner of research is required for such a prospect?

That night, while she and my husband are occupied at the parent event at school, I drop my son off with Lola and walk through the neighborhood. It's empty and quiet, and a dog barks somewhere, and somewhere else a peal of distant laughter escapes from an open window. I am aware of the sound of my own feet shuffling against the sidewalk, so I walk differently—heel, toe—so that I add no noise to the night. When a car comes, I move quickly aside and hide behind a tall bush, compelled by some instinct I shut inside myself a long time ago.

Overhead the night is cloudy, and there are no stars. If it weren't for the street lamps on every block, you could get lost on these lanes. Everything is a jungle when the light is gone. Something in my chest longs for a blackout. And then my eyes would readjust to the night, and then I could see all the helpless residents wandering, lost, feeling their ways. And I could watch them and be unafraid.

At Helena's house, the porch light is on, but all the windows are dark. I would like to get a look at her fiancé, so I put my face to the glass of the front windows, but the house looks empty. I can see the dim outline of the furniture in her living room, but the glare from the street lamps is too great. I go around the side of the house to the back, where one of the kitchen windows is open a crack. There's a fine smell coming from the kitchen, as though many healthful meals have been prepared between those walls, so I lift the window all the way, carefully remove the screen, and climb inside. Once in, I am conscientious in refitting the screen back into the window frame.

I am accustomed to dark, empty houses. I know how to navigate them. You rely on your senses. You trust your widened pupils, your outstretched fingertips, your animal nose.

I go upstairs. In her bedroom, I discover a picture of Helena and her fiancé in a frame by the bed. The picture is taken against the backdrop of some wide, forested valley — as though the only mountains worth climbing are the ones they climb together — and he is a very handsome young man with good eyebrows and an authoritative smile. She wears a baseball cap in the picture, and I wonder if I should get a baseball cap — though I would not know which team logo it should bear.

I lie down on the bed and smell the pillow and try to imagine what it is like to see, every night, the moonlight cast its particular shadow dance over the contours of this room. I imagine what it is like to be pressed under the body of that imposing man in the picture.

In her closet, I find her running shoes, set neatly beside each other, the laces tucked inside. When I put one of them to my nose, I smell nature, ruddy and bountiful. Her toothpaste, I am pleased to see, is the same brand as mine, though all the lotions and shampoos in her shower come in bottles that I've never seen on the shelves of our local grocery store. There is a little nest of her hair in the drain of the shower.

But I am drawn again downstairs, to the kitchen, because that is where I suspect Helena truly lives. The refrigerator is filled with produce, with small cartons of yogurt, with milk on the edge of souring. There are no dishes in the sink. From the smell of it, the ones in the dishwasher are clean and ready to be put away. I run my fingers over the deck of china plates standing there proudly.

In one of the cabinets, I find a jar of wheat germ that announces itself as an excellent source of folic acid and vitamin E. It suddenly feels like a tremendous oversight that I have never had any wheat germ in my house. It is clearly the source of so many good things. Wondering what new splendors might grow from the germ of wheat, I decide to take the jar with me. This will be essential to my friendship with Helena. This is what I have been missing — the key I have been looking for, the one that will unlock more conventional relationships with the world.

Except Marcie Klapper-Witt's neighborhood watch must have seen me when I climbed in through the window of Helena's house — because when I leave by the front door, the police are there waiting for me, their hands poised and ready over their holstered pistols, the lights on their car flashing pretty against the treetops.

CHAPTER 12

The name of my birth town isn't really Pale Miranda. That would be a very fanciful name for a town, and most towns are named in the service of either commerce or heritage. The town where I grew up is of the latter variety, and its real name is Polikwakanda, which is an indigenous name—supposedly from the Abenaki tribe, though I have never been able to find any reference to the word in my research of Native American languages. I don't know what it means, and maybe it means "town where monsters live" or something like that, but the only sense my young girl's tongue could make of the word was Pale Miranda, and so that's how I thought of the place where I was raised—even beyond the time when I was grown old enough to know better.

When I walked into the prom, there were banners everywhere that said, FAREWELL POLIKWAKANDA SENIORS!

Farewell, Pale Miranda.

———

DANCES IN THE town where I grew up were curious events. In other towns, the school dance is an opportunity to break free and go wild for a little while. But because our wildness was routine, because we were reminded of it monthly in cut lips and bruised thighs, our dances were tame. People stood around in compulsory clusters. They talked about dull things. No one tried to sneak vodka into the punch. No virginities were lost underneath the stage or in the backseats of cars in the parking lot. Virginities were simply not things toppled by clumsy, drunken lunging. Instead they were seized and forfeited in clawing battles under full moons while the naked apparitions of your friends looked on, howling. So it was.

When people danced at the prom, they danced slowly, pressed together and rocking back and forth with the sweet romance of dispassion. The tissue streamers wafted to and fro like underwater weeds. The students chatted pleasantly with the adult chaperones. People yawned. They went outside and looked up at the sky because they missed the moon. They sat on curbs and waited.

The previous year, I had gone to the dance with Polly. That now seemed like a very long time ago. We had already started pulling away from each other even then. I remembered seeing her across the gym, laughing at some joke told by a boy who, we had both agreed, was ridiculous. I remembered wondering about the integrity of Polly's personality, because I did not understand how people could go for so long being one thing and then, overnight, suddenly become something else. Such behavior seemed unnatural to me. A year later, though, I knew the difference between unnatural and unliterary. The natural world, it turned out, was not very literary. You could say it had poetry, but it was a rough brand of poetry.

So when I walked into the decorated gym, I entered alone.

What I realized was how far from normal my connections with other people had become. My interactions were based upon spite or jealousy or rage or strange hungers—but whatever they were, they were not dance-going relationships.

Some people said hello to me. Polly made brief conversation—and even Rose Lincoln, whose arm was still in a sling, wished me well in a way that made me think magnanimity was her newly forged weapon.

Somehow, without realizing it, I had become everyone's odd cousin. I existed as a nagging, peripheral figure in their lives—recognized only in specialized circumstances. I had become occasional. To leave a conversation with me was to return to real life.

No one asked me to dance, and I sat for a long time on the bleachers, alone on the dark periphery of the gym, watching the figures of my peers sway back and forth in each other's arms, hating them for all their pretty pretenses.

When a group of boys passed by, I could hear them talking about Mr. Hunter, who was supposed to be one of the chaperones. I hadn't seen him all night, but these boys had observed him walking the grounds of the school, cursing aloud. He swayed as he walked, said one. He was drunk, said another. The boys laughed.

"Where?" I asked.

"What?" they said. They were startled to notice me there in the dark.

"Where?" I said again. "Where was he going?"

"I don't know," said one of the boys, shrugging as though to suggest he wanted no part of whatever freakishness Mr. Hunter and I shared. "Looked like he was going toward the football field."

I WALKED DOWN to the field, the crinoline of my pink prom dress rustling against my skin. The field was not lit, but a glow reached it from the school grounds behind me. I was conscious of looking ridiculous out there, where no one was.

I didn't see Mr. Hunter at first, but I found him by the sound of a glass bottle being tapped with steady persistence against a metal rail of the bleachers. He was up in the very top row, gazing out over the field and the stars in the sky beyond.

"There she is," he called out when he saw me. I hiked up my dress and climbed to the top of the bleachers.

"Do you want to hear a story, Lumen?" he said when I reached him. "Now it's time for me to tell you a story. I quit my job. I quit it. I'm leaving. I'm going as far as I can go. Maybe Tibet. Have you ever eaten Tibetan food?"

"You're leaving? But why?"

He shook his head.

"You can't get it back," he said, "once it's gone."

"But you left once before."

He drank from the bottle.

"You have to be dauntless in this life. If at first you don't succeed at quitting, try, try again." Then he looked at my dress and seemed to notice it for the first time. "What are you dressed up as?"

I sat on the cold metal bench beside him, and the folds of my dress creased uncomfortably beneath me.

The moon was overhead, a waxing crescent, and he asked me if I weren't afraid to be alone with him.

"Jesus, girl," he said. "Didn't anybody ever tell you not to hang out with drunk, lying reprobates on emptied-out school property? You're going to stroll yourself into victimhood one of these days. Aren't you afraid?"

"I don't know."

"You should be."

He stood suddenly, wobbly with drink. Leaning over me, he gripped the bar behind me on either side of my head and brought his face down close to mine. I could smell the thick, acrid stench of alcohol. He licked his lips and smiled a threatening smile, and the bleachers tremored under his grasp.

I closed my eyes. I waited for whatever was coming.

There was another sound, and when I opened my eyes, he was standing upright, looking down at me with trepidation, even a little disgust.

"Goddamn it," he said, seething. "Goddamn you! No fear. Not an ounce of fucking fear. You invite—you *invite*—destruction. What's the world to you, huh? A place to die in? You aren't even a girl—you're a . . . you're a tragedy. There isn't a monster in the world—not a monster in the world till he meets an eager victim."

He reeled backward, and I thought he might fall, but he recovered himself.

"How come?" he said, almost pleading now. "How come you aren't afraid?"

I wanted to tell him that I was afraid. But his fury was wide—he raged against things larger than just me.

"You can't—" he started, then he used his sleeve to wipe his mouth. "You can't rub yourself against death like that. You just can't."

He wanted me to understand. There was a desperation in his eyes. He shook his head, and he collapsed onto the bench again. For a long time he said nothing but just looked out at the scattered stars.

Then he said:

"Your mother, she was the same way."

"You weren't lying, were you?" I said. "I mean, the things you said about running with my mother. Those weren't lies."

He just looked at me for a long time. I wondered what he saw in that frilled pink gown. Whatever it was, he must have deemed it fit.

He drank again and leaned forward, resting his elbows on his knees. "All right," he said then. "Time for another story. Last one. Are you ready?"

"Yes." I held my breath. I clutched at the fabric of my dress, wanting to tear it.

We sat side by side. He looked straight ahead, and I looked straight ahead, and it was no conversation. It was a kind of shared aloneness — words dropped in the void, verbal flotsam for whoever might see fit to collect it.

"She never went breach," he said. "You were right about that. That was a true thing. She was never a real breacher. It was something wrong with her maybe, her genes. Something didn't click like it was supposed to. She didn't feel the drive. No natural love of the night. But this is what you didn't know. She pretended. It was when it happened to your father. She wanted to run with him. So she pretended, and he kept her secret. Nobody knew. She took her clothes off, just like the rest of them, and she ran. You think about it the right way, it's romantic. Her and him — the night."

He paused and sniffed once.

"The problem was," he went on, "she took to it. I mean, eventually she liked it. After your father's year was up, well, she couldn't seem to stop herself. She kept going out. It had bored itself into her some way. It wasn't about instinct for her. It was about taste." He licked his lips and thought for a moment. "That's the difference. It came from a different place inside her. Your father, he tried to get her to stop. Like an addiction. She got pregnant with you, and he thought that might settle her down. But it didn't. She went out anyway, her belly all swollen up. What I heard is that people revered her, almost, like she carried the full moon inside her. I was still too young to go out myself, but I heard."

He paused again briefly.

"She was still going when I went breach," he said. "This was, you know, three or four years later. Everybody knew her secret by then. They'd all gotten suspicious when it went on so long. They figured it out—that she was a pretender. But there wasn't any . . . *disparagement* in it. See, she *chose* the thing that was forced on the rest of us. We—we loved her, even, because she loved us. I'm not saying you have to understand it. I'm just telling you how it was. Your mother, she was—she was *rare*."

I looked over briefly to see his face in the darkness, the glistening orbs of his eyes. I caught a quick glimpse, then looked away again. His story was a private one.

"You," he said. "I saw her in you. Ever since I got back. You want to know the truth? The truth is I don't want to see her anymore. It's been too long. The time comes you have to stop looking at ghosts."

It was a long time before he spoke again. For a while I thought he had forgotten I was there, but I waited patiently—as one does for revelations.

He eventually went on. "Did he . . . your father . . . did he tell you how she died?"

"Car accident," I said.

"Yeah." He shook his head. "That part's not true. But he can't be blamed. Sometimes the lie's necessary. Sometimes the truth is nocturnal. The light hurts it."

He paused again, sighing. I thought he might stop there, but then I realized the story had gone beyond him. The story would get told, as sometimes stories do, one way or the other, regardless of willful human instruments.

"It wasn't any car accident," he went on. "It was the third night of the Lacuna."

The Lacuna was the sixth full moon of the year, the still midpoint around which the rest of the year rotated. June, when the fireflies were out.

"We were down at the quarry. Your mother was there. You were at home, asleep in your crib. She was real still and quiet that night. I remember it. She had this grin, a faraway grin, like she was laughing at some joke nobody else heard. The rest of us, we were at each other one way or another. You know how it is. Foul. But she was a spark, a glistening thing in the middle of us all. She reminded us that we didn't know a thing about love. It was like that."

There was a catch in his voice, barely perceptible. A tiny tremor, the kind that means a massive fissure has quaked open somewhere deep, deep underground.

"That's where we lost her. We hunted for her. We did. The police came the next day. And firemen. But nobody could find anything. Maybe, we thought, maybe she'd come home to us. We liked to think it. Your father thought it. He thought it for a long time."

Then he was quiet, and I wondered if he was done. But after some time had passed, he rose up again, and this time he leaned over and pointed a long, wavering finger right in my face, as though condemning me for reminding him of my lost, moonlit mother.

"But this is what I'll have you know," he said, his voice hard. "She was better than us. Better than all of us. She went after the real thing of what the rest of us were just playing at. And she found it. God help her, she found it."

So there were others who felt the loss of my mother, maybe even more than I felt it, because I had only known the myth of her. Maybe that was what I saw in the eyes of those storekeepers who gifted me with free ice cream or barrettes or jars of maraschino cherries. Maybe in me they saw the reflection of my mother, whom they had lost on the narrow horizon.

And maybe that was the peculiar smell that I breathed in from the purple giraffe I had cuddled to my chest on many nights of my childhood—the odor of loss, which is like sumac and fallen leaves.

"But where?" I said, my voice small. "Where did she go? Where did you lose her?"

There was the quiver in his voice again, and a sound in his mouth like it was chewing on something—but I understood that he was only chewing on his own story, trying to swallow back down what was getting retched up.

"It was that mine," he said.

The mine. Map the mine. Hair like straw. Papier-mâché skin. Gray. A mouth that would swallow you up. I felt sick.

"She just got up and walked away," Mr. Hunter said. "That's how it was. She rose up, and everyone stopped and waited, because it seemed like she might say something—and we listened when she said things. But she didn't say anything. She stood up, and she turned her back on us, and she walked into the mine. See? The dark got her."

Those sunken eyes that looked only inward.

I wanted to run. I wanted to be split from my own skin.

"It was done before we knew it," he said. "When we realized she didn't intend to come back, we went in after her. But those mine tunnels—you've got no chance. There are shafts sunk everywhere that go straight down into nothing. You can't see two feet into the mouth of the thing. She didn't pause or turn around, she just walked forward. And then we couldn't see her anymore."

Sometimes death is a found mother.

And that's how I found mine.

———

THEN I RAN. The moon was not full, but it did not matter. Still outfitted in my papery pink party dress, I ran—I ran through town to the other side, against the headlights of the cars, into the woods, all the way to the quarry and the abandoned mine, where the wind played a shivery kind of music as it dove down into the deepest parts of the earth.

It was between moons—just before the June moon, the La-cuna—when I found my mother. I don't mean her body, which was a thing of brittle ash—I mean her voice, which one day spoke back to me from the void where I had made my meager confessions.

I was sixteen years old, and there was something gone wrong with me. I was sixteen, and I hadn't grown right, and all my friends were no longer my friends, and instead I had people I bit and who bit back. I had a beautiful, sad father and an angry drunken man who saw me as the reincarnation of a perverse angel. There was a pretty young woman with an affection for my father who picked out jewelry for me because my mother was a fantasy told to me in good-night stories. I was sixteen, and my name was light, and my body had been bloodied and torn and repaired. I did well in school. I drew maps. I wondered what my life would become—I tried to picture it. I was sixteen, and I was an animal. I was the wrong kind of animal. I didn't believe as others believed. So there must have been some evil to it. The savagery of nature minus the nature is evil. I was sixteen years old, and I had grown proud of my evil. As though the earth itself had christened me Lumen, as though the heavens had given me their imprimatur. I would take it.

And that's when I discovered my true mother.

———

THE JUNE MOON was called the Lacuna, which the dictionary told me meant "pause." Maybe because it was the halfway point in the year, a moment when time itself held its breath, waited to exhale the remainder of its months. I don't know—but it's true that there was always a kind of holy stillness about that particular moon. It's in that stillness that my mother went away many years before.

There was no light at all—no light anywhere. I ran my fingers along the walls of the caves I knew so well. My dress dragged along packed dirt. I smelled my way.

And maybe, after all, that was growing up—learning to navigate deeper territories, learning how to see in the dark. Or learning not to care that you couldn't see in the dark.

But that seemed wrong, too. The adults around me, they weren't less afraid—they were more. They were afraid of things they couldn't articulate. They had lost the power to utter themselves, and so they cowered in sheetrock houses.

Mr. Hunter. He remade himself but could never make himself unbroken. I felt guilty. I had left him behind, there on his tinny height, no one to say goodbye to.

My father, I loved him. He was a sad man, too. But my whole life he had lied to me.

Still, I didn't blame him. I would sing a song of him. I would write him into a poem. He deserved magic words to keep him safe. Miss Simons was no curse. She was not strong enough to be a curse. She was simply common. But my father and I, we were better. We cultivated ourselves on higher ground.

Maybe he had grown too afraid even to see that.

The adults, they lived in another country—a populace of scrawny fear, as far away as morning is from midnight.

———

I REMEMBER THE way your skin looked in the moonlight.

You.

Peter Meechum.

Blackhat Roy Ruggle.

Hondy Pilt.

Rose Lincoln.

Polly, pretty Polly.

I line you all up in my head, a beautiful processional, slow-motion and smiling. You are of my life.

When I point to you, stand up straight. Let me get a good look at you.

You were pale.

And you were dark.

Your ribs showed through your skin.

You were the one who always had leaves in your hair.

You wore your nakedness proudly—bathing in the moonlight as though your exposure were holy and dreadful.

You, on the other hand, always hid in bushes and behind trees. Was it shame or was it timidity?

You treated your skin before the moon came out. You were ridiculous, but you were lustrous.

You had freckled shoulders.

You had a birthmark on your right calf—I touched it once with my lips when you were sleeping.

I could draw maps of your skin—all of you. I have often, without your knowing it, traveled the topographies of your flesh.

You were brilliant in the moonlight, and I remember you all.

———

I WENT TO visit my mother. Hay for hair, paper for skin. And still just a girl. Of course a girl. It had never occurred to me—when she died she had been just a few years older than I was now. I had thought of my mother as many things: as a queen, as a bride, as a wild woman, as a prophet—but I had never thought of her as simply a girl, like me. In just a handful of years, I would be older than my own mother.

It hurt to think about that.

I could not see her in the dark, so I nestled myself against her. I spoke to her.

I said, "Hello. It's me. It's Lumen, your daughter."

Her silence was profound, mocking.

I said, "Did you wear orchid gloves at your wedding? My dad says you did, but I don't know."

She was preserved in time. I rested my head against her shoulder. Her hay hair tickled my cheek. I smelled her gray skin, and it smelled of nothing at all. Her skin was dusty.

"Did you get lost?" I said. "I got lost, too."

———

SOMETIMES WHEN YOU are looking for something, you find it.

You could call it magic.

If we name things, maybe they'll never get away from us.

———

I SLEPT, MY head in my mother's lap. It might have been five minutes. It might have been an hour. When I woke, I thought it was late. I thought about my father and my promise to be home by midnight. But when I made my way out of the mine, I found Blackhat Roy near the mouth, waiting for me. He said nothing. He looked miserable—tortured. But this boy's wretchedness felt far away from where I was.

"My mother's dead," I said.

"I know," he said. "My father's gone, too."

"I forgot that."

"I know."

"How did you know I was here?"

"People saw you. Running."

"You went to the dance?"

"No. I was looking for you."

I turned and went to my secret place, my cistern. He followed me there, but I didn't care. I had stopped hearing the world. In my head were confused, inarticulate voices. They babbled and boiled, and I drowned in them. My mother was a dead girl. There was darkness and dust and Blackhat Roy. You sometimes go wild, and you sometimes want that wildness shackled.

We faced each other, and the wind whistled up from the pit. While he looked, I undid my prom dress and let it fall to the ground. Then I took off my underwear. We're all of us naked one way or the other.

My mother was calling my name from the deep wells of the earth, and I was rotted from the inside, and my mind was a gemstone mired in murk, and I would torture the impurities out. I would sweat them out, I would bleed them out, I would suffer them out, I would exhaust them out.

For there must be order. There must be balance. For every sin, a punishment. For every shameful act, a suffering. For every impure bite, a pure tooth knocked loose.

Otherwise, what was it all for?

The earth knew, whose days and nights were perfect tides of light.

The moon knew, whose pocky face had waxed and waned by untransgressible law for billions of years.

I knew, who was yet still a girl.

CHAPTER 13

Do you want to know who I am?

Do you want to know what I do?

I live next door to you with my husband and my child.

I have done such things as would shame the devil, yet I keep my front yard tidy, the trash bins lined up neatly on trash day.

I attend the meetings of the PTA. I offer to bake cookies.

At night, after everyone is asleep, I creep downstairs to the kitchen table and write down my memories. They are the stories I tell myself when I can't sleep. Like fairy tales—or the mythos of a lost culture.

I was an excellent student.

I am an excellent member of the community. I never spit, and I always put my waste in the proper receptacles.

Do you know what else I do?

I sometimes walk out into the night. I walk down the middle of the deserted street. Our neighborhood is always silent at this hour—we comprise wholesome families. I feel the chill, as I did not as a girl. Maybe as you get older you grow into new kinds of dis-ease. Maybe death is the ultimate discomfort.

I walk to the park, which is deserted except for four teenagers who scurry away when they see me. The air they leave behind smells of marijuana. On the ground is an empty plastic bag and a box of matches with the name of a bar on it and an illustration of a woman sitting inside a massive martini glass.

The playground equipment is still and skeletal, unhinged as it is at this time of night from the fuss of child life, illuminated by what we used to call a Pheasant Moon.

I am alone. I am in love with my husband and my boy, but I am still alone.

Sometimes you want a hand over your mouth—you want to be hushed. Other times you just want to burn till there's nothing left.

———

WHEN JACK FINALLY comes, he does not speak for a while but instead just paces back and forth outside my cell. I watch him, feeling sorry that he has a wife whom he has to fetch from jail. He is a good man. All the other men in our neighborhood have wives who are properly aligned, who know how to stay indoors.

"You broke into that woman's house," he says finally, using his hands to show the concreteness of the facts. "You opened her kitchen window, and you climbed in her house when nobody was home. You did these things."

These things and others he knows nothing of. My past is sometimes so noisy in my brain. I can only remain quiet.

"Ann," he goes on. "Ann, Helena and I—we just work together. Sometimes I see her at school. Sometimes we talk. You know there's nothing between us. You know I wouldn't do that, don't you?"

"I know."

"Then why—"

He stops himself. You can see the restraint in his thin, sealed lips. He does not like to ask me why. He fears both the answer and the absence of an answer.

"They said . . ." he continues, almost pleading. "They said you took a jar of wheat germ."

I smile a little to show him that everything will be all right—that things will always be all right—but he does not smile back.

"It seemed important," I say.

Now he approaches my cage and puts his fingers on mine as they grip the bars. He looks at me as though he knows me and understands me and will be my ally forever.

"Ann," he says, "you have to be better. You have to be."

I would like to explain to him that there are worse horrors by far, that we will endure—but I don't. Instead, I just say:

"I know."

———

I STOOD BEFORE Roy—a naked little offering that he did not accept.

He seemed ashamed to see my body. And when he looked at my face, all he saw was the line of stitches.

"I did that to you," he said, swallowing hard.

Absently, I put my hand to the wound. When I brought it away, I noticed that my fingertips were coated with the peach-colored dust that Margot Simons had shown me how to use earlier.

Roy stepped away from me, as though I were difficult to be near. He moved to the other side of the pit and stood before it, gazing at me across that impossible depth. Then he looked down into it. I wondered what he saw there. Maybe he, too, had lost things to the earth. But I was unsettled by something in his eyes that was near to longing.

I was cold, and the gravelly ground bit into the soles of my feet.

"What are you doing?" I said.

"You know something?" he said without looking up. "I liked your room."

"My room?"

"It was a nice room. I wonder if I would have been different if I grew up in a room like that."

His voice was small and hollow. It echoed off the walls of the cistern.

"You grew up all right," I said.

He made a sound that echoed against the walls of the cistern and seemed to come not from him but from the earth itself.

He toed some pebbles into the black pit, and they made no sound at all.

"At the beginning," he said, "I wanted to break you. I really did. But I couldn't. Then, later, I didn't want to break you any-more. I wanted . . . the opposite. But something about me—my hands don't work that way. And I broke you instead. It was an accident."

"Roy," I said. "Roy."

"I hated you for such a long time," he said, looking up at me. He rubbed a hand across his face, and his cheek smeared with ash. That's when I noticed he was covered in it—ashy dust—as though whatever burned in him was smoldering out, leaving his skin desiccated. He smiled a smile that had no smile in it. "At least that I was good at. Hate's simple. It makes sense. You know it, too."

"Roy," I said. "Don't."

He cried now, and his bare frame shivered with his tears.

"You read all those books," he said, shaking his head. "All those fucking books."

I wanted to tell him it meant nothing. I wanted to explain that it was all I knew how to do—that I read books instead of do-ing real things. I wanted to say to him that I was different now, that I had lost who I was and that I would never get that Lumen back again, that something had gone deranged inside me. I used to think that some people are born so good they are illiterate to the languages of desolation. But we all speak the same tongue.

I wanted to tell him these things, but my heart was going too fast. I was deafened by it, muted by it. I was peaceful in my brain, viewing myself as if from above, wondering at this little monkey of a creature who stood staring.

He gazed into the pit and then back at me, and there was an awful, imploring truth in his eyes.

"Lumen," he said. "Lumen, I did something bad. Really bad. I went to your house tonight. No one was there. I tried to read the book you gave me. But I couldn't. So I wanted to bring it back to you."

He shook his head.

Something was fouled in him, and something was fouled in me, and I watched myself with him, and I could feel my own tears on my cheeks, because I knew what was coming, and I couldn't stop it. I didn't know how to stop things.

"Roy," was all I could say. "Don't. Please don't."

"Then help me, Lumen," he said. "Help me." And he put his arms out, palms up, for me to come to him.

It was a moment. I could have become one thing, but I became another. The creatures we truly are are exposed in tiny moments. This was one.

I could have saved him.

I did not save him.

"Help me," he said again.

And I said, "I can't." I said, "I don't know how."

"Lumen," he said.

I said, "Don't be afraid."

But he was. I could see that. He whimpered a little, his wild animal eyes gone all soft.

That's when I turned my back on him. I turned and closed my eyes. I could not bear witness.

I heard a brief shuffle of dirt from beneath his feet. I breathed in the dusty air. I paid attention to my heart, the stubborn beating of my dreadful heart.

When I opened my eyes again and turned around, he'd fallen. Blackhat Roy Ruggle was gone.

———

I WAITED FOR a while, and the earth was quite still. The only sound was my own breathing, and I listened to it. I persisted.

I didn't know what else to do.

I put my prom dress back on, the rustle of the crinoline echoing gaudily in that grim sanctuary. I wiped my face with my gritty hands, and I made my way outside. Walking unhurriedly back through the woods, I was aware of all the voices of the crickets and the tree toads and the owls around me. The air was cold in my lungs, the stars reflected in the still water of the lake as I passed by. I was no part of the things I saw. I was just a traveler across these fields of night, and I was alone.

I smelled the smoke when I was still a great distance from the edge of the woods. What's carried on the air can be carried a long way. I didn't see it until I was almost home, that black plume that rose behind the trees, almost invisible except for the way it blocked out the stars and gave a halo to the gibbous moon. At the same time, I became aware of the flashing lights, blue, white, and red.

I must have looked like an apparition emerging from those trees, my prom dress torn and covered with burrs. But no one noticed. No one was paying any attention, because everyone was looking at the place where my house used to be—where now blackened timbers stood upright and smoked and crackled and released every now and then a dust of ash and ember.

I looked for my father, but I couldn't see him among the neighbors who stood on the street in their nightclothes, shaking their heads and leaning together against tragedy.

When somebody finally saw me, I was seized by a team of uniformed men. Police confirmed that my name was Lumen Fowler, that Marcus Fowler was my father. They wanted to know where I had been.

"Where's my dad?" I said.

They wanted to know if I knew who set the fire.

"Where's my dad?" I said.

Then two paramedics led me to the back of an ambulance, where they put a blanket over my shoulders and performed tests on my pliant body. They told me to stay put there in the ambulance, but when they were gone I found myself wandering away

among the vehicles and lights and moving figures. I was a meager ghost. No one saw me—I was nothing to see. I heard their
voices. I heard everything. How the firemen had tried to stop
him from going inside, how they had told him they'd cleared the
house. But he had gone in anyway, saying he knew where I'd be
hidden. The coal hole. Saying he was sure I was in there because
I'd promised to be home by midnight. I'd promised.

I sat down on the ground, the crinoline bunched up underneath me, and I held out my hands to collect the ash that fell from
the sky like flakes of snow.

Margot Simons found me. She tried to lift me, but my legs
didn't work right, so instead she sat down next to me on the
road. Her face was streaky with soot and dried tears. She put her
arms around me.

"It'll be all right, Lumen," she said.

"Yes," I said.

"I'll take care of you," she said. "I'm not going anywhere," she
said.

"Yes."

"He loved you," she said. "There was nothing else in the world
for him but you."

The ash collected on my palms. Miss Simons tightened her
arms around me. She used one hand to brush away the ash that
was collecting in my hair.

"You're going to be okay," she said.

I said, "Yes."

CHAPTER 14

Jack drives. It is deep night. No moon at all. There are no streetlights out here. We are in the middle of a great black, the aperture of our headlights opening on the two-lane blacktop scrolling out before us, the margins of the trees flashing past. The only sound is the stable hum of the engine and the groan of the upholstery under us as we shift in our seats.

I glance into the backseat at our son, Marcus. Jack could not find someone to watch him when he came to fetch me from jail.

"He's asleep," I say.

"It's late," Jack says.

"It's late," I repeat, nodding.

I am very much alone, the light in the car strange, the flashes from the oncoming headlights casting shadows that make my husband look like someone I don't know.

He looks at me, earnest.

"It'll be okay," he says. "Helena and her fiancé won't press charges. They won't. I'll talk to them. You'll apologize." He makes his hand into a flat sword and cuts it through the air with each point. "She'll forgive you. It's what people do."

This is true. It requires unrelenting effort to hate. It takes strength, commitment. Most of us are not that ambitious.

"We'll…" he goes on, "we'll schedule an appointment for you. To see a psychologist. It'll be good for you to talk to someone. We'll find someone you can talk to, someone you feel comfortable—"

He stops, looking to see how I will respond.

"I will," I say simply. "I trust you."

He gives me a tentative smile. A solitary car comes from the other direction, and we squint our eyes against its headlights. Then there is a shift in his voice toward gentleness.

"How are you feeling?" he says.

"Sleepy," I say. "But okay. I feel fine."

Then we are quiet for a while. In my mind, I say a little prayer for my father, but it's a prayer I sometimes say over my son in his crib, and sometimes over my husband when he is asleep beside me in our bed. It was one of the traditional lullabies in Pale Miranda—first taught to me by Polly when we were both very little girls. It made everything seem blameless, and it went like this:

Sleep now, baby—
Sleep now, child.
See the moon, so still and mild.
Dream away
From sun's bright noon.
I'll watch you walking on the moon.
And when you're older,
Stout and true,
I will see the moon in you.

None of us is a saint, but the world is still magic.

"Just a few weeks till summer," Jack says beside me.

"It'll be nice."

"We'll have time. Maybe we should go somewhere."

"Yes," I say. "Let's go somewhere. Where do people go?"

My mother, she got lost during the Lacuna, the June moon. My father, he died just before it. Do you know what a lacuna is? It's a space. A hole. A lumen. In music, it's a pause that makes you hear silence as though it were being played by an instrument. In moons, it is the middle of the year—a hiatus. In literature, it's something left out of a manuscript. Here is a lacuna:

Do you see me there? In that empty space—that's where I got lost. It's where I went from that night to this one. It's where my father and Blackhat Roy went. I hope it's bright where they are. Bright as my aching girl-chest, where their hearts, black and white, still do dances.

Next to me in the car, Jack takes a deep breath. Then he speaks, haltingly, as though any word might cause the whole night sky to collapse.

"You know," he says, "you can . . . talk to me."

"About what?"

"I don't know. About things. Anything. Whatever's important."

After a pause, I say:

"I miss my father."

I turn and look at my husband, the way the dim light from the dash makes his face glow with a strange tint. His skin seems almost unreal, his eyes glassy. Then I look at my son, asleep in the backseat. I can see his little chest rise and fall under his striped cotton shirt, his hot breath coming slow between parted lips, his head, hair messy, cocked to one side and leaning against the cushion of his car seat. His hands rest loose on his lap, but I see his tiny fingers twitch slightly around his stuffed pet bunny.

I think of an Easter Sunday, when I was ten.

Every year my father made a special Easter egg hunt for me. He hid them in difficult places, both inside and outside the house, then he gave me clues to those hidden treasures in the form of rhyming couplets written in script on index cards.

That year I was stuck on the last one. The clue said this:

Here lies the measure of all our worth —
Look where sleeps the most precious thing on earth.

I looked in all the places in the house where we kept valuables. I scoured the sideboard in the kitchen, where we kept the china and the silverware. I looked through my father's office drawers, where he kept important documents. I sifted through the dresser where we kept all the things that once belonged to my mother.

While I looked, he watched me, smiling. He refused to help me with any additional hints.

I scowled at him. He gazed back at me with a look I'll never forget.

I finally found the last Easter egg. It was in my bedroom, under my pillow.

"Your father," Jack says now. "You never tell me about him. You never tell me anything about where you grew up, or about your school days, or about what you were like as a girl. You know I'd listen. I love you. I want to hear these things."

I look away from him toward the trees, their briefly illuminated trunks flashing by in the night. I wonder who might be out there.

"Maybe."

———

EVERYONE IN THE neighborhood will know about my breaking into Helena's house and about my being arrested and about the psychological rehabilitation I will undergo. At dinner parties, they will be nice. They are always very nice. They will offer their support. They will tell me they care about me and love me and want what's best for me. Jack will remind me, as he always does, that he loves me.

It's funny, all these people talking about love. They think love is something like a fluffy pillow where you rest your head. They think love is sweet and gentle, all hands and lips and nestling. But they're wrong. I know what love is. Love is angrier than this. It's harsher. It's tasting the world on your tongue and digging your claws deep into the underbelly of life. I know exactly what love is. It's sometimes leaning over your husband while he sleeps, while he conjures in his dreams all the fears and ecstasies he would relish if he were ever able to let himself be truly and wholly alive, breathing in the fermented air exhaled from his pink, undamaged lungs—and it's sometimes wanting to rip out his throat with your teeth.

ACKNOWLEDGMENTS

Special thanks to Josh Kendall and Eleanor Jackson. I owe them considerable gratitude. If you could read the first version of this book, you would see just how much.

ABOUT THE AUTHOR

Joshua Gaylord grew up in Anaheim, California, and currently resides in New York City. Using his own name or the pen name Alden Bell, he has authored three previous novels, including *The Reapers Are the Angels*. He received his PhD from New York University and has taught high school English as well as literature courses at NYU and the New School.